After Brett stood, he leaned down to Caprice, his hands on the table. "I can't tell you much but I can tell you this. We're looking at other suspects besides Michelle."

"Does Vince know that?"

Brett just gave her one of his I-don't-know shrugs. Still leaning toward her, he said, "I want you to promise me if you see a hint of trouble, you'll call me immediately."

"I'm not looking for trouble."

"No, you're doing worse than that. You're looking for murder suspects. I know I can't stop you, not unless I want to toss you in jail. I really don't want to do that because you do gather good information from time to time. But I want to keep you safe and I know Grant does too. If you get tempted to get into trouble, just remember, you h___ a wedding date on May 12. "

"Believe me, I'm not going ___ fr___

Brett straightened. ___ ___ ___ ___ing smile, and then a___ ___ ___ ___ be once you're mar___ ___ ___ ___ ___e to interfere in our ___ ___ ___

Before she could ___ ___ ___ the diner.

Books by Karen Rose Smith

Caprice De Luca Mysteries
STAGED TO DEATH
DEADLY DÉCOR
GILT BY ASSOCIATION
DRAPE EXPECTATIONS
SILENCE OF THE LAMPS
SHADES OF WRATH
SLAY BELLS RING
CUT TO THE CHAISE

Daisy's Tea Garden Mysteries
MURDER WITH LEMON TEA CAKES
MURDER WITH CINAMMON SCONES

Published by Kensington Publishing Corporation

Cut to the Chaise

Karen Rose Smith

KENSINGTON BOOKS
www.kensingtonbooks.com

KENSINGTON BOOKS are published by

Kensington Publishing Corp.
119 West 40th Street
New York, NY 10018

All Kensington titles, imprints, and distributed lines are available at special quantity discounts for bulk purchases for sales promotion, premiums, fund-raising, educational, or institutional use.

Special book excerpts or customized printings can also be created to fit specific needs. For details, write or phone the office of the Kensington Sales Manager: Attn.: Sales Department. Kensington Publishing Corp., 119 West 40th Street, New York, NY 10018. Phone: 1-800-221-2647.

Kensington and the K logo Reg. U.S. Pat. & TM Off.

First Printing: December 2018
ISBN-13: 978-1-4967-0979-0
ISBN-10: 1-4967-0979-9

ISBN-13: 978-1-4967-0980-6 (ebook)
eISBN-10: 1-4967-0980-2 (ebook)

10 9 8 7 6 5 4 3 2 1

Printed in the United States of America

To my husband . . .
I can remember our wedding 47 years ago as if it were yesterday—white lace and promises that began with a ring on a yellow rose.

ACKNOWLEDGMENTS

I would like to thank Officer Greg Berry, my law enforcement consultant, who so patiently answers all my questions. His input is invaluable.

Chapter One

Caprice De Luca believed in telling the truth. But as she met her sisters and her best friend Roz in the parking lot of Rambling Vines Winery, she wondered if the truth was always the best option.

Should she tell Roz now?

Should she tell her before the big day when Caprice would marry Grant Weatherford and then they would have their reception here?

Travis Dodd and his wife Michelle had decided to modernize Rambling Vines Winery two years ago with a full-out marketing campaign to promote the winery not only in Kismet but across the state of Pennsylvania. However, there was a reason Michelle had chosen Caprice De Luca Home Staging and Designs to redo the tasting room, the events room, as well as the first floor of the house on the estate. Roz didn't know what that reason was.

Her older sister Nikki pushed her blond-highlighted brown hair over her shoulder and gave Caprice a look that clearly said she should tell Roz *now*. Caprice's younger sister Bella, her tumbling black curls around her face as wayward as she sometimes could be, elbowed her as they walked toward the tasting room. Caprice delayed the moment of truth by admiring the porch that wrapped around three sides of the building housing Rambling Vines' tasting room, offices, and winery. The events room was in a separate building.

"I can't believe I've never been here before," Bella said. "The winery is only a few miles out of town."

All four women studied the entrance where stone pillars supported the porch roof. Roz held on to the cedar banister and climbed the two steps to the porch. Her violet sheath emphasized her slim figure, while her blond hair and gold earrings gleamed in the April sunlight. In response to Bella's comment, Roz frowned. "As much as Vince likes wineries, I'm surprised he never brought me here."

There was a reason for that, Caprice thought with a sigh. Was Roz's musing an opening she should take?

She was about to say to Roz, *Let's sit on the porch and talk.* There were several high-backed rockers lining the porch with short round tables between them. But before she could say the words, Travis Dodd appeared in the doorway.

Travis was about five-foot-ten, not as tall as

Grant. After all, Caprice measured everybody by Grant's height. To her, her fiancé was sexy and handsome and everything a man should be all combined in one.

Travis looked as if he were dressed for a business meeting in a suit that Caprice decided might be custom-made. The silk tie was Hermès. His sandy blond hair looked a bit too perfectly styled and he sported that new scruffy beard look as if he'd grown two days of stubble and left it there. Still, he was handsome, and in the past, he'd been nothing but charming.

Now he smiled at them, his blue eyes going from one of them to the next. "It's good to see you ladies," he said in a smoothly suave voice. "Michelle is tied up with a phone call, but she'll be here shortly."

Caprice introduced Roz and her sisters, and he shook all of their hands. "Let me show you the tasting room until Michelle arrives. I know it won't come into play for your wedding reception but your guests might wander in and out and take a look around the winery. That's what brings back repeat customers." He nodded to Bella, Roz, and Nikki and in a conspiratorial voice added, "That's how Caprice's name gets spread far and wide. You wouldn't believe how many people ask who decorated the tasting room and the events room, let alone the house."

Caprice's reputation mostly spread by word of mouth, and she was indeed grateful that the Dodds' guests and customers asked about the renovations and designs.

"She even found us the perfect furniture," Travis said as they went inside. "Exactly what we wanted."

Caprice had been a bit surprised when Michelle and Travis had wanted her to redo the tasting room with something totally different than they'd had before. Like many tasting rooms, there had been a counter and stools where a sommelier served wine and snacks. The couple had assured her over and over that they wanted something totally unique and mentioned settees and chaise lounges and a table large enough to sit six comfortably. A bar, yes, for whoever was managing the tasting room. But they'd requested a stone front and a granite surface on it. Shelves crafted of cedar like the banisters outside ran up the wall behind the counter, displaying bottles of wine. Wood and stone were everywhere.

Roz pointed across the room. "I love that teal chaise."

The teal leather also covered two club-like chairs at the other side of the room with a dark pine table between them. Another chaise in claret leather was accompanied by several uniquely designed chairs in the grouping, while a low dark pine coffee table angled between them. The teal and claret were picked up again by the glasses and dishes and cups and saucers stacked on a shelf behind the bar. Throw rugs with those same colors dotted the rust-colored ceramic tile floor.

"These pendant lights above the bar are amazing," Nikki commented, pointing to the teal hand-blown glass.

"And that chandelier," Bella said. "I'd find a place to put that in my house if I could."

The chandelier was multi-tiered copper that blended in with the native stone and the browns of the rest of the room.

All of a sudden, Michelle came running in through the front door of the tasting room like a swift wind.

"I'm sorry I'm late," she said breathlessly. "I stopped to feed the stray dog who's been hanging around on the tasting room porch."

"We didn't see one," Nikki said.

"Oh, he followed me up to the house. But I don't want to let him in. You know, fleas and all. So I put a bed around the corner on the porch and his bowls are there too. He's been hanging around since yesterday."

Somehow Michelle had come to stand beside Roz. She was wearing a two-piece cream pantsuit. Both women were fashionable, svelte blondes with green eyes. At that moment, Caprice knew she didn't want her friend to be blindsided. She had to tell her about Michelle. What if Michelle let something slip?

Travis said, "If you'll excuse me, Michelle will continue your tour. Caprice, we're so glad that you and Grant chose us for your reception."

With Grant's annulment coming through in March, they'd needed to find a reception venue quickly. That was difficult to do when those places were usually booked a year or more in advance. But when Caprice had phoned Michelle, Michelle had checked the winery's calendar and revealed that she'd had a cancellation in May. She and Travis would be glad to accommodate Caprice and Grant for the reception.

As Michelle nodded to Bella and Nikki and shook hands with Roz, Caprice suspected that Roz thought Nikki had been to the winery before and met Michelle then. And Bella . . .

"This furniture is so trendy," Bella stated. "The tasting room reminds me of those bookstores that have coffee bars and desserts. Customers can come in, sit, and talk. The atmosphere surely is inviting to bring friends along. It's much more than a wine-tasting room."

Michelle nodded. "That's exactly what we were going for, and Caprice helped us make it happen. Would you like to try out one of the chaise lounges?" she asked, pointing to the teal one.

Nikki crossed to it and flopped down. "It's comfortable. And the leather coverings are smart because you can clean them easily."

"Exactly why Caprice recommended them," Michelle agreed. "Come on. Let's go out the other exit and I'll take you over to the events building."

As they headed toward the heavy wooden door, Michelle motioned to the left. "Our offices, the winery, and the grapes receiving department are over that way. That's the business part of the enterprise. But the events room is my favorite part of the winery grounds."

After Michelle opened the door, they all followed a path lined with pansies that led to the events building. The building itself was much different than the winery. A portico reached over the entrance. To the left of the events building sat what looked like a long garage with three double-wide doors.

April wind tossed Caprice's straight, long, seventies-style dark-brown hair across her face. She didn't get much of a look at the garage as Michelle ushered them inside the room where Caprice's wedding reception would be held. It was exciting just walking in as a client of the winery rather than a designer.

In the foyer, Michelle, acting as a tour guide, motioned to the reception area with a beautiful high-gloss polished hardwood floor. The colors in this building were cream and bronze to go with almost any décor a bride would choose. Other events weren't always as color conscious.

As they strolled into the main room, Caprice's eyes automatically went to the focal point, a floor-to-ceiling stone fireplace. The cathedral ceiling added to the majesty of the room. French doors led to gardens that were now covered with daffodils. The other wall brought in sunshine through its many windows that stacked their way up to the cathedral ceiling.

"This room almost has a church-like atmosphere," Nikki noted.

"We do have many weddings take place here too," Michelle said. "Not just receptions. Weather permitting, we can also hold a wedding outside in the gardens."

"Grant and Caprice were lucky to line up a date at St. Francis on short notice," Bella said. "And then with you. I couldn't have been that patient waiting for an annulment. But it was important for them to be married in the Catholic Church."

"I imagine so," Michelle agreed. "The De Lucas' faith is important to them. It will be a wonderful ceremony, and we'll make sure we match and complement it with everything we do here. Let me show you to the alcove where the DJ will set up. It's over there next to the wet bar."

When Bella and Nikki started following Michelle, Caprice caught Roz's arm. "Wait here a minute, will you? I'd like to talk to you."

"Here?" Roz asked, looking surprised.

"I don't want to wait any longer to tell you what I have to tell you."

Now Roz looked worried. "You've changed your mind about having me in your wedding? Maybe you'd like your Aunt Marie to step in instead since she's going to be here?"

"No, nothing like that. Of course, I want you in my wedding." The other women's voices were muted now as they turned toward the bar. "I need to ask you something," Caprice said. "Has Vince told you about Michelle?"

Roz looked blank.

It didn't surprise Caprice that her brother hadn't told his present live-in girlfriend about an ex. "There's not that much to tell," she admitted. "But Vince and Michelle once dated."

With a smile, Roz gave a small laugh. "I know Vince dated lots of women before me. Kismet is a small town and running into them will happen."

In spite of Roz's words, however, Caprice saw her friend studying Michelle more carefully.

All of a sudden Travis came rushing into the events room looking troubled. He targeted his wife and ignored everyone else as he rushed to her. "I have a meeting in Camp Hill. I have to leave right now."

Caprice watched Travis and Michelle exchange a look. Michelle's chin went up and she appeared defiant. Travis was looking down at her and his eyes bore the glare of a bully.

After a tense moment or two, Travis maintained, "I don't know when I'll be back. I know you can handle everything here."

Just like that, Travis left again.

Watching Travis and Michelle, Caprice wondered about their marriage. After she'd been married for five years, she hoped she and Grant would still be acting like newlyweds. Were her expectations too high? Maybe, but whenever she considered her parents' marriage, as well as her grandparents' marriage, she knew her expectations *weren't* set too high.

Michelle shook off Travis's rudeness and his departure. Waving her hand over the large room, she explained, "Caprice has asked for round tables and tablecloths in pale aqua, rose, and yellow. She told me your dresses are all florals in different styles. We want the room to be a backdrop for her, Grant, and the wedding party. The whole atmosphere will be elegant, fashionable, and unique. We'll use white wood chairs for the guests and white plates. It will all be striking."

Caprice hoped that was true. She and Grant had come up with their ideas together. She really cared less about the colors and the state of the room than she did about her marriage to Grant.

She simply wanted the day to be special for them and their families, no matter what food they chose or the flavor of cake.

Bella closed one eye and glanced around the room, obviously envisioning it. "That's so *you*, Caprice. It will definitely work."

Nikki asked Michelle, "Did you know that Bella is creating Caprice's gown? It's a vintage style and the design is fabulous." Nikki turned to look at Caprice. "Your fitting is coming up soon, isn't it?"

"Whenever Bella wants to do it," Caprice agreed.

Roz usually had an opinion about everything, but Caprice noticed she was being unusually quiet. Was she thinking about the time Vince and Michelle had spent together? Her brother had dated Michelle for a few months and that's when Caprice and Michelle had become friendly. However, Michelle had wanted more out of the relationship than Vince, who was dating someone just because he liked to date. Michelle cut off their relationship and dumped him. Although Caprice liked to think her talent and reputation had snared Michelle and Travis's account to renovate the winery, she also believed Michelle had contracted with her because she felt a little guilty about what had happened with Vince.

After Michelle had shown them every nook and cranny of the events room, even a dressing room off to one side where a bride and her bridesmaids could freshen up before their entrance, she guided them outside to the gardens. When they'd passed through the French doors at the rear of the events room, Caprice immediately noticed the riot of color to the right around a huge fountain. The fountain was simple rather than ornate with three tiers in ombre-like colors. The top tier was rust stone, the second tier was brown stone, and the third-tier black stone. Daffodils danced all around the fountain in colorful yellow, white, and blush.

The groaning of a motor caused Caprice to take a few steps forward and look to the left at the long garage. Now two of the doors were open and another had just closed. She caught a glimpse of what looked like a late sixties MG. It was dark green with a high polish.

She pointed to it and asked Michelle, "What year is the MG?"

"That's right, you like classic cars. You own a restored Camaro," Michelle remembered. "You and Travis would have common ground there. Restored classic cars are his passion. He has several of them. That's a '65 MG."

Bella, Roz, and Nikki had walked toward the garden and the fountain. Bella was pointing to a reddish-colored ornamental grass.

Caprice's attention returned to Michelle. She understood the expense of restoring a car and what those cars were worth if they were restored authentically. "That's an expensive passion," came out of her mouth before she could catch it. Then she added, "My car took several years to restore with my dad and Vince's sweat equity along with some of their friends' time. But I do love it, so I can understand Travis's interest in classic cars."

Michelle motioned to the garage door that wasn't open. "One you can't see is a red Thunderbird con-

vertible. We rent it to just-married couples who want
unique transportation from the church to the winery. You might want to think about that."

She'd tell Grant. That was something he might
like to do.

After another exacting look at the gardens, they
returned inside the events room, all of the women
agreeing the landscaper had done a superb job.
Caprice knew Michelle hired only the best. The
winery's gardener had planted the gardens to tran-
sition from one season to the next, adding annuals
for each month. Azaleas would soon be blooming.

After a last examination of the venue, they returned the way they'd come. As Caprice glanced at
the entrance to the tasting room, movement on
the porch there caught her eye. There was a dog.
She supposed it was the stray Michelle had spoken
of earlier.

Without thinking twice, she ran over to the
porch and walked up to the steps. The dog looked
like a Schnoodle, a mixture of schnauzer and poo-
dle. He was about twenty inches high . . . possibly
twenty pounds. He tilted his face as he looked at
her, and she had to smile. His body was mostly
cream, but then he had gray floppy ears, gray
around both eyes, and a gray nose that stood out
against the creamy face. There was a blaze of gray
on his forehead too and along one side of his
flank. He was adorable.

"He's friendly," Michelle said. "I know how you
love animals. Go ahead and give him a pet."

He was wagging his tail now and coming toward
her. Caprice let him smell her hand and then he
rubbed his head against it. She scratched behind

his ears and he seemed to love that. From her guesstimation, he might be two or three.

"What are you going to do with him?" Caprice asked.

"First, I'm going to call around to all the neighbors to see if anyone lost him. He looks like a mix of a couple of things."

Caprice nodded.

"After the neighbors, I'll call veterinarians to see if anybody notified their offices that they lost him. I'm going to make another bed for him on the screened-in porch up at the house tonight. But we can't keep him because I don't have time to take care of him. And Travis . . . Travis wouldn't care about a dog."

In Caprice's estimation, if Travis wouldn't care about a dog, what kind of man was he?

The dog rolled over for Caprice and she rubbed his belly. He put all four paws up in the air and she had to laugh. Who wouldn't love a dog like this?

She knew Michelle was busy. They should probably leave. Caprice had planned lunch at her place for her sisters and Roz. From Roz's pensive expression, Caprice had a feeling her friend was going to have questions about Michelle . . . and Vince's relationship with her.

Just how much should Caprice tell her?

Chapter Two

Caprice had prepared lunch for the women early this morning. She knew they'd all want to talk after the winery tour. They always had the best discussions over food. At her house, she fed Lady—her golden cocker spaniel, Sophia—her long-haired calico, and Mirabelle—her white Persian. After eating their lunch, hopefully none of them would be interested in the food on the table.

As the women took seats around the table in her bright kitchen with its vintage buttercup-yellow appliances, Caprice first produced a basket of croissants. Then she pulled the chicken salad she'd made with its slivered almonds, dried cranberries, and celery, out of the refrigerator, setting that next to the croissants. In addition to the chicken salad, she'd prepared a tomato, fresh mozzarella, and oregano salad.

"This looks good." Nikki pulled her chair in. "Perfect for an April day."

"I'll surprise you with dessert after we've eaten

the salads," Caprice revealed with a smile as Lady sat beside her chair.

"Uh-oh," Bella said. "I have a feeling the dessert isn't low-carb."

Caprice gave a little shrug and joined them at the table. She was ten to fifteen pounds over-weight but her vintage clothes, like the turquoise-and-fuchsia crocheted-lace gauzy blouse with turquoise bell-bottom slacks that she wore today, often hid the fact. She'd long ago accepted the fact that she'd never be a size four or six.

Bella took one of the croissants and began filling it with chicken salad as did everyone. "I'll have your wedding gown ready for a fitting soon."

Nikki set her chicken-filled croissant on her lime-green plate and reached for the tomato salad. "I want to be there for the fitting. I can't wait to see your gown."

"I'd like to be there too," Roz said quietly.

Bella picked up her sandwich. "All right. But just the two of you. I want everyone else to be sur-prised. This is my first wedding creation."

When Caprice couldn't find the gown she'd liked in stores or online because she'd wanted a vintage style, Bella had shown her a design and as-sured Caprice she'd make it for her wedding. It was based on a photo of their Nana's wedding gown. But she was sure Bella would add embellish-ments of her own. Caprice hadn't seen it yet and she couldn't wait to try it on.

"Did you find shoes?" Nikki asked.

After Caprice took a few swallows of iced tea, she nodded. "I found them at Secrets of the Past. I'll show you after lunch. They're white, of course, with a pointy toe and kitten heels. They have a few crystal embellishments."

Bella poked a tomato and a piece of mozzarella with her fork. "They sound perfect. Not only will you be trying on your wedding gown, but I'll have the veil there that Mom and Nana bought you. There's a surprise with that too."

Caprice put her hand over her heart. "I don't know if I can handle any more surprises."

"This is a good one," Bella assured her, with a wide smile, her black curls bobbing.

Caprice glanced at Roz who wasn't adding much to the conversation. That was unusual for her out-spoken friend.

Nikki took a bite of her croissant and gave a thumbs-up sign to Caprice. After she'd swallowed her first taste, she put the croissant back on her plate and wiped her fingers. "Have you and Grant finalized your plans for the addition to your house?"

Caprice nodded. "We have."

Bella waved her hand at her. "Explain. Tell us your vision. I can't read blueprints worth a darn."

Everyone laughed.

Caprice loved her house and hated to think about leaving it when Grant suggested they find someplace new. However, he must have realized how she felt because at Christmas he'd gifted her with two sets of plans that added an addition for his office onto her house. She could choose whichever one she felt worked for them. His ability to compromise was one of the traits she liked best about him.

"We could have turned the garage into an office

and then added a detached garage in the back. But we decided against that."

"You wanted to keep the integrity of the front of the house and its curb appeal," Nikki guessed.

"Exactly. So we're building the addition *behind* the garage. Instead of the porch the way it is now, the contractor will construct an all-seasons room across the back. That way Lady and Patches can go out the kitchen door into the sunroom and then out to the backyard from there. Mirabelle and Sophia will have access to the room too. I'll probably find a cat condo for there so they can enjoy more sun."

Lady stood and cocked her head as if she was listening. Her ears flopped as she came over to Caprice and sat by her chair.

"Do you think Lady will be bothered by Patches living here too?" Bella asked, not as familiar with animals as Caprice was, though she had adopted a stray yellow tabby to everyone's surprise and considered Sunnybud one of the family.

"They spend so much time together now, I don't think it will be an adjustment," Caprice responded. "On the other hand, Sophia and Mirabelle simply tolerate Patches when he comes over, so there could be a few squabbles."

Mirabelle, sprawled on the dining room table since all the chairs in the kitchen were taken, meowed.

Nikki laughed. "I think she's confirming that life could get interesting."

As if she'd also heard *her* name mentioned in the conversation, Sophia walked across the kitchen like a queen. With a beautiful white ruff and more than

fluffy tail, she'd been Caprice's first rescue shortly
after she'd moved into her Cape Cod. Crossing to
Lady, Sophia pawed at her nose just because she
could. Lady didn't react. She was used to Sophia's
shenanigans. As if pointing out that the floor was-
n't a suitable place for lounging, Sophia jumped
up to the counter and leapt up to the top of the refrigerator. After settling, she looked down at them
with half-closed golden eyes.

Caprice's pets were family, and her friends and
relatives knew that. As if to emphasize that point,
Bella said, "It's no surprise that you and Grant
would think about the animals when you're building an addition. How will clients get into his office?"

Bella was the youngest of the four De Luca children and never hesitated to speak her mind. She
had a point which Caprice hoped she and Grant
had addressed. "We're going to pave a walkway
from the driveway around the side of the house to
the office. Grant will still be working from his office downtown with Vince, so he won't be seeing
that many clients here. But he will be able to work
from home. His office will also be his man-cave."

"So his office will have a door off the sunroom?"
Bella asked.

"Yes, and then an outside entrance too." Caprice
took another serving of the tomato salad.

Nikki reached over to take the serving dish from
her sister. "It sounds as though you have the bases
covered."

"We hope so. The only point still for debate is
whether we're going to put a powder room in his
office."

"Cha-ching," Bella said, indicating that would cost more money.

"I know." Caprice frowned. "But instead of a prolonged honeymoon, we've decided to just go to Williamsburg for a few days and put that money into the addition too."

As they all finished their lunch, conversation revolved around the winery and tasting room, and exactly how it would look for the wedding reception. Again Caprice noticed how quiet Roz was. Standing, she crossed to the refrigerator to produce the dessert.

When she showed the cake pan to all of them, they oohed and aahed. She set it on the table. "It's a white cake with a mascarpone and whipped cream topping. The sliced strawberries on top not only decorate it, but give it an added flavor. What do you think?"

"Let's taste it and I'll tell you," Bella said.

After Caprice cut squares for them all, Nikki was the one who took the first bite. She closed her eyes and savored it. "Heavenly. And I have an idea."

"Uh-oh," Caprice and Bella said at the same time.

"If you give me the recipe, I'll make this for your rehearsal dinner. It would be perfect. What do you think?"

"I think everyone would enjoy it," Bella affirmed.

Nikki dived into her piece with another forkful. "That's settled then."

Caprice brewed a pot of coffee to go with second pieces, smaller of course.

As the coffee and cake were finished, Nikki said,

"I'd like to stay here longer but I can't. I have to prep for a party tonight."

Bella nodded. "And I have to pick up Benny at the sitter's and work on christening outfits. I have two orders that have to be done by the end of the week."

Although Bella worked part-time for Roz at her dress shop, All About You, she also ran a costume and christening-set business from her website. Her youngest child Benny was sixteen months old now.

After hugs and thank-yous all around, Bella and Nikki left. Roz lingered and didn't seem in a hurry to leave. Still, she said, "I'd better get home too and let Dylan out. Vince jokingly said he'd take him along to the office today. He's never done that before, and I don't know how it would have worked out. I thought it was better if Dylan just stayed home until I got back."

In the fall, Roz and her brother had moved in together. They still seemed to be feeling their way and deciding whether or not they wanted to join their lives.

"Are you okay?" Caprice asked. "You were quiet during lunch."

"I didn't think knowing that Vince dated Michelle would bother me, but I guess it does."

"What bothers you?" Caprice wanted to know.

"It isn't so much the fact that they dated. It's the idea that Vince didn't tell me. After all, he knew your wedding reception was at Rambling Vines. He'll probably run into Michelle at the rehearsal dinner and the day of the wedding."

"The reason could merely be that men and women view past relationships differently. You know it took a while for Grant to share with me about his marriage to Naomi."

"But that was different. They'd lost a child. That's what made them go in different directions. Those kinds of wounds are deep. And as soon as you two became serious, you started sharing more."

"He did begin sharing, but as you said, he had deep wounds. Vince dated Michelle but that was mostly on the surface. My guess is he figured—*why bring it up now?*"

"Now that I know, I have questions," Roz admitted.

"Then you need to ask Vince. I'm positive he'll reassure you it was long over."

But Roz didn't look so certain of that.

A few hours later, Grant brought Patches along when he came for dinner. Patches, Lady's brother, was cream-colored with brown ears and brown patches around his eyes and nose as well as on his flanks. Quickly, Caprice told Grant about the winery tour and Roz's reaction to the news about Michelle.

"Do you think she's overreacting?" Grant asked as he took a tossed salad from the refrigerator and put it on the table.

Every time she looked at Grant and realized all over again she would be marrying this tall, black-haired, and handsome man, she became a bit breathless. She managed to say, "Michelle is an old girlfriend."

The buzzer went off on the stove and Caprice went to the oven to pull out the casserole. She'd made something easy tonight—rotelle with ground beef, pepperoni, and three cheeses.

"It all comes down to a matter of trust, doesn't it?"

There had been a time when Caprice had had trouble trusting Grant as he found closure to his previous marriage with his ex-wife. The annulment they'd received from the Catholic Church hadn't meant his first marriage hadn't existed. It meant the elements hadn't been there to make it a sacrament. Naomi had been pregnant when they'd gotten married and they'd married at a justice of the peace. In addition to that, Naomi hadn't been Catholic. They'd had grounds for the annulment, and because she and Grant wanted to get married in the church, they'd applied and received it.

Caprice gazed into Grant's gray eyes now. "It *is* a matter of trust. We both know that. I'm just hoping Roz talks to Vince about it instead of letting her suspicions smolder. I don't think she cares about Michelle so much. She just wishes Vince had told her about Michelle as soon as he knew my wedding reception would be at the winery."

"Fair point," Grant agreed, crossing to Caprice and wrapping his arms around her. "Everything's falling into place for our wedding and reception."

"And I checked with Aunt Marie again." She hadn't seen her aunt who lived in New Mexico for a few years.

"Is she still willing to stay here after the wedding with Sophia, Mirabelle, and Lady?"

"She is. She says she's looking forward to it. Is your neighbor still okay with keeping Patches for a few days?"

"Simon says he'll enjoy the company. I also wanted to tell you I made reservations today at a bed and breakfast in Williamsburg. I think you're going to like it."

"Can you tell me about it or is it a surprise?"

"I can tell you that our room has a huge four-poster bed with a canopy." He wiggled his eyebrows at her.

She and Grant had made the decision to wait until their wedding night to have sex. Sure, they were attracted to each other, and most of the time their kisses could easily explode into much more. But they'd decided the anticipation would prolong the excitement and give them even more to look forward to.

"Are you nervous about our wedding night?" Grant asked.

"If I say I am, will you be disappointed?" she asked with some trepidation.

"No. But I can tell you that you have nothing to be nervous about." When he kissed her, she was reassured again that he was right.

On Wednesday afternoon, as Caprice walked into the six-thousand-square-foot stone-and-brick home with ivy covering many of its walls, she considered how much she liked it. Many of the houses she staged were for buyers. She wouldn't live in one herself. This house, however . . . Sure, it was too much square footage for her and Grant and the animals, but she loved the style. The problem was the house was going to be extremely difficult to declutter. Her assistant, Juan Hildago, was supposed to arrive in a little while. She would depend on his help to create the declutter list.

Althea and Dustin Bassani had opened the big wooden door and now ushered Caprice through the foyer into the living room. "We found the perfect house in Carmel," Althea said, her red-blond hair in a straight cut swinging as she walked.

Her husband Dustin, about six-foot-four and thin as a rail, nodded until his long brown hair tied back with a leather band bounced on his shoulder. "It's stucco with trellises and a courtyard in the back. It's about half this size, but we can't wait to decorate with our favorite colors."

Dustin was a forensics accountant well known in his field. CEOs of companies from oil to electronics consulted with him and hired him to go over their books. Since he flew across the country at the whim of CEOs, he could live anywhere—anywhere he and his wife would be happy. They'd decided on the seaside town of Carmel, California.

"It will be hard to leave this house though." Althea looked longingly at the turquoise curio cabinet in the foyer. The wall behind it was wallpapered with a teal, and navy pattern. One of their fireplaces was located in the living room and it was the most unusual one Caprice had ever seen, done in flower mosaics in turquoise, mauve, and yellow. The hearth was upended pink bricks.

The same room had one wall painted turquoise, built-in white bookshelves full of books, and sofas and armchairs in splashes of color that included coral, sky blue, white, and orange. The *boucherouite* rug from Morocco on the pale oak flooring was beautiful. The same colors danced throughout the house, in the parlors, studies, and bathrooms and were even included in the shower curtains. The sunroom boasted a macramé chair that hung from the ceiling, while the staircase leading upstairs was a pathway to photographs, about twenty of them in various sizes, arranged together like pieces in a puzzle. Most were of family. The one that had taken Caprice's attention was the handprints of one of their children.

"It's always hard to leave a home that you've loved," Caprice sympathized. "But I imagine you'll be taking a lot of the furniture with you."

"We will move our favorites," Dustin assured her.

Althea pointed out, "As you decide to declutter, we'll tell you the ones we aren't taking and those we can send to the consignment shop."

"That's a great idea. Juan should be here in a little while to help me develop a list. But before he comes, maybe you can start that list with the pieces you're certain you want to keep."

"I love the theme you've decided on for the house," Althea commented. "'Bohemian Rhapsody' is perfect. Dustin and I have always considered ourselves fans of the boho lifestyle. And as far as that list goes"—Althea pulled a folded piece of paper from the pocket of her brightly flowered maxi-skirt—"I already made it. Dustin and I went through room by room last night."

There was another reason Althea and Dustin were moving besides Carmel's beach and artistic lifestyle. "You said one of your children lives in California?"

"Yes, our daughter. She's in Sacramento, and

our son lives in Arizona. So we'll be closer to both of them." Althea motioned to the living room. "Why don't you have a seat and I'll pour us some iced tea until your assistant arrives."

Caprice smiled. "That would be great since you already have half the work done."

"I only wish," Dustin groaned.

Soon Althea was back with glasses of iced tea and Caprice began looking over her list. "I do like your pops of color and pieces of turquoise and teal in this house. They are my favorite colors. In fact, when I redecorated the tasting room at a winery, I used teal in the chaise lounges."

"Chaise lounges in a tasting room?" Dustin asked. "Which winery?"

"Rambling Vines. Do you know it?"

"I've been there over the years but not since it was redecorated," Dustin said.

"My wedding's in May, and Grant and I will be holding our wedding reception there."

"Are you getting married there?" Althea wanted to know.

"No. We'll be married at St. Francis Church."

"I'll bet you're so excited," Althea said enthusiastically. "Try not to stress over every detail and really enjoy the day. Dustin and I had a destination wedding before they were even popular. We were married in Hawaii on the beach. It was beautiful."

"Grant and I want everything to be meaningful. We're just fortunate Rambling Vines had a cancellation. We're putting our wedding together on more short notice than most weddings have these days."

"I'm not surprised they had a cancellation." As soon as he said it, Dustin looked embarrassed. "Maybe I shouldn't have said that."

"Why did you?" Caprice asked.

"I've heard that quite a few weddings over the past six months have had complaints. One of my local clients who had his reception there felt cheated. He didn't have the food layout he expected, and the flowers weren't fresh."

When Caprice frowned, Dustin warned, "Just stay on top of it. Put someone in charge of making sure everything is exactly the way you want it, especially those flowers."

"I don't think it's just the winery having problems with receptions," Althea chimed in. "Michelle and Travis dropped their membership to the Country Squire Golf and Recreation Club."

Caprice knew Roz had a membership there and it was expensive. "So all of that put together means the winery isn't doing well?"

Dustin shrugged. "Maybe the new image they tried to develop hasn't gone over as well as the old-fashioned image that old William Dodd, Travis's father, had built up at the winery over the years. Either that or Travis and Michelle have mishandled organization, wine development, and bookkeeping. Sometimes there's more than one problem at the root of it."

Caprice was already thinking about what she could do for quality control when the doorbell chimed through the house.

"I'll get it," Althea offered. She rubbed her hands together. "I can't wait to get started."

Caprice would have to stop thinking about her wedding reception and begin the task of decluttering the Bassani home. She'd discuss what she learned with Grant and maybe Nikki to find out if they'd heard anything about the rumors. That old adage, *Where there is smoke there is fire*, was often true.

On Saturday morning, Caprice and Grant waited for Vince, Uncle Dom, and Brett Carstead at a tuxedo rental store. As they sat in chairs in the small reception area, Caprice caught Grant up on what Althea and Dustin Bassani had told her.

She said, "I phoned Nikki last night to ask her if she'd run into any catering difficulties there, but she said she hadn't catered a wedding reception or anything else at the winery in about a year. After I told her about all of it, Nikki assured me that she'll oversee the flower delivery and make sure everything's perfect. And you know she will. She's like a general commanding her minions when she's running a catering event."

"No wonder she and Brett get along so well," Grant joked.

Caprice playfully nudged his arm. "Brett's a good guy and you know it."

"I do know it. That's why I asked him to be a groomsman. But you've got to admit, being in a relationship with a cop has to be tough."

"If anybody can handle it, Nikki can." Caprice believed that to the bottom of her heart.

Even though Caprice knew she only had a few

minutes until their groomsmen arrived, she didn't want to postpone the subject that was important to both of them. "Have you gotten in touch with your brother about being a groomsman? We'll have to rent him a tuxedo if he wants to be in the wedding party."

"I e-mailed him and I've left messages for him, but he hasn't gotten back to me yet."

Caprice could see Grant was troubled by that. She knew he and Holden didn't have a close relationship. She gave a shrug. "Renting a tuxedo isn't like finding a bridesmaid dress or having fittings. If he wants to join us, all you have to do is get his measurements."

"Right. All I have to do," Grant repeated.

Since she'd plunged into this discussion, she decided to plunge in further. "Have your parents decided whether or not they'll stay with my parents while they're in town?"

"They haven't decided yet, either. You're going to get the feeling that Weatherfords can't make a decision."

Grant's parents weren't the affectionate warm people Caprice was used to. When she and Grant visited them for a few days after Christmas, they got along okay. Yet Caprice didn't feel as if she'd deepened her relationship with them. His brother had been out of town. Grant's family was the one aspect of the wedding that she was worried about.

Grant was a perceptive man, and he must have heard the concern in her voice. He took her hand between the two of his. "Whatever happens, whoever comes, whether or not my parents stay with your parents, our wedding's going to be perfect simply because we're getting married. If you concentrate on that, everything else will fall into place."

"Is that what you're telling yourself?" she asked with a hint of amusement.

"I am. If I say it often enough and I get you to believe it too, it will happen."

"So I've convinced you affirmations are a good thing."

"There's never anything wrong with positive thinking."

That wasn't quite the same thing as the affirmations Caprice tried to do every morning, but she'd take it.

Glancing out the window, she broke into a smile. "Your best man is on the way in, and Uncle Dom and Brett are right behind him. Now let's see if we can decide on tuxedos."

"We?" Grant asked with a raised brow. "It seems to me I didn't have any input on bridesmaids' dresses or your wedding gown."

"Do you think all of you can come to a decision on your own?" she teased.

"I'll tell you what. You can be the tie breaker."

Marriage was all about compromise. She supposed they might as well start now.

Chapter Three

Late on Sunday afternoon, Caprice and Grant were sitting on a bench at the dog park appreciating the warm April day when Caprice's cell phone played.

"Go ahead," Grant said, waving to her skirt pocket where she usually kept her phone. "It could be your mom needing you to bring something along to dinner."

Yes, it could be. Today was one of the monthly De Luca Sunday dinners when everybody contributed food to the meal. For this dinner, Caprice had made her rotelle casserole because Grant had liked it so much.

However, when she plucked her phone from her pocket, she saw Michelle Dodd was calling. "It's Michelle," she said to Grant, and then answered. "Hello, Michelle."

"I'm sorry to call you on a Sunday," Michelle apologized.

"No problem. Grant and I are at the dog park.

We'll be heading over to my mom's for dinner shortly."

"Ah, the De Luca family dinners. Vince never invited me to one of those."

Michelle's comment told Caprice once again that Vince hadn't been serious about Michelle.

"They're always boisterous and noisy," Caprice responded because what else was she supposed to say—*I'm sorry my brother never invited you?*

"This is kind of awkward," Michelle finally said.

Talking about the De Luca family dinners? Caprice wondered, but she waited.

"I have to ask if you and Grant can pay the second half of the reception charge now instead of after the wedding. The truth is, the winery usually takes a percentage of the catering cost but with Nikki catering for free, the winery is out that money. I'd like to do a few extras for you and Grant like a flowered arch to make your entrance into the reception hall. I can do that if I have the whole amount."

The request seemed unusual to Caprice. On the other hand, she didn't have a wedding reception every day. "I'll talk to Grant about it and we'll get you a check. I'm glad you called because I wanted to tell you that Nikki is going to oversee not only the food but the flower delivery too. It would be great if you could stay in contact with her about it."

"Sure, I can do that. Just give me her e-mail address."

Caprice rattled it off.

"I really appreciate this, Caprice. Having that check will enable me to do the best for your wedding reception."

After Caprice ended the call, she said to Grant, "That was odd."

"What did Michelle want?"

"She wants the balance of what we owe for the wedding reception."

"I thought we didn't have to pay that until after the reception."

Caprice explained why Michelle had asked.

Grant's dark brows arched as they usually did when he questioned something. "That doesn't seem right to me, but I can understand if she's not getting a cut of the catering. On the other hand, if the reception isn't everything you paid for, I can always send out a legal warning so they return funds for whatever they didn't do. We do have a contract with them."

"I hope we haven't made a mistake booking our reception there. I don't want to be embarrassed in front of your parents."

Grant took her hand. "We could have the reception in the backyard of your mom's house."

"Her yard is on more than one level. That would be difficult."

"But not impossible. We can always have it in *your* backyard."

"I wanted something special for us."

"Our reception will be special no matter where we have it. Stop worrying, honey."

"What about *your* family? What will they think if something goes wrong?"

Amusement danced in his eyes. "You mean like not having a flowered arch to announce us at the reception?"

After she punched him in the arm and glared at him, he circled her shoulders and brought her close. "My parents know as well as anybody that life can throw curveballs. So whatever happens happens. Think of it this way. If we have it in a backyard, Patches and Lady could be there."

"I forgot to order them bridal wear," Caprice mumbled.

Grant laughed. "And I'm sure they're grateful for that. Come on, let's head over to your mom's."

"We have to go back to my place to pick up the casserole, and I think I want to change before dinner."

"Your denim skirt won't make a fashion statement?"

"Nope. I found a dress I think you'll like. It's lime green and pink, and perfect for an April day."

"I like everything you wear. Maybe after we're married, we should coordinate. I can try to find a lime-green shirt," he joked.

"As if you ever would." Caprice just rolled her eyes, stood, and called, "Lady and Patches, come. Time to go."

As the dogs ran toward them, Grant tapped Caprice on the shoulder. When she gazed at him, he said, "I really do want you to stop worrying. Worry will only spoil your enjoyment of the day."

Grant was right. She'd stop worrying right now.

Grant didn't have much to say as they drove to her parents' house, the dogs in the kennels in the back of his SUV. Although he'd advised Caprice not to worry, she wondered if *he* was worrying. Or maybe he was getting fidgety about the wedding. Cold feet? Maybe later she'd ask him. She wanted him to feel free to tell her his concerns. His just-go-with-the-flow attitude might be on the surface, but what was underneath?

The usual cars were parked at the side entrance along the curb of her parents' house. Caprice had so many good memories about her childhood home. Every time she walked inside, one of them came rushing back. She'd played hide-and-seek with Bella in back of the barberry bushes alongside the side porch. She and Nikki had often snuck out onto her parents' balcony off their bedroom and pretended they were in a Shakespearean play.

The house was unusual for Pennsylvania because it was a California-style stucco, and had a red barrel tiled roof that always seemed to need repair. Even when her brother Vince was small, he'd asked their parents, "Are you fixing up again?" It seemed the house usually had something to fix. But that's how her parents had been able to afford it when they were first building a family. They'd kept unique features that were sometimes high maintenance, like the casement windows, the yellow stucco exterior, and of course the roof. When Caprice's Nana—her dad's mother—had moved in with them, they'd added on a suite for her. Caprice had special memories about Nana's suite too. She and Nana had a habit of having tea together every few weeks. Delicious aromas always emanated from either Nana's suite or her mom's kitchen.

Grant carried the casserole in one arm and encircled Caprice's shoulders with the other as they

went up the porch steps. Patches and Lady ran by
them past the dark-brown rope-style pillars that
supported the porch.

After Grant opened the screen door, they stepped
inside to the foyer. The dogs ran into a long living
room that was dark now. A sunroom stretched off
that. The library behind the living room had its own
little balcony as well as a fireplace that had a mate
in the living room.

The cuckoo clock in the dining room struck
four and Caprice heard voices coming from the
kitchen. Caprice started to head in that direction
but Grant stopped her by snagging her arm. He
kissed her hard and then grinned.

She smiled because sometimes Grant wasn't so
predictable. As she went to the archway in the
kitchen, a crowd of people flooded out, all of them
saying some form of "Happy wedding shower."

Nikki had brought balloons with her and they
floated to the ceiling. Lady and Patches met up with
Blitz, her parents' white Malamute, and barked at
the balloons. Everyone crowded around Caprice.

She was surprised to see so many people had fit
in the kitchen. Besides Nana and her mom and
dad, Bella, Joe, and their children, Vince and Roz,
Nikki and Brett, Uncle Dom and her neighbor
Dulcina, Ace Richland, a rock star who had become Caprice's friend, his daughter Trista, and his
ex-wife Marsha were among those congratulating
her. A few of her high school classmates were there
too. She'd been involved on the reunion commit-
tee with them.

She was absolutely overwhelmed, even more so

when they all began bringing dishes into the dining room and setting them on the table.

Grant added Caprice's casserole to the mix.

She turned to him. "Did you know about this?"

"Of course. I was supposed to get you here at four o'clock on the dot."

Caprice spotted Isaac Hobbs, the owner of Older and Better, Kismet's antique shop. Tall and husky and in his early 60s, his thinning hair was almost completely gray. He was hanging back in the kitchen along with Suzanne Dumas, who was the owner of Secrets of the Past, Caprice's favorite dress shop . . . next to Roz's All About You, of course. Petite Greta Hansen, manager of Perky Paws, Kismet's all-around pet supply store, waved at Caprice as she pulled a pitcher of iced tea from the refrigerator and brought it to the table. Soon they were all enjoying the food, sitting around the large dining room table on chairs at its perimeter and even in the living room.

Conversation was lively—about the wedding, about the reception, about the garden society and church, and anything else that had to do with Kismet. Caprice paid particular attention to Roz and Vince, and they seemed to be fine. That was a relief. Roz must have accepted the fact that Michelle Dodd was in Vince's past, and he hadn't thought that history was important enough to tell her.

"We have a whole table full of presents for you," Nana said as she patted Caprice's shoulder. "They're all in the library. Why don't you go sit on the sofa in the living room and we'll bring them to you."

"You want me to open them now?"

"Sure, we do," Caprice's dad said. "Then everyone can see the joy on your face when you open their present."

That made sense, Caprice thought, although present-opening could get boring for the guests.

"We'll just keep passing around the chocolate cake and the cannoli," her mother assured her. "And your dad will pour more coffee. If anyone wants wine, we have that too. We'll have a fine time counting all your toasters."

Everybody laughed.

Caprice made a point of thanking each one for coming before she settled in the living room.

Grant told her, "I'll help with the presents."

She found herself sitting on the sofa with Greta on one side and Isaac Hobbs on her other side.

Isaac gave her arm a nudge. "I noticed the wine came from Adams County Winery instead of Rambling Vines. Any reason?"

Caprice gave a little shrug. Isaac often teased her. "Dad's more familiar with Adams County Winery wines. I imagine that's why."

"I know your brother thinks he's a wine connoisseur but I enjoy my wines too."

"More than coffee?" Whenever she stopped at Isaac's and he wasn't busy, they had coffee together, and he had a treat for Lady. The coffee often tasted like sludge, but it was the companionship that was important.

"Definitely more than coffee. I've been thinking about getting one of those machines that makes one cup at a time," he offered.

That would definitely be an improvement because his coffeepot wouldn't sit all day heating coffee residue.

"Actually, I heard that Rambling Vines didn't enter the Farm Show wine competition this year," Isaac revealed. Then he went on, "I also heard they didn't do workshops or have a booth at the Pittsburgh Wine Conference either."

"Maybe they're concentrating on national competitions," Caprice offered.

Greta, overhearing their conversation, said, "No, I don't think so."

"No nationals either?" Caprice asked her.

"Rumor has it the winery couldn't meet payroll demands. My sister worked for them in the distribution department and they cut her job about three months ago. She said they were going to cut two more assistant positions."

Well, if that was true, Michelle asking for money sooner rather than later made sense. She'd have to have a heart-to-heart with Michelle when she delivered her check tomorrow.

Grant, Nana, and Roz all brought presents in and set them on the coffee table. Caprice began opening them, reading cards, and passing everything around. After a short while, Isaac got to his feet and said to Grant, "You sit here too. These presents are for both of you."

Grant did as Isaac suggested. He and Caprice opened everything from a set of cocker spaniel salt and pepper shakers to a cat-decorated sugar and creamer. There were placemats in Caprice's favorite colors, a leather desk set for Grant's new office after they put the addition on, a French press coffee maker along with a milk foamer to go with it, and other presents that were unusual enough that Caprice and Grant didn't already own them. Finally, while Joe rocked Benny to sleep in the rocking chair, Bella stood by supervising while Megan and Timmy brought Caprice a large box. When Caprice checked the tag, she saw it was from her mom and Nana.

"Do you know anything about this?" she murmured to Grant.

"Not me," he said. "No one told me anything. I was just supposed to get you here."

Bella said to Grant, "We're going to ask you to do something unusual."

Uh-oh.

"Can you go into the kitchen and stay there until Caprice opens this one? I'll call you back in then. I promise."

"Why does he have to leave?" Caprice asked.

"Not leave," Bella assured her. "We just don't want him to see this."

"Okay," Grant said, after a hand squeeze for Caprice, and a questioning look at Bella. Caprice heard Bella murmur to him, "Some things you're just not supposed to see until the wedding."

"Got it," he said with a smile and left the room.

Caprice's fingers shook a little as she opened the box that was as big as a coat box. She couldn't imagine what it was. After she tore off the silver wrap, she lifted the white lid and pushed back the tissue paper. She lifted out a beautiful finger-tip-length veil that was embroidered all around the edges.

Nana sat forward on her chair. "That, *tesorina mia*, is the veil you can wear at your reception. It's just the right length not to get in your way."

"It's beautiful! Thank you." She went and gave her mom and Nana a hug and a kiss. "I don't know what to say."

Her mother explained, "You can wear the cathedral-length veil for the wedding and to make your entrance at the reception if you'd like. The shorter veil is for the reception itself so you can move around freely and have fun."

"I don't know how to thank you."

"No thanks necessary," Nana and her mom said at the same time.

Bella assured her, "I'll keep the veil at my place along with the other one and your gown. Then you don't have to worry about Grant getting a look at anything."

Bella helped Caprice fold the veil while her mother and Nana passed around another tray of cannoli. Once the veil was boxed, Bella took it out to her car. That's when Roz brought Grant back in.

"And no one's going to tell me a thing, are they?" Grant asked.

"Not a thing," Ace assured him. "We're all sworn to secrecy. Caprice won't decorate any more houses for us if we let it slip."

The group laughed.

As all of the guests stood, stretched their legs, and nibbled some more, Ace approached Caprice and Grant. His stiff, spiked brown hair was short enough that the two-carat diamond earring was obvious. Now in his early fifties, the rock legend was making a comeback with more than his career. His green eyes sparkled. "I just want you to know I'll make it a point to be home the weekend of your wedding," he assured them.

Caprice said, "I know you have commitments for your tour."

"I blocked out a couple of weeks in May, hoping one of them would be your wedding. My luck held because one of them is. Besides, that will give me a block of time to spend with Trista and Marsha. I understand there's going to be construction at Caprice's house."

"There is," Grant said. "We'll have to figure out how to make my townhouse home base until the construction is finished. We don't want to subject the pets and ourselves to all the noise and the smells and the bedlam."

"That makes sense," Ace confirmed and added, "If you get through this wedding and then the construction of an addition, and you're still together after that, I'd say the rest of your marriage is smooth sailing."

Caprice hoped Ace was kidding. But when she snuck a look at Grant, she saw the expression on his face and knew that Ace was right. But they *would* get through it. She and Grant had been through tough times before. A wedding, a reception, family involved in both, and construction on her house that would change it forever wouldn't be difficult as long as they loved each other.

Right?

Chapter Four

In the early afternoon on Monday, after Caprice had finished with client appointments, she drove to Rambling Vines Winery with her check. She parked where she'd parked before because Michelle had told her she'd be in the winery office.

Again, Caprice spotted the adorable dog on the porch. He was lying in a bed Michelle had obviously fixed for him there. He had a water bowl and a food bowl, and the food bowl still had kibble in it. The pooch ran over to Caprice as she climbed the steps. Holding out her hand first again, she let the Schnoodle smell it. Crouching down, she rubbed him behind both ears and he seemed to love that.

"I don't think you're allowed inside, are you? Actually, I'm surprised you're still here." Maybe Michelle had decided to keep him. "I'm going to have to go inside without you."

The dog looked at her sadly as if he knew exactly what she was saying.

"When I come back out, I'll give you a belly rub. How's that?"

The Schnoodle gave a little yip. Caprice patted him a last time and then went inside.

The tasting room was empty. She knew the offices were located down the hall. At the head of the hallway, she called, "Michelle, are you here?"

Michelle appeared a few seconds later and beckoned to her. "Come into my office. We can talk there."

Once Caprice was inside the office and Michelle sat behind the desk, Caprice asked her, "So the stray is still hanging around?"

"He's so cute. When Travis isn't around, I let him in here. But Travis is here today, so he has to stay out on the porch or in the screened-in room down at the house. I called all the vets and I put an ad in the community paper. No one has claimed him yet."

Caprice took the check out of her purse and laid it on Michelle's desk.

Avoiding her eyes, Michelle said, "Thank you. I really appreciate this."

Caprice might be mistaken but she thought Michelle almost looked ready to cry.

"Michelle, Grant and I are worried. We've heard rumors about the winery. We want to make sure our wedding reception isn't going to be ruined."

Michelle shook her head. "I promise you all will go well, though I do have to admit your reception might be the last one at the winery."

Before Caprice could follow up on that statement, a loud male voice yelled, "Michelle, come here."

"That's in the winery," Michelle muttered. Without even an "excuse me," she took off running down the hall.

After Caprice followed her through swinging metal doors, they could both see that Travis was the one who had yelled. He was holding a teenager by the scruff of his neck. The blond boy, who was wearing jeans, an oversized T-shirt, and scuffed up sneakers, looked to be about seventeen or eighteen. What held Caprice's attention, as well as Travis's and Michelle's, was the vial the boy held in his hand.

Travis gave the boy a little shake, and Caprice wanted to stop him from doing that. Travis's face was red and he looked about ready to explode. "I caught him trying to dump whatever is in that vial into the vat. It would ruin the wine."

"I didn't know what I was doing," the boy said. "I thought it was a joke."

"A joke? It would ruin my business," Travis shouted back angrily.

Caprice didn't know if she could intervene, but she had to try. "What's your name?" she asked the boy.

"It's Andy. Andy Sprenkle."

"I don't care what his name is," Travis protested. "If he doesn't start talking, I'm calling the police."

Michelle put her hand on her husband's arm but he shook it off. Still, she suggested in a calm voice, "Travis, go easy. There was no harm done. Unless you want him arrested for trespassing."

"I want answers," Travis insisted. "What do you mean, you thought this was a joke?"

"I just answered a post online at a job website," Andy maintained. "My instructions were to pick up the vial and the directions about what to do with it from a locker at the gym. The key was waiting for me at the desk. If I took a picture with my phone of pouring the vial into the vat, I'd earn five hundred dollars for doing it."

Caprice noticed a thunderous look cross Travis's face. "I know who's behind this and I'll kill him when I find him."

Andy looked downright scared now. "I didn't mean any harm. Honest."

"Come outside with me," Travis ordered the boy. "We're going to talk and then I'll decide if I'm calling the police."

Travis took the teenager out through a back entrance. Michelle and Caprice followed and peered out the door.

"I want to make sure he's not going to hurt him," Michelle said.

"If he tries to, *you* might have to call the police."

"I have my phone in my pocket," Michelle assured her.

Caprice checked her watch. "I'm going to have to get going. I have a video conference with a client in about twenty minutes. But is there anything you want to talk about before I go?"

"No, not really."

"Do you know who might have wanted to ruin the wine? I know Travis is right about it hurting your business. If you're already having problems, that sure wouldn't help."

"I don't know who he has in mind."

An instinctive feeling in Caprice's solar plexus told her Michelle was lying. But that really *wasn't* any of her business. There were obvious problems at this winery that she couldn't solve.

However, after she said good-bye to Michelle, gave the Schnoodle his belly rub, climbed into her Camaro and pulled out of the parking lot, she wondered just how those problems were going to affect her wedding reception.

Caprice traveled to Baltimore the next day to meet with a contractor about decorating his homes. On her way back, she stopped at Nana's to pick up Lady who'd spent the day with her and her cat Valentine. After Caprice visited with Nana while stroking Valentine, a gray tabby, she gave her Nana a hug and a kiss and Lady followed her to her car.

When she motioned Lady inside the passenger side, Caprice asked her, "How does takeout sound tonight?"

Lady barked.

"Exactly what I was thinking. I'll text Grant and see if he can pick up Chinese." They hadn't had dinner together last night because they'd both had work to do. She'd called him, though, to tell him what had happened at the winery. He was coming over tonight so they could discuss it again and spend time together.

Grant arrived about an hour after she got home with five cartons of Chinese, a sampling of three main dishes and two cartons of rice.

"You're hungry, I take it?" Caprice asked.

He grinned that grin that made her heart flutter. "I am. But I also know how you like to taste some of each one." After he set the food on the table, he wrapped his arm around her and gave her a long kiss. Patches had already run to Lady and they were both at the cat tree annoying Sophia who lounged halfway up.

"We could let them play outside while we eat," Grant suggested. "That way they can run off energy and settle down when they come in."

Caprice nodded as she pulled yellow and turquoise plates from the cupboard and placed them on the bright placemats on her table. While Grant let the dogs out, she scooped up utensils, positioning them at each place setting.

After Grant returned, she asked, "Water, iced tea, or coffee?"

"How about iced tea with the meal and coffee afterward?"

"You were reading my mind."

"I'd better become an expert at that. I hear it comes in handy when you're married."

His smile and the darkening of his gray eyes made her feel warm, but most of all loved.

"How did your meeting in Baltimore go?" he asked as he pulled out a chair at the table.

"It went well." She poured glasses of iced tea as she went on, "I prepared my budget and a list of furniture I can either rent or buy, depending on Roland Vaughn's plans. He told me to go ahead and purchase it. That way he can sell the homes as is. I have to refrain from being too unique. I can't decorate them as I would stage one of my houses."

"You don't think anyone would buy a house decorated in lime, fuchsia, and turquoise?"

She'd told him about her "Bohemian Rhapsody" client. "Not for the model homes, though I hope to give each one a unique touch with either antiques that fit in or else a standout decorative wall piece. And I'm not doing taupe and gray. I talked to Nolan about that. Color is okay with him as long as I keep it muted. So I'll probably go with tones of sage and cream, a touch of yellow and blue."

"Seaside colors."

"Possibly for one of the houses. After all, we *are* near the Chesapeake Bay. How was your day?" she asked as she sat across from him.

"Nothing unusual. A few wills. I drew up powers of attorney—that sort of thing."

"Did you talk much to Vince?"

Grant narrowed his eyes. "What about? When you ask that, I know you have something in mind."

She tapped her temple. "Reading my mind already. You're ahead of the game."

Grant shook his head. "What do you want to know?"

After a brief hesitation, she said, "I just wondered if Vince mentioned if Roz brought up Michelle."

Grant cast a narrowed-eye look in her direction. "And you really think we talk about that?"

She twirled lo mein noodles onto her fork. "It's a possibility."

Grant spooned half of the sweet-and-sour chicken onto a mound of rice on his plate. "Vince was in court most of the day, so I hardly saw him. When I did see him, we talked about baseball."

Caprice frowned. "That's no help at all."

Her phone buzzed. She'd set it on the counter to charge. "That could be Juan. He was going to check in on availability of a few rental pieces for the bohemian house."

Grant nodded. He was used to her business calls and she was used to his. But when she pulled her phone from the plug and saw that Vince was calling, she was puzzled. "It's Vince," she told Grant.

"Were your ears burning?" she asked him. "Grant and I were just talking about you."

"Caprice, this is serious."

She heard a note of panic in her brother's voice. "What's serious?"

"Travis Dodd was found in the tasting room at the winery this morning. He was stabbed in the neck with a double-bladed cheese knife. Michelle finally called me to help her because she's at the police station being questioned. They've kept her for hours. I'm on my way there. Roz's phone keeps going to voice mail. Can you find her and tell her what's happening?"

"Exactly what *is* happening?" Caprice asked.

"Michelle didn't know who else to call, so she called me. For the time being, I'm going to act as her lawyer."

Caprice frowned, knowing this was a mistake on so many levels. "Vince, you shouldn't."

"Don't even go there," he ordered. "Just find Roz for me, will you? Tell her what's going on. I'll get home as soon as I can. I'm going to cut off the questioning. From what Michelle told me, she's already been over what happened too many times."

"I'll find Roz," Caprice promised. "But, Vince, don't you think Michelle needs to hire another lawyer . . . a criminal defense attorney?"

"One decision at a time, Caprice. One decision at a time."

Chapter Five

"Where do you think Roz could be?" Grant asked Caprice as they filled Kong balls for their dogs which would disseminate treats when the dogs played with them. Lady and Patches started nosing the toys with kibble as soon as Grant rolled them onto the kitchen floor.

Caprice didn't bother with a coat, just grabbed her purse. Grant took his keys from his pocket. "Let's take the SUV."

As Caprice thought about the question Grant had asked, they climbed into his vehicle. "Roz usually keeps her phone on no matter where she goes. The only place that she might be unreachable would be at the Green Tea Spa. They won't give information about their clients whether they're there or not, but we can drive by their parking lot and see if Roz's car is there."

Since Grant thought that was a good idea, that's what they did.

In the parking lot of the Green Tea Spa, Caprice pointed out the window at the little red hybrid. "That's Roz's. Do you want to wait here while I run in?"

"That's probably a good idea. I don't think Roz would want me to see her with mud all over her face."

Caprice groaned at his attempt at humor, unfastened her seatbelt, climbed out and dashed toward the entrance to Green Tea Spa. Now and then she went to the spa herself on special occasions, like the time she gave Bella a gift certificate for her birthday and Bella wanted company, or if her mom decided they all needed a spa day.

Fortunately, Caprice knew the receptionist who sat at the desk. She quickly glanced around what was supposed to be a relaxing atmosphere. On a side wall, a black fountain dripping water down at least five tiers played its own liquid tune and somehow fit in with the soft instrumental music in the background. The reception area was painted seafoam green, somewhere between aqua and blue. Ergonomic furniture upholstered in shades of blue surrounded large hassocks where anyone waiting could put up their feet and relax.

Caprice said "Hi" to the receptionist who sat at a Plexiglas desk that looked as if it was floating in air. It wasn't, of course, because it held a computer. But it gave a light airy affect to the rest of the décor. The metal sculpture of a yin yang symbol that hung on the wall reminded clients that everyone had a masculine and feminine side. One of the other walls held a grouping of photographs from the purple and blues of the Grand Canyon, to the red rocks of Sedona, to the beach at Big Sur and the rocky shore of Maine.

The receptionist asked Caprice, "Can I help you?"

"I come here for treatments sometimes," Caprice said honestly.

The receptionist suddenly recognized her. "You're Caprice De Luca."

"I am and I have an emergency, or rather one of your clients has an emergency. Roz Winslow is having a treatment. I wonder if you could send her out as soon as possible."

The receptionist said, "Give me a minute," and scooted down the hall. A few minutes later she came back and said, "Danielle is with Roz. She says she knows you. She's been to your open houses. She'll tell you where to go."

Caprice had taken yoga classes here too, as well as a self-defense course. She supposed it was a good thing the staff remembered her . . . or maybe not.

Danielle, a petite blonde, motioned to Caprice from a set of double doors. Once Caprice reached the doors, Danielle said, "Roz asked for you to come back instead of her coming out. She finished the body wrap and massage and is now having a facial. But you can talk to her."

Caprice hurried in and found Roz in a motorized lounge chair that was laid back. She had white goop all over her face but Caprice could tell it was Roz from her slim figure in the robe and her green eyes.

"What's wrong?" Roz asked. It seemed as if her

lips were moving but her face wasn't. "Danielle said it was an emergency. Is someone hurt?"

"That depends on how you look at it," Caprice answered.

"Don't talk to me in riddles, Caprice, while my face is getting stiff as a board. Soon I won't be able to ask questions."

"Maybe you'd better sit up."

"Some of the mask could fall off her face," Danielle said quickly.

"I don't think that's going to matter when she hears what I have to say. She might get a few more wrinkles."

That did it. Roz pressed the button to raise the back of her chair.

When she was staring at Caprice, totally perplexed, Caprice explained, "Travis Dodd was murdered. I don't have all the details yet, but apparently the police have been questioning Michelle for hours and she called Vince. Here is where I don't want you to over-react."

Roz waved her hand so Caprice would continue.

"Apparently she didn't know who else to call and Vince went to the police station to advise her."

Although Roz didn't comment, she picked up a towel lying over the arm of her chair and started rubbing at her face with it.

"Wait a minute," Danielle said. "You'll scratch your face. Let me get a moist towel."

Roz was already on her feet.

But Caprice stopped her panic. "There's no reason to hurry. Vince is at the police station, and he asked us to find you and tell you what was happening."

Danielle handed Roz a moist towel and she wiped the rest of the goop from her face. Although her face was buffed red, at least she looked like herself.

Roz said to Caprice, "All I can do is to go home and wait for him. Do you want to come with me?"

"Grant drove me over. Are you sure you want us there?"

"You need to find out the details too. Maybe you'll have to move your reception."

At the moment, Caprice wasn't worried about her reception. She was worried about Vince and Roz's relationship.

Caprice really liked the split-level home that Vince had bought and Roz had moved into with him. It had a few unique characteristics that gave the house charm, from a stone fireplace to a renovated kitchen with quartz countertops. Like most split-levels, it had three—a bedroom level, a living room and kitchen level, and a family room level.

Now as Caprice and Grant followed Roz into her home, she was silent. Grant clapped Caprice's shoulder and nodded to Roz who seemed to be walking in a daze to the kitchen.

"I'm going to give you and Roz time to talk. I'll go to your place and make sure the animals are okay."

"My place will soon be *our* place," Caprice reminded him with a smile.

He gave her a soft kiss on the lips. "Yes, it will, and I can't wait. Call me once Vince gets home, okay? And I'll come over."

Caprice went into the kitchen with Roz after Grant left. "Why don't I make us tea? Do you want herbal or do you need caffeine to be alert?"

"I don't want to mellow out now. Let's go with caffeine."

Caprice took the teapot and set it on the stove burner. Because she spent some time here, she also knew where Roz kept her tea. She took two mugs from the mug tree and put a teabag in each.

Finally Roz said, "I know Vince is your brother, so sometimes it's hard for me to talk to you about him."

Caprice's family was loyal to each other. But when there was a problem, they preferred to face it head on. "Tell me what you're thinking. We're friends, Roz. You can do that."

"Ever since Vince bought the house and wouldn't let me put any money into it, I've been concerned about his level of commitment."

"That's not news. I suspected you'd feel that way. Did you talk to Vince about it?"

"I tried but he just insists this way is simpler. That's what his lawyerly advice would be to any couple like us. How am I supposed to argue with that?"

Sometimes her brother's education got in the way of good sense and feelings. She hoped that wouldn't be the case.

Vince came home an hour later. As soon as Caprice heard his car, she called Grant. After all, they only lived a few blocks away. Grant arrived before Vince even had time to make himself a mug of coffee in the one-cup brewer.

Her brother wasn't talkative, so Caprice just let the moment settle. Roz didn't go to him and kiss him. He didn't go to her. The silence between them was a tension as taut as a charged electric line.

Vince motioned to the sofa in the living room. "Let's sit down and I'll tell you what I know."

While Vince sat next to Grant on the sofa with Caprice by his side, Roz sat in an armchair.

Vince, his handsome face troubled, his dark-brown hair mussed, turned to Caprice. "As I told you when I called, Travis was murdered in the tasting room with a cheese knife to the neck. It severed his carotid artery. Michelle found him sprawled over the chaise lounge."

"Is she a suspect?" Grant asked.

Vince ran his hand through his hair. "I'm sure Detective Jones thinks she is. He was the one questioning her. You know the spouse is always suspected first. I'll tell you, though, his attitude needs an adjustment. I felt like doing it for him but knew better."

"So you think the killer knew what he or she was doing?" Caprice asked. "I mean, did they know if they hit his carotid, he'd die? Or do the police think it was a lucky shot?"

"The autopsy might tell the detectives more, but for now they're focusing on Michelle and any other suspect they can find."

Finally Roz spoke. "Did you take Michelle home?"

Vince sighed with resignation, as if he'd expected the question. "The police picked her up so she didn't have a car. Yes, I took her home. I wanted to make sure she got home okay."

"Did you go in?" Roz's gaze was like a laser, focusing on Vince.

He obviously knew he was under her scrutiny and he didn't like it. He tersely stated, "Yes, I went in until she turned the lights on. Someone was murdered in their tasting room. I wanted to make sure the house was safe."

"I'm sure they have a security system," Roz said.

"Yes, they do. But even security systems can be breached. I might as well tell you, I'm meeting with her again tomorrow." His gaze was locked with Roz's, but then suddenly he broke it and turned toward Caprice. "Michelle requested that you be there."

"Me? Why?"

"I don't know. Maybe it has something to do with your wedding, but I'm supposed to bring you along."

Grant sat forward on the sofa cushion. "Vince, we're not criminal defense attorneys. She needs to retain somebody who is."

"It isn't going to come to that," Vince protested. "She's innocent."

But from the look Roz gave Vince, Caprice could tell her friend wasn't so sure. From the looks Roz and Vince were giving each other, they needed to talk, fight, and communicate somehow. They wouldn't be able to do it with other folks present.

Caprice elbowed Grant. "We'd better go."

Grant appeared to want to protest, as if he wanted to convince Vince finding another lawyer for Michelle would be the best thing to do. But the subject of lawyers just wasn't the topic Roz and Vince needed to talk about right now.

Caprice took Grant's hand and stood. "Vince, text me on what time you'll pick me up tomorrow."

"I'll do that," her brother confirmed. "Michelle's going to call me with the best time for her."

Caprice felt like rolling her eyes. That was exactly the wrong thing to say in front of Roz. Men!

First, she gave Vince a hug, then she went to Roz and did the same. She whispered in Roz's ear, "Try to listen, but make your feelings clear."

Roz gave a nod and, as Caprice pulled away, she saw her friend's eyes were moist with emotion. This whole situation wasn't going to be easy for anyone, not unless Vince had nothing more to do with Michelle.

Outside on the sidewalk, Grant took Caprice's arm. "You should have let me drill into Vince's head that he's not equipped to handle this."

"I'm not worried about whether he is or isn't," Caprice said. "I'm worried about Roz and Vince."

"They'll get through this," Grant assured her. "And when they do, their relationship will be stronger."

"Maybe so, but there's a reason they have a problem. Roz isn't convinced that Vince is committed to her since he wouldn't let her pay for part of the house. If she'd invested in it, she'd feel he trusted her and they were reaching the next level in their relationship."

"You already know why Vince decided not to," Grant reminded her.

"Oh, I know why. But common sense has nothing to do with this, feelings do. And there *is* a problem, a big one, if Vince is still attached to

Michelle by either guilt or affection . . . or even friendship."

As they reached the curb, Grant pulled Caprice into his arms and leaned his forehead against hers. "We have to let this play out. You know we do."

She nodded. "I know. It's just hard to stand by and watch them struggle."

"Roz and Vince watched us struggle. Let's give them the chance to figure this out on their own terms. We might have a worry of our own. We might have to look for a new venue for our wedding reception."

"If the murder was in the tasting room, the police will have the crime scene cleaned up in a few days. That really doesn't have anything to do with the reception hall."

"Except for the fact that there will be publicity. Do you think our guests will want to attend a wedding reception where a murder took place?"

The following morning Caprice found herself sitting in one of the parlors at the winery house with Vince and Michelle. After Travis's father died and Michelle and Travis rethought how they wanted to renovate and run the winery, they'd decided to let Caprice decorate the tasting room as well as the two-story brick Colonial with its east and west wings. They'd wanted the traditional out and contemporary in. The contemporary look Michelle had chosen consisted of silver and black and lots of glass. The rug on the floor was a geometrical black-and-white design. Every time Caprice had suggested pops of color in the room, neither Michelle or Travis had approved. So they'd gotten exactly what they'd wanted.

Right now, sitting across from Michelle in a black leather armchair, she paid attention as Michelle told Vince, "The police are riding me hard because I was alone when Travis was killed and I don't have an alibi."

"Where were you?" Vince asked. He turned to Caprice. "I didn't let Michelle answer that last night."

"I took a drive." Her chin went up and Caprice knew there was more to the story than that.

"Why did you take a drive?" Caprice asked.

"Travis and I had an argument," Michelle said with a sigh.

"What was the argument about?" Vince queried.

"I had talked to Travis's CFO, Neil Allen, about increasing the amount of a severance package that Travis had put together for Fred Schmidt, an employee he'd let go. The older man was furious that Travis had fired him after he'd been working at the winery for twenty-five years."

Although Caprice had supervised the decorating of the tasting room, she'd never met Fred Schmidt. He must have worked in the back where the grapes were unloaded and the wine was created.

"Why did Travis let him go?" Vince asked.

"Because of budget cuts," Michelle answered, shaking her head.

"And you spoke to this Neil Allen because you felt sorry for Fred?" Vince queried.

"It wasn't just that. His wife has been ill and this

is the worst time for him to lose his job. But Travis wouldn't even consider increasing it and he was angry that I'd gone to Neil."

Vince must have had a list of questions in his head because he asked next, "Where did the argument occur?"

"We were in Travis's office in the winery."

"Did anyone overhear?"

Looking worried, Michelle shook her head. "I don't think so. I think all the employees were gone by then."

"But you don't know for sure." Vince's words were a statement, not a question.

"Not for sure," Michelle admitted.

Michelle addressed Caprice this time. "I asked you to sit in because I want your help in figuring out who killed Travis. I know you and Grant can't want the suspicion of murder hanging over my head at the time of your reception. Will you help me?" There was a pleading note in her voice and maybe one of fear too.

Before Caprice could answer, Vince jumped in. "Grant won't like it if you do."

Caprice said factually, "My guess is Roz doesn't like you helping either."

Vince's face turned a little ruddy.

"This is Grant's wedding reception too," Caprice told Vince. "He's going to want this cleared up as much as I do." That was one reason she should help, but there was another. She needed to do it for Vince and Roz's sake. The sooner the murder was solved, the sooner Vince and Michelle would have no connection.

"I'll help you any way I can," Michelle said. "Ask me any question you want. I really have nothing to hide."

Famous last words, Caprice thought.

"I'm going to need you to think about a place to start," Caprice directed. "I need to know anyone who you think would be a possible suspect. You can think about it this afternoon and e-mail me tonight. Can you think of anybody off the top of your head, besides of course, Fred Schmidt?"

"Fred was a gentle soul who only cared about making good wine."

"Even when he was fired? Did he threaten Travis?"

"From what I heard, he was pretty angry," Michelle confessed. "He went toward Travis with his fist raised and Neil stopped him."

Suspect number one, Caprice thought. A cheese knife wasn't a heavy weapon to wield. "Anyone else off the top of your head?"

Michelle was thinking about Caprice's question when the doorbell sounded through the house. "Excuse me," Michelle said, standing and exiting the parlor into the marble-floored foyer.

Caprice could only see Michelle's back. When Michelle opened the door, she straightened and froze.

"Jarrett! What are you doing here?" Michelle's voice was filled with surprise and maybe dismay.

The Schnoodle darted in the door, obviously taking advantage of no one keeping him out. Michelle turned to see where the dog had gone but Caprice noticed her face had gone pale, and she looked . . . stunned.

"Do you want me to catch him?" Caprice asked.

"No, he's probably headed for the kitchen. Nancy's in there making lunch. She'll give him something to eat."

"Do you want me to take him to my vet to have him scanned and see if he has an owner?"

Michelle shook her head. "I was going to do that, but then everything happened. Give me another day or two."

The gentleman at the door wandered in. He looked to be about Michelle's age. He was dressed in pressed khakis and wore a Ralph Lauren shirt. His loafers looked like Italian leather. He had dark-brown hair, parted to the side and gelled a bit, but not so much that it looked like a fifties style or fake. His handsome features reminded her of somebody . . . and then Michelle made who he was very clear.

"Pardon my manners," she said to all of them. "Caprice and Vince, this is Jarrett Dodd, Travis's brother."

From the look still present on Michelle's face, Caprice knew this brother was going to be one of the suspects too.

Chapter Six

The following morning, Caprice, her mom, and Nana had been paging through an album of floral bouquets at Posies Flower Shop for a half hour. Along with Jeanie Boswell, the florist, they discussed flowers for the church as well as for the reception.

"I want it all to look vintage," Caprice reminded them. "Yet I'd like the flowers to complement my color theme of floral pastels for the reception."

"Maybe we should have waited until Bella and Nikki could join us here," Nana suggested.

"I think we're going about this all wrong," her mother said. "You're looking at all these photos and getting confused. Just tell us what *you* want in your bouquets."

Thinking about Travis's murder in spite of herself, Caprice tried to concentrate on flowers. What *did* she like best? "I like roses," she said. "But I'd like something more unusual to put with them to make the bouquets and arrangements unique."

Caprice looked toward her Nana. "When I say *vintage,* what flowers come to your mind?"

"That's easy for me," Nana said. "When I think of vintage I think of roses and peonies. I've always had them in my yard. They're in your mother's yard now."

"I never thought about peonies." Caprice looked at Jeanie. "Would they be possible?"

"*Anything* is possible," Jeanie said with a smile. She pulled a scrapbook from the shelf behind the counter. "This is my personal scrapbook of favorites that I've found in magazines or online, even in advertisements. I want to show you one particular arrangement for the unity candle. I imagine you'll be using that at St. Francis?"

"Yes, we will," Caprice said.

Jeanie paged through her scrapbook until she came to what she wanted. Then she turned the book around and placed it in front of Caprice. "Take a look at that arrangement as a whole. Think about roses and peonies replacing the mums and using Queen Anne's lace for the white-and-frill aspect."

Studying the arrangement, Caprice could easily envision her wedding bouquet. "How about pale pink peonies and white roses in my bouquet? For my bridesmaids, we can use pastel colored roses— yellow, lavender, pink, and white. I can see a white rose boutonniere for Grant and maybe lavender for the other groomsmen."

"I can picture it," her mom said. "I think your flowers will be unique and very pretty."

"For the unity candle, I'd use the pink peonies and white roses, Queen Anne's lace, and ferns,"

Jeanie explained. "The other table arrangements can be a combination of those and pastel roses."

"And how about white tulle bows on the church pews?" Jeanie asked.

"I like that idea," Caprice agreed. "I'll have to check this all out with Nikki, Bella, and Roz when I can reach them. They didn't come today because they said the flowers were my choice. The bridesmaid dresses are florals and different styles in the same pastels."

Nana and her mom exchanged a look. Her mom said, "About the table arrangements. Are you sure you don't want to change your venue from Rambling Vines to somewhere else?"

"Oh, right," Jeanie said, "because of the murder there."

Caprice sighed and explained her reasoning for keeping the reception at the winery. "The murder was in the tasting room. The reception building is separate. Besides, I don't think it's right to take business away from Michelle if she's innocent."

"*If* she's innocent?" Nana asked.

"After speaking with her, my gut tells me she is," Caprice said. "But that's certainly not proof. She's going to have a hard enough time keeping the winery afloat without me taking business away. Besides, there aren't any other venues available at this late date. Our wedding is only three weeks away."

Her mother patted her elbow. "It's your choice and Grant's. We just want everything about your wedding to be perfect."

"Nothing is perfect, Mom. You know that. Grant and I decided no matter what happens, no matter

who trips over what, or who spills what or who
ruins what, our vows are what matter. Being happy
that day is what matters. I don't want to be nervous
about my dress or my shoes or my veil. I just want
to think about starting my life with Grant."

Nana gave Caprice a hug. "That's the way it
should be. Why don't you see if you can get hold
of your bridesmaids right now? Then we can order
exactly what we want."

Moving her scrapbook back to the shelf, Jeanie
turned toward the counter once more. "Who will
be overseeing your flower order, and who will be at
the wedding venue in order to receive it?"

"Nikki will be checking on the flowers with you
and making sure everything's there."

"She'll be handling the catering too," Nana reminded Caprice. "Are you sure that won't be too
much for her? I can certainly go over the flower
order with Jeanie."

"I think Nikki is going to let her assistants handle the catering. She knows exactly what we want
and she trusts her staff. But she will be checking
on everything as soon as Mass is over and she arrives at the winery. So it would be great if you
could handle the flowers, Nana."

"Before you make a final decision on the flowers," Jeanie said, "will the mother of the bride's
dress, the mother of the groom's dress, and your
Nana's dress all tie in?"

"Mine is rose-colored," Fran said. "No problem
there."

"And mine is a beautiful aqua," Nana chimed
in. "It will fit in with the pastels."

Both her mom and her Nana looked toward

Caprice. Finally her mother asked, "What about Grant's mother?"

"She hasn't found a dress yet," Caprice told them. "Their town in Vermont doesn't have a bridal shop so she needs to go farther afield."

"In a way that's good," Nana commented. "You can tell her your color scheme and she can either fit in or not. She shouldn't have a problem finding a dress in a spring color. You're making this easy with the pastels."

"I know what Caprice is thinking," Fran whispered to Nana.

"What am I thinking?" Caprice asked warily.

"You're thinking that nothing might be easy with Grant's mother."

"Mom—" Caprice had a warning note in her voice. Grant's mother wasn't anything like her own mom. Caprice's parents were emotive and huggers and good communicators. Grant's parents were, well, reserved. Caprice didn't know how his mother would take the news of a color scheme, but she'd never know if she didn't call her and tell her.

"I think I'll call Grant's mom before I call Nikki and Bella and Roz. Then there won't be any mistake about exactly what we want to order."

Caprice knew if anything went wrong with this wedding, it would have something to do with Grant's parents not liking what she and Grant had planned. Grant's father had already told him that adding the addition onto her house wasn't the best idea. He believed Grant should pick out the house and they both should live in it. Thank goodness Grant's ways weren't his dad's.

It might be a good thing his parents lived in Vermont and she and Grant would live in Pennsylvania.

That afternoon, as Caprice drove up the winding drive to the winery, she peered out at the fencing, the green grass, the grapevines already starting to produce. Even the house, tasting room, offices, and reception hall fit in with the surroundings. How could a place that looked so peaceful be a setting for a murder?

She was hoping she could find out more about that with Michelle. She didn't want to put a time cap on this visit, but she was supposed to meet Juan to discuss another house staging. She trusted him when he placed orders for rental furniture as well staging a house, but he always wanted her final okay. He insisted that was because she had a different touch than he did.

She supposed that was true. She'd brought her van today in case they needed all of her sample books. She'd told him what she was doing this morning, and he said to text him if she was going to be late. He really was the best assistant.

Caprice spotted the Schnoodle penned on the sunporch at the house. He was napping in a bed that easily fit him. Instead of disturbing him, Caprice walked down the brick lane to the front door.

When Michelle answered the door, she looked as if she hadn't slept. She invited Caprice inside to the same parlor where they'd sat before. "I have to let Nancy go," she said. "I've given her two weeks' notice."

Caprice remembered that Nancy was the Dodds' housekeeper and cook.

"You can't pay her salary?" Caprice guessed.

"Travis was the one who wanted her here. It doesn't make sense to have a housekeeper for just one person, let alone a cook. I know how to cook perfectly well. It was just that Travis said he liked Nancy's dishes better than mine. She'd been his father's housekeeper and Travis had known her since he was a teenager. It's not as if I'm turning her out in the cold. One of my friends is going to hire her. She has two kids and Nancy will love that. I'm sure she'll be happier there."

"It's nice of you to find a job for her."

"She's been here for years. I couldn't just let her go with a minimal severance package. This way she'll have severance and a new gig. Would you like coffee or iced tea?"

Caprice shook her head. "No, I'm fine. Thank you. Did you make a suspect list for me?" Michelle had never e-mailed her names.

Michelle leaned back in the black leather club chair. "I didn't need to make a list. I have the names in my head. But it's not like I know anything for sure."

Caprice took her electronic tablet from her purse. "I understand that. Just tell me your thoughts and we'll go from there."

"The first person I thought of was Neil."

"Travis's CFO?"

Michelle nodded. "There has been tension/between Travis and Neil over the past few months, but neither would talk about it."

Caprice tapped in Neil's name. "Next?"

"I'm more sure about this one," Michelle noted. "Our closest neighbor hasn't liked being in proximity to the winery since we built the events room. He's especially been protesting about increased traffic on the rural road. He even took his complaints to the town council. The traffic might bother him but I think there's a bottom line to his thinking."

"Something to do with the winery itself?"

"Oh, yes. He doesn't drink, and he doesn't want anyone else to drink either. He definitely doesn't approve of our dance events whether it be square-dancing or ballroom dancing. What puts him high on my list is that he monitors his property carefully and he has a shotgun he pulls out if anyone trespasses on his land. Andrei Moldovan has been a widow for a long time and he's gotten crankier and crankier each year. If he came over here to confront Travis and they got into an argument, I can easily see him reaching for the cheese knife in a rage."

Caprice typed an asterisk next to Moldovan's name. He definitely had to be looked into. "Anyone else?"

Michelle wouldn't meet her gaze.

"Michelle, I can't help you if you're not honest with me. I saw your expression when you opened the door to Travis's brother. What caused the shock?"

"It's complicated."

"Family matters usually are."

With a sigh, Michelle met Caprice's even stare.

"Jarrett has always been the prodigal son. Travis was the one who, from a young age, was involved in the wine making business and wanted to be."

"Jarrett wanted no part of the business?"

Michelle shook her head. "I don't think he did. Still, he didn't want to flat out tell his father that." Michelle's fingers tapped on the arm of her chair as if she was restless . . . or anxious. But she continued with, "Jarrett left home after college to backpack through Europe. He used the excuse that he wanted to experience vineyards there. The truth was, he was never really interested in making wine. After Europe he moved to Hawaii, worked in a restaurant and surfed. He kept in touch with Travis on and off, a call at Christmas, that type of thing. He usually didn't hold a job longer than a year."

"I hear a 'but' coming," Caprice determined.

"Everything changed after William died. I don't know if Travis asked Jarrett to come home or Jarrett volunteered on his own. But in their dad's will, they both inherited the winery. Neither of them realized that their father had been sinking all of his money into the winery for years and not getting a decent return. Since the two of them were in it together, they made the decision to take the cash they'd inherited and rejuvenate the wines and the winery. William did have stocks and bonds and a retirement account. But after a year of working with Travis, Jarrett had had enough of the business and he was ready to roam again."

"No reason to stay? Or was there an inciting incident that made him want to leave?" Caprice guessed.

Michelle's eyes misted a bit. "Oh, there was an inciting incident all right. After a rough day of Travis being difficult to get along with while I worked on the PR and event planning, Jarrett was comforting me. Travis walked in and accused Jarrett of making a pass at me which wasn't true. That day, Travis decided to buy Jarrett out so the winery would be his and his alone. He sold one of his restored cars, mortgaged the property, and made a settlement with Jarrett without consulting me."

"Was that usual for him not to consult you?" Caprice was beginning to get a picture of a man who liked to be in control of everyone around him.

"Yes, it was usual for him to make decisions without me, at least after we were married for about a year."

Caprice circled back to what she wanted to discuss. "Let's get back to Jarrett. Did he and Travis part on friendly terms?"

A deep male voice suddenly interrupted the discussion. "My brother and I were *never* on friendly terms." Apparently Jarrett had come down the stairs and overheard what they were saying. Caprice hadn't realized he was at home, but certainly Michelle had known that. Was there a reason she hadn't told Caprice?

No matter. Now she could question Jarrett herself. She motioned to him. "Come on in and join our discussion."

Jarrett appeared to be more curious about her than defensive. "Michelle told me about you. You help the police solve murders."

"Circumstances have just happened that way.

One of the detectives and I have a decent relationship, so if I find important information, I share it with him," Caprice explained.

Michelle asked, "The detective dating Nikki?"

"He's the one—Brett Carstead. He's a good guy with no ax to grind. He just wants to get to the bottom of the investigation and find the truth."

"How quaint," Jarrett commented.

That comment irked Caprice in a way. Jarrett had taken a seat on the loveseat. She turned to him and asked, "Do you have an alibi for the night Travis was killed?"

To her surprise, Jarrett didn't seem perturbed at all by her question. He shook his head. "No, I don't. Like Michelle, I spent the evening alone in my apartment in Maryland."

"I understand you have a long résumé of different jobs." Caprice intended to keep up a bit of pressure to throw him.

But he wasn't thrown. His comeback included a tone of amusement. "Michelle, have you been sharing my history again?"

Michelle looked a bit embarrassed but she didn't comment.

Swinging his focus back to Caprice, he admitted, "Yes, I have taken a lot of different jobs. Before you ask, yes, I'm working now. I work in a crab shack on the bay. I'm doing some of the cooking and I'm thinking about going to culinary school. I actually have a benefactor who will pay for it."

For obvious reasons, Caprice guessed the benefactor was a woman. She wouldn't go there . . . yet.

After another half hour of conversation, Caprice

decided she couldn't learn any more from Michelle or Jarrett.

Jarrett said to Michelle, "I'm going to take that dog for a walk. Okay with you?"

"He'd probably like that," Michelle answered.

Maybe Michelle had changed her mind about keeping the Schnoodle.

After Caprice said her good-byes, Michelle walked her to the door. Caprice was strolling down the brick lane to the parking lot when she saw someone she wasn't sure she wanted to see. Brett Carstead was exiting his car. She hesitated, then continued down the walk until she met Brett at the entrance to the parking lot.

Brett's sunglasses hid his eyes as he said, "I'm sure you're at this winery on wedding reception business, not for any reason involving the murder, right?"

Caprice wasn't going to lie to him so she kept silent.

He shook his head and lifted his sunglasses to the top of his head. She supposed he wanted her to see the seriousness in his eyes.

"I know you have a stake in this investigation because of the wedding, but you need to stay clear of it," he commanded her.

"Don't give me a lecture," Caprice advised him. "Because I'm going to tell you the truth. I won't stay clear of it, and it's not just because of the wedding."

Brett gave her an odd look.

If she told Brett that Michelle and Vince once dated, would Vince be a suspect? Still, *anyone* could spill that bit of history. She'd trusted Brett before to do the right thing and to keep confidences. She had to trust him now.

He must have seen the debate inside her head because he asked, "What do you have to tell me, Caprice?"

Before she analyzed the situation too much, she revealed, "Did you know that Vince and Michelle once dated?"

Brett rubbed his hand over his face. "Now that you told me, I'm going to have to talk to Vince."

Caprice shook her head. "You can't. You know Vince is Michelle's lawyer, don't you?"

Brett's jaw jutted out and Caprice knew that stubborn look and probably what was coming. She was right.

"Michelle and Vince's client privilege isn't going to stop me from asking Vince about his former relationship with her. And you know who else I'm going to have to tell, don't you?"

"No, you don't."

"Yes, I do." He pulled out his phone.

With a sinking feeling in her stomach, Caprice knew he was calling his partner, Detective Jones.

She hurried to her van, unlocked the door, and then pulled out *her* phone.

Her brother's secretary answered the call. "Hi, Caprice. Grant's not here."

"I'd like to speak to my brother. Is he there?"

"Vince is in his office so I can put you through. Are you ready for your wedding? We're all so excited about that. I just can't wait to see you and Grant married. My hope for you and Grant fifty years from now is as Gene Perret once said, *Our wedding was many years ago. The celebration continues today.*"

"I can't wait to get married," Caprice assured her.

"That's as it should be. I'll patch you through to Vince."

Vince picked up immediately. "Hi, Caprice. What's up? Don't tell me you changed your mind about the tuxedos we picked out."

"No, this is serious, Vince. I made a mistake."

"What kind of mistake?"

"I told Brett that you'd once dated Michelle. He's calling Detective Jones as we speak. They're going to invite you in to talk about your relationship with her."

Vince was silent for a few heartbeats.

She rushed to say again, "I'm so sorry. I never should have told him. I have to remember he's a detective first and sort of a friend second."

Vince's response was immediate. "You can be friends with Brett when he's not involved in a murder investigation. But I understand why you told him. Full disclosure, right? Face it, Caprice. He would have found out soon enough. It would have looked bad if it hadn't come from one of us. So don't fret about it."

While she had Vince on the phone . . . "How are you and Roz?"

"That's a subject I don't want to talk about."

"Vince—"

"I mean it, Caprice. I don't need interference from you or Nikki or Bella."

She looked toward Brett and saw he was still on his phone. "Are you and Roz going to work things out?"

"There's nothing to work out. Michelle is consulting with me as a lawyer. Period."

"And Roz won't believe that?"

Her brother sighed. "She doesn't believe it's a lawyer-client relationship. But she has to trust me, Caprice, or else we don't have anything."

"Do *you* trust *her*?"

"Of course, I do."

Caprice could have asked then why he didn't ask Roz to buy into the house with him. Yet she didn't. Not now. Not yet. She'd find out from Roz if Roz talked to him about it because she had the feeling that Roz's distrust was based mostly on that fact. It had more to do with Vince's commitment to her than with Vince's past relationship with Michelle.

She could be wrong. She'd been wrong before. Time would tell.

Chapter Seven

When Caprice's doorbell rang that evening, she suspected who it might be. She checked the video monitor on her computer desk and she was right. It was Vince. She almost hated to answer the door but she knew she had to face him.

Lady ran with her to the door.

"Maybe *you* could talk to him instead of me," she said to Lady.

Lady tilted her head and stared straight at Caprice. Caprice thought she gave a little nod.

She'd definitely been at her computer too long.

After she opened the door, Vince opened the screened storm door. He looked rough. He was still wearing his office white Oxford shirt and black dress slacks, but he'd opened the top three buttons of his shirt and his tie hung down from the collar. His shirt was wrinkled and the truth was, sometimes in the middle of the day, Vince changed shirts so he could keep his starched look. It was the lawyer façade. Or the "appearances counted" motto. She wasn't always sure which.

But now it was more than his clothes that looked bedraggled. It was his face. He didn't just look tired, he almost looked defeated. She was afraid to hear what he had to say.

"Come on in," she said. "Coffee, iced tea, water, or wine?"

"I'd like some of that bourbon Dad likes so much, but I'll take the water. Better yet, give me black coffee. I still have work to do tonight."

"You have it with you?" Caprice asked. He wasn't carrying his brief case.

"No, I stopped in to give you a report, and to get a reprieve before I go home to Roz."

That didn't sound good. However, she didn't question him about Roz just yet. "Living room or kitchen?" she asked him.

He stooped down to pet Lady and spent a good long time doing it. "The kitchen. If I sit in your living room I might fall asleep."

"Sleepless nights?"

"What do you think?"

"I think you need a cream puff with peanut butter cream filling. I made them for tomorrow when Grant comes for supper."

As they walked into the kitchen, Lady between them, Vince asked, "So I get one before Grant? What an honor."

Caprice slugged his shoulder as she'd often done when they were kids.

He rubbed his arm. "Ow. You pack too much of a punch. It must be all that swimming you do at the gym."

She'd gotten back into her swimming routine with the warmer weather. Come to think of it, she really should go tomorrow morning. Maybe.

Caprice brewed a pot of strong coffee. She didn't know how long Vince would stay but he might need more than one cup. He took a seat at the table and, all of a sudden, Mirabelle appeared and hopped up on the chair next to him. She peeked at him from under the table and gave a soft meow.

He ran his fingers through her long, soft white fur. "She's really at home here now."

"Yes, she is. She's part of the family." Caprice took a cream puff shell from the container and filled it with pudding from the refrigerator. Then she set it in front of Vince. "Okay, now that you've caught your breath, tell me what happened."

"Detective Jones called me to come in for questioning."

"Oh, Vince. I thought Brett might do it himself."

"Not a good idea since he's dating Nikki. This was the right way to do it."

"And how was Jones? Brash and mean?"

"I didn't give him a chance to be brash and mean. I didn't tell him much more than the time period I dated Michelle and the reason we broke up. When he asked me if I'd seen her since then, I told him I had—once."

Caprice had been in the middle of filling her own cream puff when her head snapped up so she could stare at Vince. "You *have* seen her since then?"

"Don't you become an interrogator too," Vince groused. "Around Christmas we ran into each other at the Koffee Klatch when she was shopping. We spoke for a few minutes and then she went on her way. That was it."

When Vince said that was it, then that was it, Caprice hoped.

"Does Roz know you ran into her around Christmas?"

Vince took a large bite of the cream puff before he answered. Then he licked his lips, wiped his mouth with a napkin, and grimly said, "She does now. I told her before I went to the police station, knowing it would come up."

"Do I want to ask you about that discussion?"

"There wasn't much discussion and, as I said before, I don't want to talk about it."

When Vince didn't want to talk about something, he didn't. At this moment, she'd respect his privacy. All she could do for tonight was ply her brother with cream puffs and coffee and hope from now and going forward he made wise decisions about Michelle . . . *and* about Roz.

The following morning Lady decided to wake Caprice by chasing Sophia down the stairs. How eight paws could be as loud as thunder, Caprice didn't know, but they were. Mirabelle, who was stretched out next to Caprice on the bed gave a soft purring sound as Caprice petted her.

She ran her hand down Mirabelle's body enjoying the feel of the cotton-soft fur. "Some people clip their Persians," Caprice told Mirabelle.

Mirabelle opened one golden eye as if to say, *Don't you even think about it.*

After Caprice rubbed Mirabelle under her chin, she received another purr. "Okay, kitto," she said. "Time to rise and shine. I think I'll feed you girls breakfast and take Lady for a walk before I get a shower today. We'll work all morning, but this afternoon I might have to be out and about."

Mirabelle yawned, opened both eyes, and then slowly rose to her paws.

In the doorway to her bedroom, Caprice asked Mirabelle, "Are you coming?"

Mirabelle gave another yawn, stretched, and then jumped off the bed to follow Caprice down the stairs.

A half hour later, as soon as Caprice and Lady went out her front door, she could tell the temperature was about fifty-five. But the sun was shining brightly and the sky was blue. It was a perfect spring day.

As Caprice walked Lady along her street, she noticed daffodils blooming in neighbors' yards. Some forsythia bushes had burst into bloom already, and she realized hyacinths wouldn't be far behind. They walked two blocks on her side of the street, crossed over, and strolled down that side under the maples and elms that were budding with leaves.

Usually Lady heeled and Caprice didn't have to worry about her tugging on her leash. As a plus, she'd taught her to stay in that square beside her with treats and praise. But now Lady did start tugging and Caprice soon saw why. Her across-the-street neighbor Dulcina was sitting on her porch drinking a mug of coffee.

Caprice hurried along with Lady up the steps to say good morning to her neighbor. Dulcina was dating her Uncle Dom. She'd be handling the guest book at the wedding and reception.

"Would you like a cup of coffee?" Dulcina asked. Her pretty black hair laced with strands of gray was drawn back into a ponytail. She worked at home doing medical transcription for a pediatrician's office.

"I'll take a rain check on the coffee. I have a lot of work to do this morning if I want to run errands this afternoon."

Lady had gone to Dulcina who was petting her with a fondness that made her a good pet sitter when Caprice needed one. "Did Uncle Dom ask you about coming to the rehearsal dinner at the Country Squire Golf and Recreation Club?"

"He did, but are you sure you want me there?"

"Of course, I want you there. Uncle Dom is a groomsman and you're handling the guest book. You're both part of the wedding party."

"Thank you for thinking of me that way. I'd love to come. I was surprised when I heard Roz was giving you the dinner. Doesn't the groom's family take care of that?"

Caprice and Dulcina often gave each other honest feedback. They were that kind of friends.

"When Roz heard that Grant's parents hadn't said anything about the dinner yet, she insisted on giving it to us as a wedding present."

Dulcina rocked back and forth on the high-backed rocker while Lady watched the motion of the rungs. "You know, instead of going to the church, I could go to the Country Squire while everyone is at rehearsal to make sure it's set up properly. Would you like that?"

"That sounds like a great idea. I'll have Roz call you to iron out the details."

Dulcina studied Caprice over the rim of her coffee mug. "Should I ask about the wedding reception? Will you still be having it at the winery?"

Caprice was trying to stay optimistic. "We're hoping to. Everything's already decided—tablecloths, centerpieces, the DJ. The only thing that would make us move it would be if the winery had immediate financial problems and had to shut down. But I don't see that happening before the wedding. Michelle told me we could be the last wedding reception there, and that was before Travis was murdered."

"Do you think there's any way she can succeed on her own?"

"I don't know. Travis's brother came back to town, and he's staying there with her. He ran the winery with Travis for a year not so long ago. Maybe he'd have ideas to get it on its feet again. It's possible."

"Does that give him a motive for murder?" Dulcina asked.

Caprice hadn't found out more about Jarrett . . . yet. "Possibly. I don't know enough about him."

"Are you looking into this murder in spite of getting married soon?"

"Because Michelle asked for Vince's help, I got involved. Vince once dated Michelle and Roz isn't too happy that he didn't tell her. I'd like to see this solved quickly before Vince gets more involved, or Roz gets perturbed enough with him to move out."

"You don't think that will happen."

"I don't know. I just want to see them have smooth sailing again."

"You know as well as I do that relationships are never smooth sailing."

That was true, she supposed. She and Grant had certainly had their bumpy road. "So are you and Uncle Dom having smooth sailing, or are you bumping along?"

Dulcina smiled. "Both, I think. But we're okay with that. He has his issues because of his ex-wife; and me, my marriage was what every woman dreams of. Then it was suddenly taken away from me when Johnny died. It was what I wanted and it was good. But I think over the years I've built it up in my mind to be even more than it was. Do you know what I mean?"

"Yes, I know what you mean. That was your way of memorializing it and remembering Johnny."

"That's true. Your Uncle Dom is the one who pointed that out to me and I wasn't too happy when he did. But we worked through it. We both decided we're not in any rush. I know neither of us is getting any younger but that doesn't mean we should be reckless and make a mistake."

"You mean like the mistake I almost made with Seth?" Seth Randolph had been a handsome and charming doctor whom she'd dated for a while.

"You didn't almost make a mistake. Your heart knew Seth wasn't ready to settle down and that his career was more important than anything else. You also realized he'd probably never put you first. I think your heart was trying to tell you all along that you'd decided Grant was the one for you ever since you met him when he and Vince were room-mates at law school."

"But I was too young and he was four years older. Then he found a job in Pittsburgh and married Naomi."

Lady rubbed against Dulcina's leg and Dulcina studied her. "Have you ever asked him if he thought of you while he was married to her?"

"No!"

"Why so vehement? Grant has gotten an annulment on the grounds that his marriage was never a true sacrament because Naomi was pregnant, because they were married by a justice of the peace, because there were probably lots of doubts."

Caprice tried to think about Dulcina's question with less emotion. "I still don't know if it's a question I'd ever ask him."

"What I'm saying is that maybe he never forgot about you, just as you never forgot about him. It took you two long enough to find each again after he was back in Kismet. But you did. He was your destiny and you were his."

Caprice smiled. "You make it sound very romantic."

"Isn't it?" Dulcina countered.

"It didn't feel very romantic when we were going through it, but now it does. And now I just want to be Caprice De Luca Weatherford. I might keep my maiden name for business purposes or maybe I'll hyphenate the two names. I haven't decided yet."

"You don't have too much time."

"No, but it's an important decision in lots of

ways. I do want Grant's input on that to see how he feels."

"Then you'll make the right decision."

Lady moved away from Dulcina to snuffle around the porch as if she was looking for food.

"I'd better take her home and feed her breakfast."

"And have some breakfast yourself?"

"At my desk."

Caprice said good-bye and walked Lady down the steps, but she was already thinking about the rental furniture she wanted to use for her next house staging.

After Caprice left her felines napping and she'd rolled Lady her treat ball and said good-bye, she drove to the winery. As she veered onto the winding drive, she considered everything she'd learned about Travis's murder. It wasn't really much. That's why today she wasn't here to see Michelle. She intended to visit Neil Allen.

Caprice parked and went to the tasting room entrance. No one was in the tasting room again and she supposed news media reports were keeping tourists and even locals away. The room had been cleaned up from whatever mess had been there, including fingerprint powder and possibly luminol.

Caprice easily noticed that the teal chaise lounge was missing, probably the one that Travis had been discovered on. She supposed he had fallen on it when the murderer killed him. Would Brett give her details about that? Probably not.

She continued through the room into the hall that led to the offices. Neil Allen must have heard her footsteps because he came out to the doorway. When he saw her, he said, "Michelle's not here."

"I'm not here on wedding business today. I actually came to see you." There was no point prevaricating because when she began asking questions, Neil would know what she was about.

"Me?"

"I'm trying to learn a little more about Travis. I'm helping Michelle stay clear of charges. If the police don't have another suspect, you know how that goes."

Neil was middle-aged, probably in his late forties. His hair was thinning on top and he had a mustache, maybe to make up for what he was losing on top of his head. He had a long nose and thin lips.

His hazel eyes were piercing as they studied her. "I don't know what I can tell you that Michelle doesn't already know."

Neil was dressed in a polo shirt and jeans today as if he didn't expect to be doing winery business. Were things really that bad?

Instead of asking that, however, she said, "I'd like somebody else's perspective. Do you think you could give me that?"

Neil motioned down the hall to his office. Caprice followed him and sat on the chair across from his desk. Her lime bell-bottom slacks nestled against her espadrilles as she crossed one foot over the other. Neil was studying her, from her fuchsia-and-lime Peter Pan–collared blouse to the ring on her finger.

He gestured to it. "That's a beautiful ring. Michelle told me it was unusual."

Caprice looked down at the heart-shaped pink diamond set in a band of alternating pink sapphires and diamonds. "My fiancé picked it out. He has good taste and he knows what I like."

"That's a good start," Neil acknowledged with half of a smile. Sobering he asked, "What do you want to know?"

"Tell me why you think Travis was murdered."

Neil's eyes widened a bit as if he hadn't expected *that* question. He took a few moments but then he answered her. "Travis could be ruthless in business and he made enemies. Yes, he could be charming when he wanted to be, like when he courted Michelle. But it wasn't long before she saw his true colors."

"True colors?"

"He courted her as if she were the most important woman in the world. Do you know what I mean? Flowers, candy, jewelry. Even more than that, he gave her his time. But as soon as he had her, he changed."

"I don't understand why he'd go to all that trouble if he wasn't going to follow through."

"He went to all that trouble because his father wanted him to marry well. And not only well, but a woman who was accomplished. Michelle is. Although she was a nurse, she could hostess a party and make everyone a friend quicker than you can say winery. It wasn't long after they were married that Travis was at the winery eighteen hours a day. He was always wheeling and dealing promotions and opportunities. Not that they ever did much good. He had no time for his marriage."

Caprice shifted her straw purse on her lap. "Certainly, he would go home at night."

Neil shook his head. "Michelle would set up dates for them and he'd always bail out."

"He couldn't have wanted Michelle just as a hostess," Caprice protested.

"Marriage looks good on paper. Travis could claim he was a family man. Michelle handled the events so it looked as if they were a team."

Caprice thought about all that. "Michelle mentioned that Travis had an interest in old cars."

"Not simply old cars. It wasn't just a hobby. Travis's true passion involved antique cars that he had restored. Why don't you come over to the garage and I'll show you around his cars?"

"I'd like a tour."

Neil grinned. "Come on then. You probably haven't seen anything like the cars he has in the garage."

Caprice followed Neil through an outside door at the end of the hall. They turned right at the garage. Neil took a remote control from his pocket. One of the garage doors went up.

"Do you recognize the first one?" Neil asked.

Caprice did recognize the body. "It's a Dodge Coronet."

"You've got a good eye." Neil seemed surprised at her recognition.

"My father and my brother taught me well."

"It's a 1969 Coronet RT, completely restored with original parts."

The car had a high-gloss finish and looked as if it had never been driven.

"Do you recognize this one?" Neil asked.

The yellow car was almost the same color as her yellow Camaro. "That's a Plymouth Duster."

"Ding, ding, ding. The lady is right again. It's a 1973 coupe with a V-8 engine and a five-speed manual."

Caprice could only imagine the price of these restored cars. She could only imagine the money that Travis had sunk into them to restore them.

"Then there's this one," Neil said proudly.

"I'm not familiar with that one," Caprice said. "Is it rare?"

"It's a 1971 Hemi 'Cuda. This little baby cost Travis around ninety thousand dollars to restore."

"What was the original cost?"

"Around one hundred and fifty thousand."

Caprice whistled as she would when she was calling Lady. "So even though the winery might be in the red, Travis's personal accounts were stoked up by these cars."

"That's right."

The two of them kept staring at the cars, appreciating the restoration.

"Who did Travis's work for him?"

"The guy's name is Leon Wysocki." Neil checked his watch. "I'd better get back to work. The books have to be in order for the lawyer and the accountant. I wouldn't want to be in Michelle's shoes."

Caprice stepped out of the garage. "Because the police consider her a person of interest?"

"Not just that. Settling the estate in general. And now with Jarrett here, I don't know if that will help or hinder her." Neil pressed the remote and the garage door came down.

"Were you and Travis friends?" Caprice asked, remembering that Michelle had said there had been tension in the men's relationship lately.

Neil started walking toward the winery. "We worked together. It was uncomplicated."

Caprice didn't know of any relationships that were uncomplicated.

Turning toward her, Neil asked *her* a question. "Are you trying to gather information for the police?"

"If I can."

"Who's next on your list to talk to?"

"The man Travis fired—Fred Schmidt."

Neil shook his head. "That was such a shame. Fred only had a year until retirement. He and his wife really need his salary. I tried to tell Travis that, but he wouldn't listen. He said it was merely business."

Merely business. Travis's philosophy could have been what had gotten him killed.

That evening while Caprice and Grant were in the backyard with Patches and Lady, letting the cocker spaniels run off some of their energy, Caprice caught Grant up on everything she'd discovered. She explained about the cars in detail.

"Wow," Grant said. "And the thing is, if someone sees one of those classic cars, or even a garage full of them, they don't realize how much they're worth. You have to know cars to know that."

"Imagine, a hundred and fifty thousand to buy

one, and another hundred thousand to restore it. I'm not sure why Travis didn't sell more cars to buy out his brother. Rambling Vines might not be in the trouble it's in if he had."

Grant's cell phone buzzed. He took it from his windbreaker's pocket and said with lots of enthusiasm in his voice, "It's Holden. He's finally calling me back. I'll put him on speaker."

Hoping beyond hope that this was good news, Caprice waited beside Grant, tilting her head toward his so she could hear the conversation too.

"Hi, Holden. It's good to hear from you. Did you call to give me your measurements for the tux?"

"Not exactly," Holden said. His voice wasn't as deep as Grant's. Caprice had seen pictures of him. He didn't have the maturity in his face that Grant did. But then maybe he hadn't had the heartache either. His hair was dark-brown instead of black, and his eyes were green instead of gray. She could picture him now.

"Exactly why did you call?" Grant asked warily.

"In order to tell you I'll be coming to the wedding," his brother responded without much enthusiasm.

"That's great. You can be a groomsman along with my partner Vince, Caprice's brother-in-law and her sister's boyfriend Brett. Her uncle too."

"That's the thing, Grant," Holden explained. "I really don't want to be in middle of all that. Is it okay with you if I just come as a guest?"

Caprice glanced at Grant's face and could see he was disappointed. He didn't let that emotion show in his voice. "Certainly it's all right. I'll just be glad to have you here."

"On the happiest day of your life?" Holden asked a bit cynically.

"I hope it will be one of them," Grant answered. "Don't worry about booking a hotel or anything like that. You can stay in my townhouse with me."

"I don't want to put you out or make things too tight."

"It won't be tight. I have two bedrooms. It should be convenient for you. If you don't leave right away after the wedding, you can have the place to yourself."

"Mom and Dad said they're not sure where they're staying yet—if they're going to stay in a motel or at your fiancée's parents' house."

"I'm hoping they'll stay with Caprice's parents." Grant gave Caprice a look that said he meant that. She knew he wanted their in-laws to get to know each other in more than a superficial way.

"Dad won't want to put out the money so they probably will. If you're sure it won't be a bother, I'll stay at your place."

"That's great. I'm glad you called, Holden. We should talk . . . more."

"About our lives?" Holden asked. "There's not a whole lot to tell with mine. I'll text you when I know I'll be arriving. I'm thinking about driving."

"Whatever's most convenient for you. Mom and Dad are going to fly because I told them there are plenty of people who can pick them up at the airport or chauffeur them around if necessary. They don't even need to rent a car."

"I'll probably drive so I have my car. I'm going to take time off from work and maybe drive down to Hilton Head while I'm at it."

"That sounds nice."

"I'll let you know if anything changes. I've got to run. I'll text you before the wedding."

Grant hardly had a chance to say good-bye before Holden ended the call.

When Grant turned to her with a shrug, Caprice wondered if their wedding could bring these brothers closer together. She put her arms around Grant and gave him a huge hug. After that conversation, she suspected he needed it.

Chapter Eight

Painted with swirling psychedelic colors and a few large flowers, Caprice's van advertised in large turquoise lettering CAPRICE DE LUCA—REDESIGN AND HOME STAGING. Even more noticeable than her yellow Camaro, the van promoted her business. Today she *wanted* to reinforce her identity. She was driving to an out-of-the-way location outside of Kismet to the home of Fred Schmidt.

Following her GPS and the Australian male voice that guided her, she found herself on a gravel lane leading to a cottage-style house off of one of the rural roads. This was one of those times—going to visit a stranger in an out-of-the-way location—that Caprice was going to take Grant's advice. She'd brought along Lady. She was also going to dial Grant and keep her line open.

As Caprice parked, she reminded herself not to be nervous. To distract herself, she thought about her wedding gown fitting tomorrow afternoon at

Bella's and knew her heart was beating fast out of excitement, not fear. Still, Fred Schmidt had been fired by Travis before retirement and he could be furious. He could have been the one who killed the winemaker.

Caprice went to the back of her van, opened it, and let Lady out of her kennel. Her cocker eagerly hopped down from the van and looked up at her mistress, proud of herself for doing so.

Although Caprice didn't use treats as rewards as much as she had when she was training Lady, today she took one out of the pouch on her belt and held it up before her cocker. Lady sat without the command.

"I want you to keep your eyes open. You know I trust your judgment on whether someone is trustworthy or not, or nasty or not. So help me out here today, okay?"

Lady cocked her head and then raised her paw. Caprice shook it and gave her the treat. Afterward, she attached Lady's leash, walked around to the side of her van, and dialed Grant.

"I'm here," she told him.

"And I'm too danged far away. You should have let me follow you and park on the road."

"You're my fiancé, Grant, not my keeper."

"And you remind me of that every chance you get," he grumbled.

"I'm putting you in my pocket."

She didn't wait to hear his reply, but she knew he probably had one. She'd worn a maxi-length denim skirt today with pockets deep enough for her phone. Her peasant blouse was embroidered

with a riot of colors and her jeweled sandals completed the outfit. After all, her fashions today
matched her van pretty well.

The cottage was small, sided in narrow white
lengths. Black shutters hung at the windows, and
window boxes under those acted as colorful deco-
ration with the purple and yellow pansies that
filled them. The well-tended lawn around the cottage and the trimmed boxwood shrubs spoke of
care for the outside of the property, as did the
white trellis at the side of the house. Caprice liked
the homey feeling of the little house. But she also
knew looks could be deceiving.

She pressed the doorbell and heard the *ding-
dong* so she knew it worked. An older man opened
the door with a grumpy look on his face that could
have wilted the pansies. He had an oval face with
lots of wrinkles, a bald pate with a fringe of gray
hair on each side. He was wearing a plaid shirt and
jean overalls, and his feet were bare.

She held out her hand. "I'm Caprice De Luca."

He peered around her to see her van. "If you're
selling something, I'm not buying." He seemed
about to shut the door in her face but then he saw
Lady. His expression changed and he almost
smiled.

"I assure you, I'm not selling anything," Caprice
said. "I know Michelle Dodd, and our wedding reception is supposed to be at the winery. I'd like to
ask you a few questions about Travis, if you don't
mind. We could do it out here if you don't want
me inside. Let me show you ID."

She fished in her pocket, the opposite one from

her phone, and pulled out a small wallet. Fred
Schmidt could see her driver's license through the
plastic window on the front.

The man scowled. "I don't know why you want
to talk to me. I don't have anything good to say
about him."

"Michelle told me that he fired you. I'm afraid
she's the police's number one suspect, and I'm
hoping to clear her of that suspicion, even if I
can't figure out who killed Travis."

Fred Schmidt tilted his head first one way then
the other and backed up a step. "I don't have my
glasses on but I've seen your picture and your name
isn't common. You're the one who helped the police with solving murders."

"I am. Does that mean you'll talk to me?"

Fred stuck his hand out to her. "I'm Fred."

Caprice smiled. "This is my dog Lady."

"Will she behave if we go inside?"

"She certainly will. I've had her since birth and
still run her through her training."

"The reason I ask . . . my wife's resting. She went
through chemotherapy and radiation for breast
cancer and she's recovering."

"I'm sorry to hear about the cancer, but glad
she's recovering."

Fred motioned Caprice inside. When he did,
Lady stayed right by Caprice, but she didn't seem
afraid of Fred at all. She just cocked her head and
watched him.

The living room's furnishings were definitely
dated, but the green-and-white-patterned slipcover
on the sofa looked fairly new. There were two re-
cliners—a dark-brown leather one that showed

signs of wear and a newer one upholstered in fabric that had a control hanging over the arm. Side tables were maple and had Colonial-style legs. The only thing that wasn't dated was the small flat-screen TV that was as big as Caprice's computer monitor. Caprice guessed the beautiful lead crystal dish on the middle of the coffee table that held rose petals was an antique.

"Have a seat," Fred said, motioning Caprice to the sofa. He headed for the recliner.

"Tell me about Travis," she prompted.

Fred snorted. "Travis was a SOB who only cared about the bottom line. Yet he couldn't do even as well at the winery as his father had. Pouring all that money into redecorating and promotion was downright stupid."

"You don't think promotion works?"

As if he was unburdening himself, Fred blurted out, "Not the way *he* went about it. There are ways to sell wine and there are ways *not* to sell wine. He did everything all wrong and wouldn't listen to anybody. If you're going to spend money on ads, it has to be the right ads where wine buyers and connoisseurs will see them. He went flitting around the Internet and paid good money for ads on way too many sites. But those ads, those sites, didn't even target wine buyers."

"You mean like social media?" Caprice asked. Fred sounded as if he knew what he was talking about and Travis hadn't taken advantage of his experience.

Fred's heavy brows knit together. "Where messages are called tweets? How stupid is that?"

"Some people do sell their products that way."

Shaking his head, Fred admitted, "Maybe so. But Michelle kept telling him they needed to build up a good following first, that the new ways were fine, but you had to spend time on it before you could sell on it. She wanted to post pictures of the winery, the tasting room, the reception hall, to interest customers. He just wanted to post ads."

"I suppose the two could be combined."

"Sure, they could. But he wasn't open to her advice, and he wouldn't let her design the ads or target the audience. He spent too much money on everything. Some graphic designer he'd met somewhere charged him big bucks for the winery website and designing ads. I'll tell ya, I have a soft spot for Michelle. She tried to save my job, and she was always good to me—polite and respectful. Travis had no respect."

That assessment seemed to parallel what others had told her about Travis. "Did you know that Jarrett is back in town?"

Lady stood and went over to Fred, sitting by his feet. She'd apparently assessed his character and decided she liked him.

Fred reached down and petted her. "I didn't know Jarrett was back. That's interesting."

"Can you tell me what the winery was like when Jarrett was helping to run it? I understand he worked there for about a year."

Stooping lower, Fred ran his hand down Lady's flank and she rolled over. "Unlike his brother, Jarrett was an okay guy, just not very focused. They really were opposites. Their dad always considered Jarrett the black sheep."

"But his father never really saw him work at the winery."

"Jarrett returned for a visit now and then, but that wasn't often. He was close to his mom and when she left, he was devastated."

That was new information and Caprice wanted more of it. "When did she leave?"

Fred closed his eyes for a moment to think about it. "Travis was about fourteen and Jarrett was twelve. The settlement William gave Vivian with their divorce stipulated that he had full custody of the boys and she had no say in their upbringing. She was a weak woman with no backbone. After the divorce, she went home to New Hampshire. I think Jarrett always stayed in touch with her, and he blamed his father and Travis for her leaving. He confided in me once that they made her life miserable. I'm not exactly sure how, but I imagine if two people in the house were against you, and you're not very strong, you'd soon cave in to their demands. But I don't know that for sure."

Caprice suddenly heard a door open. When she looked toward the rear of the cottage, she saw an older woman coming out from the bedroom. She had very short white hair. She was wearing navy sweatpants and a zip-up jacket in the same material. She looked pale and frail.

Fred hurried to her immediately. "Agnes, honey, you should have called for me."

It was easy to see from the expression on Fred's face that he would do anything for this woman.

"I didn't need you to help me out of bed, and I can walk on my own. Remember the doctor said that's good for me."

Still, Fred tucked his wife's arm around his and walked her to the fabric recliner. She sat and then shooed him away. When Mrs. Schmidt's eyes fell on Caprice, Caprice thought she saw fear there. What did she have to fear? Whatever questions Caprice might ask?

Lady was perceptive about moods. As if she could sense the older woman's emotions, she went to her, looked up at her, and then sat at her feet.

"This is Agnes, my wife," Fred told Caprice. And then he introduced Agnes to Caprice and Lady.

When Agnes stooped to pet Lady, some of that fear seemed to vanish from her expression. Pets always seemed to give comfort.

Fred briefly explained why Caprice was there.

Relaxing a little, Agnes said, "Michelle was always kind to me and good to Fred when she could be. While I was having chemo, she would come and sit with me for a while. She sent us baskets full of fruit or goodies. I know she mailed Fred coupons for takeout after Travis fired him because she knew I wasn't cooking."

Yet Agnes's face suddenly turned determined. Straightening in the recliner, she shook her finger at Caprice. "I'll tell you, young lady, you need to be careful."

"Of anyone in particular?" Caprice asked.

Agnes and Fred exchanged a look but neither of them answered. So Caprice proceeded on her own. "Can you tell me how well you know Neil Allen?"

Agnes ruffled the fur along Lady's neck and wrinkled her nose. "I don't like the man. He's as slimy as Travis was."

Caprice wondered if Agnes thought that because Neil couldn't keep Fred from being fired. But she knew better than to assume anything. "Tell me why you think that."

After another look at his wife, Fred explained, "I overheard several arguments between Travis and Neil. During the most recent ones before I left, I heard Travis telling Neil he should fire him. Neil shot back that Travis couldn't do that because Neil knew too much about the winery and sabotaging the competition."

"Do you think someone was sabotaging Travis?"

"I never saw any signs of that," Fred said.

Following her instincts, Caprice revealed to Fred and Agnes what happened with the teenager who'd tried to spoil the wine in the vat. "Do you have any idea who might have planned to ruin Rambling Vines Wines?"

Fred gave a huge sigh as if talking about all of this was a relief somehow. "Well, we know it wasn't a teenager. Do you know if it was a man's or woman's voice the boy heard on the phone?"

"There are machines that can change the sound of any voice," Caprice informed them.

Agnes shook her head. "What's the world coming to? This tech age is passing me by."

"Remember, I got you a medical alert system and a smart phone so we can be in touch all the time," Fred reminded her.

"Those medical alert people are too nosy. I have to press that button every night or they call to ask if I'm all right. No privacy."

Caprice held back a smile.

Sitting to the front of his recliner, Fred said,

"You asked who I think would ruin Rambling Vines wine. That could be anyone from Jarrett, who didn't feel his settlement when Travis got his half of the business was just, to the owner of Black Horse Winery near Hanover. I'm not positive, but I think it was Travis who bribed the reviewer to give Black Horse bad press. Everyone in the local wine business had a niche carved out. When Black Horse received that bad review, Travis stepped right into that gap, promoting his wine wherever he could, spending outrageous amounts to ensure he got their business. Maybe competition was what killed him."

Agnes was leaning her head against the chair back now. She looked even paler and exhausted.

Caprice didn't want to overstay her welcome. Taking a business card from her pocket, she laid it on the coffee table next to the crystal dish. "I'm going to leave my card with you. If you think of anything else that might help, just give me a call. You can call my landline and leave a message if I'm not there, or just call my cell. Either is fine."

Agnes roused herself and again stooped down to pet Lady. Lady turned her head toward Agnes and then licked her hand.

"I think you've made a friend," Caprice said.

"If you come back again," Agnes said, "Please bring her with you. And remember, we like visitors. I know I get tired quickly but that's going to change in the coming months."

Caprice went over to Agnes, stooped down and patted her hand. "I'll be glad to bring Lady along when I visit again. She likes coming with me instead of staying at home with my two cats."

Agnes laughed. "I suppose she would."

Fred stood and walked Caprice and Lady to the door. "I hope we helped you," he said as he opened the door.

"You gave me leads to follow and I'm thankful for that. Both of you take care."

Fred watched from the open door as Caprice put Lady in her kennel in the van and shut the door. He was still watching as she jumped into the driver's side and started the ignition. She liked the Schmidts. She just hoped she and Lady were reading them correctly and they'd had nothing to do with Travis's murder.

Caprice climbed the steps of Bella's house on Sunday afternoon, noticing the pristine white porch railing that Joe had recently painted. The white trim and shutters went well with the yellow siding. The old-fashioned door had sidelight windows and the white storm door was decorated with a black emblem of a carriage with a horse. She heard women's voices through the storm door.

She and her sisters had an open-door policy. As she stepped inside, her sandals tapped on the parquet floor in the foyer. Through the wooden pillars on her left, she could see the small living room and, through French doors, into the family room beyond. Sunnybud, the yellow tabby cat that Bella had adopted, lay across the seat of Joe's comfy chair. Rousing a bit, he blinked green eyes at Caprice. She blinked back.

Nikki, Roz, and Bella were standing in front of the built-in birch bookshelves in the family room.

"Am I late?" Caprice asked as she walked through the kitchen and into the family room through that doorway.

"No, we're early," Nikki said. "Want a glass of iced tea before we get started? You can't drink it when you have your wedding gown on. We're not taking any chances with spills."

Caprice laughed. "I agree. No chances with spills."

She studied Roz who had pasted on a bright smile. But Caprice didn't see that smile in her eyes. She gave all three women hugs. "I'm ready when you are."

Bella pointed toward the kitchen and the door that led to the basement. "Let's go down to my workroom. I have a dais there that you can step up on to check the hem."

Fifteen minutes later, she was standing on the dais in her wedding gown and white bridal shoes. "Bella, I love it."

Bella had designed the gown, replicating their grandmother's wedding gown. There was ruching across the waist and hips. The sweetheart neckline did not show cleavage. Sleeves reached to her elbows but had a flutter to them which would be great if the day was hot. Caprice's train was detachable. Attached to the dress now, it flowed at least six feet behind the gown. For the reception, Caprice could detach it to move around more easily.

Nikki and Roz both said at the same time, "The gown is perfect." They looked at each other with tears in their eyes.

Bella produced the lace-edged cathedral-length bridal veil that had been a Christmas present from her mom and Nana. Flower appliqués that matched the lace were strategically placed on the bottom third of the veil.

Bella noted, "The veil is attached to two pearl-studded combs. Are you wearing your hair up or down that day?"

"I'm not sure. I usually wear it down and that's how Grant knows me. On the other hand, I wore it up for that Valentine's Day dance and I think that's where he first decided he might want to get closer."

"Then up it is," Bella said. "We can keep the combs or . . ."

From her worktable Bella produced a headband that didn't look anything like a headband. It was decorated with pearls and tulle and tiny crystals. "If I use this, that veil will be a lot more secure on your head. It seems light but that's plenty of material to have flowing down your back. What do you think?"

"I love the headband," Caprice said. "I think it will be perfect."

"Give me a few minutes to attach it, and then we can see the whole picture."

While Bella worked, Caprice asked Roz, "How are you doing. Really?"

"I hate to talk behind Vince's back," Roz murmured.

"We're his sisters," Nikki protested. "Who better to vent to? If you want to hold in your feelings around his business associates or your friends, that's fine. But you can be honest with us."

Roz tried to smile. "That's what I like about the three of you. You're always so tactful."

They all laughed, breaking the tension.

Nikki touched Roz's arm. "Tell us what's really going on. I don't know if we can help but you might feel better if you talk about it. You know what happens if you keep it in. You'll explode."

"Have you exploded with Brett yet?" Roz asked with a raised brow.

"No, of course not. I try to be straight up about any issues. I told him last week he's got to get over this idea that I won't stick by him because of his job. I think he's beginning to realize that his *attitude* is a turn-off, not his police life."

Bella added her two cents. "Okay, Roz, you deflected the question. Tell us what's going on."

"I'm worried," she confessed. "I'm not sure where our relationship is headed. Not a day goes by that Vince doesn't talk to Michelle. And now I found out that he saw her at the coffee shop before Christmas."

Caprice was worried about that supposed run-in too. Vince said it was happenstance. Was he downplaying it? "Is he open with you about the phone calls?"

"Yes, he is. Some of them are about winery business. Apparently, Michelle doesn't know who to trust so she's trusting Vince."

"You know, don't you, that Vince would never have asked you to move in with him if he didn't want a future with you."

"I remember he used to be a speed dater," Roz said.

"But not after he met you," Bella reminded her.

Roz wasn't buying it. "If he trusted we could have a life together, I still don't understand why he didn't let me pool my money with his and put my name on the house title."

The women all exchanged looks. "Have you told him how you feel?" Caprice asked.

"Not lately. There's tension between us, and I don't want to make it worse."

"I think you're making it worse by not talking to him about it," Caprice said.

"Maybe," Roz finally admitted.

"I'm done," Bella announced, carefully folding the veil over her arm. She stepped up onto the dais and then fitted the headband on Caprice's head, even though she was wearing her hair down. The veil softly floated over the gown's train.

Roz began to cry. Tears came to Caprice's eyes too, because she was so eager to be married to Grant, so thankful they'd found each other, so grateful they didn't have long to wait to become one. She loved him so much that sometimes she felt as if her heart would burst with it.

Everyone had tears in their eyes now.

"That's it," Bella said with a sniff. "Take it all off, Caprice. We need to go up and sit with Sunnybud in the family room. I have iced tea and Nana's biscotti and we can simply yak about nothing that matters."

"Amen to that," Caprice agreed, also thankful that her sisters were her friends, and that Roz was like a sister. That's why she would help her and Vince by solving this murder.

Chapter Nine

Ever since Caprice was around ten, she'd cherished her teatime with Nana Celia. She guessed their teatime dates had started when she was sick and had to stay home from school. Since her mom was a teacher and her dad was at work, Nana took care of her and always brewed tea. Whenever she'd visit Nana with news to share, her grandmother would bring out a box of flavored teas. When she was little, the idea of strawberry or peach had been a treat like a piece of candy. Even better than candy, though, were her Nana's stories.

As Caprice had gotten older she'd asked her Nana more than once why she'd married when she was only seventeen. She'd inquired about her grandfather's barbershop and studied the old photo albums. Nana was all about tradition, family history, and old-world charm. She was smiles and joy, encouragement and love.

Now as Caprice followed Nana into her parlor—in other words, her small living room—Nana's cat

Valentine, a gray tabby, darted in and out between their legs. Lady, who was very familiar with Valentine, darted after her in a pretend chase. Valentine ended up on the top shelf of her cat condo with Lady sitting on the floor underneath her.

"You two are going to behave, aren't you?" Caprice asked them.

Valentine hung her paw over the shelf. Lady cocked her head, stared at Caprice, then looked back up at Valentine.

"I'll take that as a *yes*," Caprice said with a smile.

It seemed as if she always smiled when she came into her Nana's parlor. Her grandmother's taste ran to antiques, lace, and flowered patterns in lilac, yellow, and pink. A regal woman, Nana was only five foot three, but she always held her head up high and her shoulders straight.

Nana's small table between two wing chairs near the window was already set with delicate teacups, a plate of biscotti that Nana had made herself, and a teapot wearing a tea cozy.

As Caprice sat in one of the chairs, Nana poured tea into their cups. "So tell me, what did you think of your wedding gown? Your mom and I can't wait to see it."

"I love it! It looks like yours in some ways, but then Bella added her own design to it. And the veil . . . Oh, Nana. That veil is just beautiful. We were all in tears."

"Hopefully you'll be wearing a smile on your wedding day and the rest of us will be in tears."

Caprice laughed.

"Tell me, *tesorina mia*, are you ready to get married?"

Caprice didn't hesitate for an instant. "Oh, yes. I'd run off with Grant today if a church wedding didn't mean so much to us and the family."

"Anticipation is good," Nana told her. "On your part and his part. Does Grant seem nervous?"

"Not about the wedding."

"About something?" Nana prompted as she seated herself in the other chair.

"He's nervous or anxious about his family. His brother has agreed to come but he doesn't want to be in the wedding party. I know that upset and disappointed Grant, but he *is* glad Holden is coming. And his parents . . . They haven't decided yet whether they're staying here with Mom and Dad, or if they should reserve a room at the bed and breakfast. They also haven't made any arrangements for the rehearsal dinner, but Roz has. Do you think it would be all right if Mom calls them to tell them that?"

Nana thought about it, took a sip of tea, then set her cup down carefully. "It might be better if Grant calls them, honey. You know, it *is* the groom's family's tradition to host the rehearsal dinner."

"Yes, I know, but he doesn't want to put them in an uncomfortable position if they haven't thought about it."

Nana touched the bun at her nape as if she were thinking about what she wanted to say next. "So I suppose what you're telling me is that Grant and his family don't communicate well."

With anybody else but Nana, Caprice might not say anything at all or answer her question. But this was Nana who always gave her wise advice.

"The truth is—I think they avoid conversation

about subjects that matter . . . difficult subjects. I don't think Grant ever talked to them about his marriage to Naomi or his divorce or what he felt afterwards."

"That's such a shame."

"I think his decision to get engaged to me was a surprise to them too," Caprice admitted.

"Did he think they would disapprove?"

"Most probably. And disapproval was the first feeling I got from them when I met them at the restaurant. Not that they disapproved of me so much, but they didn't like the idea of the annulment and Grant marrying again."

"I can understand that," Nana said. "But on the other hand, I don't think men and women were meant to live alone. Grant's marriage was a mistake and then he had tragedy on top of that. If anyone deserves a fresh start, he does. And I think he'll have it with you."

Nana's support meant so much. "The contractor is going to start on the addition as soon as we return from our honeymoon. Depending on the disruption, we might be staying at Grant's townhouse. It depends. We have the animals to consider." She glanced over at Lady and at Valentine who were both snoozing.

Changing the subject, Caprice asked, "Have you spoken to Vince since the murder occurred at the winery?"

After a bite of biscotti, Nana frowned. "No, I haven't. You girls confide in me but Vince not so much. Your father did tell me that Vince was helping out Michelle Dodd and Roz wasn't happy about it."

To distract herself, Caprice lifted a biscotti from the plate and took a bite. Nana's biscotti weren't twice-baked biscotti like you found in stores. Hers were soft and biscuit-like with a lemon icing.

Caprice finished the biscotti and wiped her fingers on her napkin. "I don't know what's going to happen between the two of them. I don't think they're communicating very well right now. I'm trying to gather some information to get Michelle off the hook. If she doesn't need Vince, then he and Roz can go back to normal."

"Maybe they can't get back to normal when there's a disruption in a relationship that's not easily forgotten," Nana advised.

That was true. Caprice remembered when Grant had spent time with his first wife Naomi so they could have closure. It was definitely a rough patch. But they'd come through that okay. Surely Roz and Vince could too.

"Do you have any other suspects besides Michelle?" Nana asked.

"A few," Caprice responded. "There's Travis's brother Jarrett. The two of them didn't get along well. There's Travis's chief financial officer Neil Allen. Someone overheard Neil threatening Travis with blackmail." She didn't consider Fred a real suspect.

"An odd incident happened when Travis was still alive and I was at the winery." She told Nana about the teenager trying to ruin the vat of wine.

"Do you know this young man's name?"

She remembered it. "His name was Andy Sprenkle."

"Then you have another place to investigate," Nana suggested.

As always, her Nana was right.

Since she'd been involved in murder investigations, Caprice was learning nifty computer skills as well as how to search databases. It wasn't long before she found a couple most likely to be Andy Sprenkle's parents. If she was wrong, then she was wrong. But she had to try.

The one thing she could do to make sure the address she'd found was correct was to park on Andy's street for a while and see who went in and out of his house. If it *was* his house. She could be patient.

Thankfully the afternoon was warm but not too warm. She'd driven her yellow Camaro because she didn't think anyone on Andy's street would recognize it. His house was at the north end of town on Maple Avenue, nowhere near her neighborhood or her parents' neighborhood . . . or even Bella's.

She'd brought along her earphones and iPad. She intended to listen to music while she was waiting. Her oldies-but-goodies playlist would do. She had to choose songs for the DJ. This was her way to multitask.

She'd been sitting there for about an hour and was getting antsy wondering how policemen actually survived stakeouts, when a young man came zooming by her on his bicycle and rode up the driveway. As she watched, the teen took off his helmet.

It was Andy Sprenkle. She hadn't seen anyone else go in or out of the house. If she was lucky, he'd be there alone.

She waited ten minutes and climbed out of her car, went up the walk, and knocked on the door.

Andy himself opened the door, and his eyes widened when he saw her.

"I don't want to talk to you," he said.

"Why not, Andy? Obviously, you recognize me, and I know what you did at the winery."

"I didn't do nothing."

"Drop the act. Travis practically hung you up by the neck of your shirt. The police are looking for anyone who knows anything about Travis and who might have had a grudge against him."

"It wasn't me." Andy started to shut the door.

Caprice set her palm on the door. She wasn't going to force entry, but she wanted to convince him to talk to her. "If you're smart, you'll talk to me. I know the detective on the case and I can turn your name in."

At that thought, Andy went pale. He also looked scared. "What do you want to talk about?"

"I want you to tell me how you were hired and who hired you to pour the vinegar bacteria into the wine."

"How do you know that that's what it was?"

"Because I've spoken to Michelle. Travis didn't even have to have it tested. He knew what would ruin his wine. A murder happened, Andy."

"I'm telling you, I don't know nothing about that."

"Then tell me what you *do* know. You said you

were supposed to take a selfie when you poured the vinegar into the tank. How did you know where that photo was supposed to go?"

"I had a number to text the photo to."

"And how did you and Travis settle this?"

The teen shrugged. "We didn't settle it exactly. Travis made me take the photo of me pouring the mixture into an empty tank and then send it. Travis said he had a friend who can trace where it went. I was supposed to get five hundred dollars by going to a drop-off point a mile out of town. The envelope with the money would be in the hollow of a tree at noon the next day. Travis scouted out the area and he waited there. When I got there to pick up the envelope, no money was there. So I don't know whether or not Travis found out who was supposed to leave it. But the next thing I knew—Travis was dead. I really didn't have anything to do with it."

It was easy for Caprice to see that Andy was shaken up.

"As I told you, I know the detective on the case. I think you should go to him and tell him exactly what happened." Michelle might have already done that as far as she knew.

"I don't want to go to the police station and I don't want to tell my parents."

"How old are you, Andy?"

"I'm nineteen."

"Then you're old enough to do this on your own. Maybe your parents don't have to know. That depends."

"On what?"

"On what Detective Carstead has to say to you."

She could see he was still frightened, and there was only one way she knew how to alleviate that. "If you'll talk to the detective, I'll go with you to the police station."

"Will you be in there with me?"

"I doubt if the detective will let me stay, but at least you'll have an escort there, and a friendly face to introduce you to Detective Carstead. Let me call the station and see if he's there."

"You have his number?"

"I've worked with him before." She pressed the icon for contacts and found Brett's number. Fortunately, he answered.

"Carstead."

"Brett, it's Caprice."

"Uh, oh. Am I going to like this?"

"You might. You might not."

He gave an amused chuckle. "That's just like you. Is this about Nikki? Or about the murder?"

"It's about the murder."

"You know something?"

"Michelle might already have told you about this. Did she say anything about the teenager who tried to ruin a vat of Travis's wine?"

"She mentioned it, but she didn't know much about it other than he tried to do it. Why?"

"Because I'm with Andy now. I told him I'd bring him to the police station and introduce him to you. That's if you want to talk to him. Someone hired him to do it. Maybe you can learn a clue about that."

Brett was silent for a few heartbeats. "You're too involved in this because of Vince," he said with a sigh.

"It's not just Vince. I'm supposed to have my wedding reception at the winery, remember?"

"You can't find another place?"

"Obviously you don't know much about weddings. The alternative would be to have the reception in my backyard."

"Would that be so bad?"

"Brett," she said impatiently.

"Okay, I'll butt out of your wedding stuff. But let me tell you, Caprice, once you bring this kid into the station, I'll want you out of it. You can't tell me Grant wants you involved either."

"Whether or not I want to be involved, I am. And don't warn me about obstruction of justice. We've been through this before. I'm not doing anything wrong. I just Googled Andy Sprenkle and his parents. I found him. Did you have his name?"

"Michelle couldn't remember it," he admitted.

"And she didn't tell you I was there?"

"I was going to talk to you. I just hadn't gotten around to it yet," he said defensively.

"Brett, you're going to be Grant's groomsman. I don't want to argue with you."

"I don't want to argue with you either," he said begrudgingly. "Bring the kid in. But once I meet him, I want you to leave."

"He has to get home again."

"I'll take him home."

"He's going to hate that."

"I'll use an unmarked vehicle. No patrol car."

"You'll give me your word on that, even if you get tied up with something?"

"If I get tied up, I'll call you back and you can pick him up. How's that?"

"You're a good guy, Detective."

He was silent.

"I'll see you in about ten minutes."

"Ten minutes," Brett confirmed, and then ended the call.

Andy was watching her. He'd obviously heard the back and forth between her and Brett. "You sound like you know him."

"I told you I've worked with him before. Besides that, he's dating my sister."

At that news, Andy looked a bit relieved. Maybe now he wouldn't just see Brett as a detective, but as a regular guy.

"He's good at what he does, Andy. He'll ask you the tough questions, not give you a pass on anything. So be prepared for that."

Andy thought about it. "All right. Let's go. I want to get this over with."

Caprice just hoped with the information Andy gave Brett, they could all get the murder over with too.

Caprice and Grant were sitting on the sofa in the living room going over the notes they had made for the contractor. They'd planned a meeting with him for tomorrow night and they wanted to be prepared. Yes, they'd had the plans drawn up, but there were details to be ironed out. He'd have questions for them and they'd have questions for him. The biggest one was—could they stay in the house while the renovations were going on?

Caprice was using her electronic tablet. Grant was using a legal pad and a pen. They had just agreed that they wanted a bathroom off of Grant's office. They might as well do it now. It would be convenient to have one there.

"Do you think Lady and Patches will mind when the yard is smaller?" Caprice asked him.

"You have a big lot. They'll still have enough room to run and play. Besides, we walk them and there's the dog park too. They'll be fine." He reached over and put his arm around her shoulders. "Are you getting nervous about the wedding and the construction, so you're concentrating on details?"

"Could be. Maybe I'm thinking about the honeymoon."

Grant gave her a crooked smile. "Nothing to be nervous about with that. We'll be good together, Caprice. You know we will."

Yes, she did. But wasn't a bride supposed to have jitters before her wedding? Some of them were caused by pure excitement and anticipation.

Grant had just leaned over to kiss her when her cell phone played. She'd set it on the square coffee table that was inset with colorful ceramic tiles. The antique silent butler sat next to her phone. That was where she'd placed her affirmations every morning.

When she picked up the phone, she saw Michelle was calling. She said to Grant, "Do you mind if I take this? It's Michelle."

"I hope nothing else has happened to complicate the situation even more."

So did Caprice.

"Hi, Michelle."

"Caprice, I need your help."

"What do you need help with?"

"You find homes for stray cats and dogs, right?"

"Yes, I do." She suspected what was coming.

"That Schnoodle that's been hanging around here. I'm having trouble taking care of everything else, let alone caring for a dog. I took him to the vet. There isn't a chip. He checked him over and said he's healthy."

"What vet did you use?"

"Marcus Reed at Furry Friends."

Marcus was the vet who'd often helped Caprice. She always took animals to him to get them checked or for necessary appointments. "I trust Marcus. If he said the dog's healthy, that's a good thing."

"He gave him a rabies injection and some other stuff, but now he needs a home. No one has responded to my ads or my notes on bulletin boards. Can you help?"

"I might be able to." What she was thinking was a bit unorthodox, but that didn't mean it couldn't work. "Are you going to be home in the morning?"

"I have errands to run. I'm meeting with the loan officer at Kismet Community Bank. But Neil can be here."

"I'll pick up dog supplies and drive to the winery to pick him up. If what I have in mind doesn't work, you might have to keep him a little longer until I can find him a home."

"That's fine. I just want to know he'll be having good care."

In spite of herself Caprice could see Michelle was a little attached to the dog. "I'll see Neil in the morning about ten."

"That sounds good. And thank you, Caprice. I really appreciate this."

After she put her phone back on the coffee table, Grant asked, "You're going to try to find a home for the dog at the winery, aren't you?"

"I have something in mind. If it works out, it will be win-win-win for everybody, including the Schnoodle."

Grant just shook his head but then he kissed her.

Before Caprice drove to the winery the following morning, she called Marcus and asked him about the Schnoodle. Marcus had told her that he was probably about two. He'd given him a flea treatment and vaccinations he deemed necessary. Michelle had told him she wanted the dog to stay healthy. He'd also explained to Michelle that the dog had a good sense of commands.

Caprice wanted to find that out herself. As Michelle had told her, she wouldn't be at the winery that morning but Neil was. He was waiting at the house when Caprice arrived.

"So you're going to take him," he commented.

"I'm going to find out if someone would like to foster him. If they foster, they might decide to keep him."

Neil shook his finger at her. "That's sly."

"No, it works to see if an animal and owner are a good fit. I'm going to play with him a bit and see what commands he knows before I take him."

"That's fine, but he's in your custody now. If he runs off, it's not my fault."

"I'll take responsibility for him," Caprice assured him.

After Neil went back into his office, Caprice took the Schnoodle around to the gardens. She'd brought along a ball and she tossed it for him. He ran after it, ears raised, tail wagging. He obviously liked someone to play with him. After he'd worked off energy, she tried basic commands—*sit, stay, come.* When she hooked him up to the leash, she said, "Heel" and he did. He walked right beside her.

Just where had he come from and why hadn't anybody claimed him? But that was a question she'd had to ask too often.

"Let's go see if we can find you a home," she said to him.

His bright brown eyes were sparkling as he tilted his head as if he was listening.

"Do you like that word *home?*"

He barked.

"All right. Let's see what we can do for you." She opened the passenger side of her Camaro and he hopped in without hesitation. She unhooked the leash and went around to the driver's side. "I'm not going to let you hang out the window," she told him.

He gave her a soulful look, then he sat in his seat peering straight ahead out the windshield.

This might just work.

At a red light, Caprice braked. She glanced over at the Schnoodle. He was watching her.

"How do you feel about trying out an experimental home if who I'm thinking about will take you?"

He cocked his head at her with enough vigor to make one of his ears flop over.

Caprice smiled. "You are too cute for words. Let's see if I can find you a home with someone who needs you as much as you need them."

Caprice set her radio on an oldies-but-goodies channel. She was trying to find more songs to give the DJ for their reception playlist. She'd found a few—*Our Day Will Come* by Ruby and the Romantics, *For Your Precious Love* by Jerry Butler and the Impressions, *I Love How You Love Me* by the Paris Sisters, *Only You* by the Platters. But she needed to find a lot more. She was humming along to *Dream Lover* as she took first one road and then another and finally the gravel lane that led to Fred and Agnes Schmidt's cottage. Agnes and Fred both had seemed to enjoy Lady. A dog could be good therapy for both of them. It all depended on whether the Schnoodle and the couple would bond. That's what she was here to find out.

Fred opened the door to her again, but this time Agnes was sitting in her recliner, watching TV.

Fred looked down at the Schnoodle. "Who's this?" he said, crouching down. "Another one of yours?"

Apparently familiar with dogs, Fred held out his hand to the canine. The Schnoodle smelled it all over, even each finger and then licked it.

Fred laughed. "He probably still tastes bacon from this morning."

As Fred stood, Caprice said, "No, he's not mine, and the thing is he needs a home. I thought maybe you and Agnes might like to foster him for a while.

My fiancé has a cocker spaniel who is Lady's brother and with my two cats, we have a full house of animals. Do you think you'd be interested?"

Fred started shaking his head. "Oh, I don't think so. A dog takes care. We would have to let him out and take him for walks . . ."

Agnes called to her husband. "Fred. Let Caprice in. Is that another furry friend she brought with her?"

Caprice could hear the interest in Agnes's tone. She looked at Fred with raised brows.

He just shook his head. "Come on in."

Instead of nosing everything in the room like some dogs might do, the Schnoodle went straight over to Agnes. He even waited by the side of the chair while she lowered the footrest.

"Isn't he just too adorable?" Agnes remarked. "What's his name?"

"It's like this," Caprice said. She wasn't going to hide the facts. "He's a stray. Michelle found him at the winery, and she's been taking care of him for about two weeks. She called all the veterinarians in the area and even put an ad in the newspaper but no one's claimed him. A few days ago, she took him to her veterinarian who also happens to be mine, and he checked him out and gave him a flea treatment. He's healthy, neutered, and probably about two or three years old. He needs a home. I know you probably haven't thought about getting a dog but I wondered if maybe you'd foster him on a temporary basis."

Agnes was using the electric control on her chair to raise the seat so she could stand much easier. After she did, she stooped down to the Schnoodle looking into his eyes. "If you stay, we'd have to give you a name."

"What do you mean if he stays? Agnes, you can't be serious!" Fred's eyes were wide and his stance defensive.

Agnes addressed Caprice. "Sometimes my husband is a little too pragmatic . . . realistic in the sense that he can't see outside of his box."

"What box?" Fred mumbled. "You're still recuperating."

"That's my point exactly," Agnes said. "If we take in this adorable fellow, he would be good company for me. You could leave more often and not worry so much when you run errands, even just working out in the yard. Besides that, the doctor said I'm supposed to walk. What better way to motivate me than to have a dog to walk. And speaking of walks, why don't you and Caprice take a little walk on this beautiful day and let me get to know him. When you come back, if he and I are good friends, then I think he should stay."

Caprice lowered her voice in a conspiratorial tone to Fred. "Does she often argue with you?"

"She doesn't call it arguing, but somehow she gets her way."

Agnes was talking to the dog in soft murmurs. Finally she petted him. Caprice could swear he gave a little doggie sigh as Agnes's fingers went through his curly hair.

"We can stand right outside the door if you don't want to go too far," Caprice said. "And actually, I'd like to ask you something."

"So you didn't just come over to deliver the dog?"

"The dog was my main reason."

They stepped outside and walked around the trellis out of earshot of Agnes. Nevertheless, Fred left the door open so he could hear what was happening with the dog.

"Can you tell me where you were the night Travis was murdered?"

"Do I have to?"

"Do you have an alibi?"

"Yes, I do, but I don't really want Agnes to know about it."

Uh, oh. Did that mean he was involved in something illegal?

Fred scowled. "I know what you're thinking, and I'm sure you couldn't possibly guess what I was doing."

"So fill me in."

"We need money. The night Travis was killed I met a friend at Suzie Q's to talk to him."

"Was this about a job?" Caprice guessed, following a logical track.

"Yes, it was." Fred's voice lowered. "It was a janitorial job. My friend works for the company and says he has good benefits and that's what we need." Fred was obviously embarrassed.

"Why don't you want Agnes to know?"

"I don't want her to think about me being a janitor to pay the bills."

"So your pride is keeping you from being truthful with your wife?"

He looked toward the living room. "Put like that, I guess it's not a very good reason. But I don't have much left but my pride."

"You do. You have your house, you have your wife, you have your health. Nobody knows what's going to happen tomorrow."

Fred appeared chagrined. "That's true, I suppose. I mean, after all, look at what happened to Travis."

"What time did you meet your friend at Suzie Q's?"

"Do you still not trust me?" Fred's voice was angry.

"Trust doesn't have much play in an investigation. Have the police spoken to you yet?"

"I got a phone call. I have to go in and see them tomorrow."

"You can bet they'll ask the same question. They'll want to know about your alibi."

With a resigned sigh, Fred explained, "It took me about a half hour to get there, and I was at Suzie Q's about an hour. A half hour to come back. So I was gone from seven to nine, longer than I like to be away from Agnes."

"But now if she has a friend to keep her company, that might change," Caprice suggested optimistically.

Fred's scowl was even more ferocious this time. "Having a dog will be an added expense. I need to buy dog food, a leash, a collar."

"No, you don't," Caprice assured him with a smile on her face. "I just happen to have all that in my car, including bowls and a bed. All of that comes with him."

"Michelle bought him those things?"

"She bought the beds and bowls. She just had a little bit of food left, so I stopped to pick up that . . . and a few toys."

Once more he looked toward the living room. "Come on. Let's see if they're getting along."

Caprice wished she could take a picture of the scene she witnessed when they returned inside. Agnes was sitting on the recliner again. However, she'd pulled over a straight chair and set it right in front of her. The Schnoodle was on the chair, facing her. They looked as if they were having a discussion.

"He's so responsive," Agnes said as soon as she saw her husband. She held out a country magazine. "This was on the floor over there. He fetched it for me." Demonstrating further, she told the Schnoodle, "Lay down." He did and put his paw on Agnes's knee then dropped his head onto his paws.

"See, Fred? He loves me already."

"This is temporary, Agnes, just to see if things are going to work out."

"You can believe that if you want to. But I know he'll fit in perfectly, just as I knew I'd recover from my breast cancer. You have to have some faith, honey."

At the endearment, Fred's cheeks reddened. He gave Caprice a resigned look. "So I guess this is happening. Go ahead and bring in the supplies. But I won't take charity. I'll be donating to an animal shelter as soon as I find a good one."

"I'll bring the supplies in." She quietly went to her Camaro.

After Caprice carried in the dishes and Fred placed them in the kitchen, after he hoisted up the bag of kibble, and she managed the bed, they stood back watching Agnes and the dog. The

Schnoodle had crept farther and farther front and now half his body was practically on Agnes's legs. She didn't seem to mind a bit as she cooed to him, fussed over him, and scratched around his ears.

A loving look in Fred's eyes as he watched his wife almost brought Caprice to tears. She was hoping the Schmidt home would be more than a temporary place for the Schnoodle to stay.

Chapter Ten

Caprice had called Derek Gastineau and asked him to be their contractor because she had a professional history with him. He'd built the model homes that Caprice had decorated the year before. She knew he was a developer, as well as a contractor, and she trusted him and his crews. She'd seen their work and it was top quality.

Derek laid out the plans for the addition to Caprice's house on the coffee table. "This is exactly what you told me you wanted. However, I want you to take a good look at it and make sure. If we start and we have to make changes, it will cost you more because we might have to tear something out, put something else on hold, and spend more time on it. I'd like both of you to initial the right-hand corner."

Derek was sitting beside Grant and Caprice on the sofa. She and Grant moved to the edge of the couch cushions to study the architect's renderings of the structure that portrayed all the requirements on their list.

Caprice traced her finger over each line of the addition, each wall, each door, each window. She'd started with the planned sunroom. They'd be using the same entrance from the garage into the sunroom, from there into the kitchen. They could also access Grant's new office from the sunroom as well as from outside.

Beside her, Grant studied the plans too. He must have been following her tracing because she stopped when she reached the powder room.

Grant asked her, "Are you sure you want the expense of installing a bathroom?"

"I'm sure. It will be convenient for you and any clients who come in. Not only that, if we have guests and need another room, we can put a pull-out couch in your office and then the bathroom would be there. I think it will pay for itself in convenience."

Derek nodded vigorously. "Caprice, as well as my builders, knows that bathrooms and the kitchen often sell a house. I know you're only thinking about now, but think about the future too. Whether you stay here forever or whether you sell it eventually, in a buyer's mind, the two bathrooms down here could make up for only having one upstairs."

"Do you think we should put a shower in down here?" Caprice asked.

"It wouldn't be a bad idea," Derek agreed. "Especially if at some time you want to use it as a guest bath. If you plan to stay here during your retirement years, the house would have everything you need on the first floor."

Caprice automatically turned toward Grant. "What do you think?"

"That sounds good," Grant said. "But how much will it cost?"

"We'll be working with the same size room. That won't change," the contractor said. "There's plenty of space in there for a decent-sized shower. Knowing Caprice and how her tastes run . . ." He wrote a figure down on the small notepad that he'd laid next to the plans. He turned it so Caprice and Grant could see it.

"Now remember, Caprice, I'll be giving you a ten percent discount on materials because we've worked together in the past and I'm sure we'll work together in the future. But the labor cost is the labor cost, unless of course, you want to do anything yourselves."

Grant seemed to think about it for a long minute, but then he shook his head. "You know the materials. You know how they fit together. The truth is, I don't want to mess something up by doing it myself and then paying for the cost of redoing it. Painting, Caprice and I can handle. But the floors and the skim plaster coat, experts need to do."

"Grant's right," Caprice said, nodding. "And we do want this done as quickly as possible."

"Are you sure you want the skim coat of plaster rather than inlaid wood panels. It *is* an office."

Grant answered him. "Caprice and I have agreed that we want the addition to complement the features we already have in the house."

"You have old-fashioned plaster in the rest of the house. A skim rough coat on blueboard will give you the same look. I do have one more suggestion you might want to consider."

"I can see the dollar signs," Grant murmured.

Derek smiled and Caprice was sure he had this conversation with all of his clients. "I'd like to suggest you put in a gas stove. We're updating your heating system so the office will be warm enough. However, you know Pennsylvania winters. You know the electricity has often gone out, especially with ice storms and heavy snowstorms. If you put in a gas stove, you would have a remote to turn it on and off, and you don't need electricity to fire it up. I know you have a fireplace in the living room, but it's certainly not going to give you a lot of warmth with the hot air escaping through the chimney. If you want to make it more efficient, you should put a wood-burning insert in your fireplace."

Caprice was already shaking her head. "I always wanted a real fireplace and I'd like to keep it."

"That makes my suggestion even more important. You can have your fireplace going, but you could also keep the office warm and sleep there without worrying about putting out a fire or stoking it. The office can have its own self-sufficiency. You have gas appliances now. We can just run a gas line to the stove."

"You make it sound so easy." Grant obviously wasn't sure about the stove.

"I like the idea," Caprice assured Derek. "But if Grant's not sure, then we need to think about it and we can let you know."

"All right then," he said.

Caprice had served coffee and her chocolate loaf before they'd started. Derek took his mug from the side table, took a healthy swallow as if to fortify himself, and then suggested, "Let's look at the figures. I included the stove, but I can easily deduct it if you don't want it. I'd rather start out with everything you might want and then go from there."

He stooped to his messenger bag and pulled out a stapled set of pages. He handed them to Grant and Caprice.

After both of them had gone over the contract, Grant said, "This only came in a little higher than what Caprice estimated it would. It looks fair."

Caprice was smiling now. "I told you Derek was one of the good guys."

"I think I'll have to prove that to Grant," Derek confirmed with a smile. "But you can watch the work every step of the way, as long as you don't get in the way."

They all laughed. They both signed the contract.

Ten minutes later they'd said good-bye to Derek and seen him out. Then they returned to Caprice's living room. Lady and Patches were sleeping under the cat tree where Sophia and Mirabelle dozed on separate shelves.

Grant took Caprice's hand. "We have to talk about something."

His voice was somber and she wondered if he was having second thoughts about the addition. "Was there something you didn't like on the plans?"

He shook his head. "No, not at all. I want to make

a suggestion, and I want you to really think about it before you react."

Uh, oh, what could be coming?

Grant went on, "I want you to remember how Roz feels about Vince's house. I want to pay for this addition. I want to feel invested in our marriage and in our property."

Caprice just stared at him wide-eyed until tears filled her eyes. "Did you think I'd fight you on this?"

He was as serious as she'd ever seen him. "I didn't know."

She quickly assured him, "I'll add your name to the deed after we're married."

"No, not after we're married. I want you to wait until after the addition is completed."

She realized that sometimes a man's pride was everything. This was Grant's pride talking, as well as his love for her. She wouldn't fight him on it, but she would like to pay for something herself. "How about if I buy us the stove? Then every time you turn it on to be warmer, you'll think of me."

He laughed. "My guess is you want to buy the stove to pick the color."

"If we get one with a ceramic coating, they actually do come in colors."

Grant groaned. "Don't tell me you'd decorate my office around the color of the stove."

"That's quite possible," she teased. Then she grew serious. "I do understand your feelings about this."

"Now that that's settled, we can concentrate on the wedding." He tugged her back to the sofa and pulled her down beside him.

"I have a list of everything we have to do yet."

He wrapped his arm around her shoulders. "I know you still don't have an answer from my parents about where they're going to stay. I'll call this week and ask again, and also tell them about the rehearsal dinner."

"Will you feel comfortable doing that?"

"I hardly ever feel comfortable with my parents. I'll try to be tactful and honest. If they object to Roz planning it, we'll figure out how we can include them."

Caprice had thought a lot about brothers lately, not only about Grant and his brother Holden, but about Travis and his brother Jarrett. She was lucky to have good friendships with her sisters, but that didn't mean they didn't have complications now and then. She had gone through a spell when she and Bella's husband Joe hadn't gotten along at all. That had caused mounds of tension. Grant had started sharing with her more and more, but he'd never shared what kept him and his brother at arm's length.

"Can you tell me why you and Holden don't have the best relationship?"

Grant didn't say anything for a good little while, and Caprice had decided she wasn't going to push . . . just wait. Finally, the waiting paid off.

He blew out a breath and turned to face her. "Part of the problem has always been that Holden is five years younger than I am, so our interests never overlapped. I've always thought Holden was wasting his life by not going to college. He could have gone to a community college and then taken out loans for two more years at a state college. He had average grades but he also had ability and intelligence."

"How did *you* get through school? Was it a breeze?"

"No breeze. But I had been lucky. My grades were high enough and, along with my track trophies, I earned scholarships. I also worked while I was in school so I could take as little as possible from my parents. Even though Holden had the smarts, he was tired of books and school. When he graduated from high school, his main interest was working to buy a car. After he did, he drove to Canada with friends. Then he drove to Florida, and next Minnesota . . . just because he wanted to. Eventually he found a position with a medical supply company. He's the head of a division now and he travels a lot in that work. But I don't know if he's happy."

Taking Grant's hand and leaning tighter against him, she concluded, "So the main problem between you is that Holden doesn't believe you approve of his life and that you haven't approved of his decisions."

"I suppose that's right," Grant admitted.

"When Holden arrives for the wedding, you can find out if he's happy. Maybe you can mend anything that's broken between you."

"You don't want much," Grant muttered.

"Just a kiss," she said sweetly.

A smile turned up the corners of his lips. Tipping up her chin, he gave her a kiss that told her their wedding couldn't come soon enough.

* * *

Caprice walked through the gardens at Rambling Vines Winery looking for Michelle. Hyacinths were blooming now around the fountain and their sweet scent seemed to linger over the area. The beautiful flowers and their aroma seemed incongruent with the idea that a murder had been committed here. The crime scene tape was gone now and that meant the York County Forensic Unit had finished with the crime scene.

Caprice heard a garage door go up. When she looked in that direction, she spotted Michelle with a man standing by the Dodge Coronet.

As she approached them, Michelle began introductions. "Caprice, this is Leon Wysocki. He restores cars. He did all of Travis's."

Leon was a short man, easily in his fifties. He had thick, gray-brown hair that was parted too far over on one side. A bit stocky, his ruddy cheeks seemed to complement his bulbous nose. His forehead was high and his lips thin.

Leon extended his hand to her. "It's good to meet you, Miss De Luca. I understand you have a Camaro that I could probably sell for a good price."

"My Camaro isn't for sale. Too much sweat equity invested in it from my family."

Leon nodded. "These cars do take time and attention, upkeep too. Well, I'll let you two ladies talk." He gave Michelle a steady stare. "Remember what I said. Call me any time."

Leon didn't leave through the gardens but rather began walking toward the large bay where the grapes were unloaded at the back of the winery. Caprice knew that road wound through the vineyards and then out to the main road.

"Are you thinking about selling the cars?" she asked Michelle.

"I am. Of course, Leon would get a commission from the sales but it would be worth it to unload them. The sale of the cars could stake me until the winery sells. Eventually I can return to nursing to support myself."

Caprice remembered now that Michelle had been a nurse when Vince dated her.

Michelle mused, "I met Travis in an ER. He'd had an accident during planting season."

Caprice could see that Michelle's memories seemed to be fond ones.

Suddenly Michelle seemed to shake herself free of them. "Let's go to the house. The dog isn't with you so you must have found him a home."

After they emerged from the garage, Michelle pressed a remote in her pocket and the door went down.

"I took him to Fred and Agnes's house," Caprice revealed. "He and Agnes got along immediately. I told them it was a foster situation. But I'm hoping he'll wiggle his way into their hearts."

After Michelle thought about the match, she smiled. "He could be good for both of them."

As they strolled toward the house, Caprice explained why she'd come. "I wanted to talk to you about Andy."

"Who?" Michelle asked, obviously not connecting the name with anyone.

"Andy Sprenkle, the teenager who snuck in here determined to ruin Travis's wine."

Recognition dawned on Michelle's face. "What about him?"

Caprice explained about her conversation with Andy and her drive with him to the police station.

"Did you hear anything from the detective after he questioned him?" Michelle wanted to know.

"Brett doesn't share information with me unless he has to. But if I hear anything, I'll let you know."

When they'd almost reached the house, Michelle tapped Caprice's arm. "I got a call from Chief Powalski. They released Travis's body. His funeral will be the day after tomorrow."

Michelle looked devastated by the thought. A funeral always seemed to make reality harsher.

"I'll be there," Caprice assured her. She had to be there to support Michelle as well as her brother. In addition, sometimes a funeral was the best place to find a suspect with a motive for murder.

Chapter Eleven

As soon as Caprice entered the funeral home, she realized the seats in the viewing room this morning were almost filled. She was later than she wanted to be. She also realized the outfit she'd chosen was appropriate. She'd worn high-waisted wide-leg navy trousers with a pale-blue long-sleeved blouse and an embroidered navy vest. Some men were dressed in suits but a few wore jeans. The women's attire was springtime casual. There wasn't going to be any type of service here because the graveside service and the reception at the winery would take place afterward.

The funeral director motioned Caprice toward the guest book. She signed it, briefly scanning the other names there. It seemed Vince had been here earlier. She wondered if he was still here. If he was, that meant he was doing more than paying his respects.

A copper-colored casket was positioned in the center at the front of the room. It was closed with a picture of Travis on top. Displays of flowers spread across the floor and on tables on either side. She imagined many of the people here had put in an appearance for Michelle as much as Travis. From what Caprice had heard, Michelle was well liked among the winery's clients.

Caprice spotted Michelle halfway up the side aisle. As always, she was impeccably dressed. Today she wore a green skirt suit with gold hoops at her ears.

As Caprice progressed up the aisle, she noticed Jarrett on the other side of the room, speaking to a couple.

Caprice decided to talk to Michelle first. An older, bald gentleman with wire-rimmed glasses was speaking to her. Should she interrupt or shouldn't she? If she got close enough to listen to the conversation, maybe then she'd know whether Michelle would like to be rescued or not. Sometimes at viewings, a friend who knew the deceased would latch on and monopolize the relatives. On the other hand, in this case, people who came to pay their respects could be questioning Michelle about what had happened. In poor taste? Certainly. But that didn't stop people from doing it.

As Caprice approached Michelle, she heard the older gentleman say, "You need to keep the winery and run it."

Michelle responded with a smile. "I was the event planner. I didn't make the wine or handle the business."

That didn't dissuade the advice the gentleman was giving her. "Maybe you should have been involved in that. Don't you know you could hire the right people if you really want to keep the winery open?"

The man was getting a little too animated. Caprice took a step closer and he noticed her. His face turned red. He patted Michelle's arm. "I'm sorry I was monopolizing you, but think about what I said."

"I will," Michelle told him pleasantly.

Close to her now, Caprice leaned in so no one could hear her. "I didn't know if you needed to be rescued."

"Mr. Lewis would have explained the whole business plan if he could have. Thank you."

"Are you considering running the winery yourself?"

"I just don't know. My head's still swimming from everything that happened."

Caprice asked, "If you would keep the winery would you still hire Neil as the CFO?"

"No, I don't think I would. He was Travis's hire, and the two of them usually got along just fine. But Neil and I—I don't know. I think we're just on two different wavelengths."

Caprice wondered what those wavelengths were.

"Whether I keep Neil or not, there is still a problem. I don't have the funds to keep the winery afloat. I would need an investor. Who would want to invest in a winery where someone was murdered?"

A young woman with a chic, short hairstyle and dressed in a gray business suit made her way toward Michelle. Caprice was going to step away but

Michelle grabbed her arm. "Hi, Leanne," Michelle said. "Caprice, this is Leanne Colbert. She's my former assistant. Leanne, meet Caprice De Luca."

"I remember Caprice," Leanne said. "She's the one who redecorated your tasting room and house too."

"That's me," Caprice said. She would have extended her hand but Leanne didn't seem to expect that.

Leanne explained, "I worked on event planning with Michelle before Travis fired me. Believe me, I'm not here for Travis. I'm here for Michelle." Her voice trailed off as her gaze went across the room. "I'm here for Jarrett too." She said to Michelle, "I am sorry, though. Travis's death probably leaves you in the lurch in a lot of areas. If you'll excuse me, I'll go talk to Jarrett."

After Leanne was out of earshot, Michelle kept her voice low. "I think Leanne had a crush on Jarrett when he was at the winery. Maybe now that he's back, she'll want to resurrect it."

"Did she find another job after she was fired?"

"Oh, yes. She was hired for one of the paid positions at the community center. She plans events for kids and adults. The salary isn't great, but from what I understand, she's enjoying the work and doing a good job of it."

Grant entered the room, saw Caprice, and came toward her. She couldn't help but smile. Every time she saw him, she got butterflies.

"Sorry I'm late," he said, wrapping his arm around her waist, leaning close and kissing her cheek. "Simon had some questions for when he keeps Patches when we go away on our honeymoon. I didn't have the heart to tell him I didn't have time to talk. He's like Patches' grandfather."

Caprice smiled just thinking about it. She was glad Grant was close to his neighbor. She hoped they'd stay friends even after Grant moved. Simon's townhouse wasn't that far to visit or drop Patches off if Grant needed him to pet sit.

Caprice's gaze fell on Jarrett and she thought that he looked uncomfortable, even jittery maybe. What was that about?

She leaned close to Grant. "The times I met Jarrett he was calm, cool, and collected. He doesn't look that way now. In fact, he just took out a handkerchief and wiped his brow."

"Maybe he had real feelings for his brother and this is difficult for him."

Caprice had to wonder if Grant was talking about himself and Holden.

Michelle moved away to talk to someone she knew, but Neil rose from his seat and came over to Grant and Caprice. Did he have something to tell her that might help in the investigation?

As he moved toward them, she noticed Leon, Travis's car mechanic and restorer who had been sitting near Neil. She spotted Fred Schmidt too in the row behind him. She was sure he was here for Michelle and not Travis.

Something she had forgotten came back to her now—the neighbor whom Fred had mentioned. The man didn't like the winery events since Michelle and Travis had redecorated and redone the winery. He was going to be the next person Caprice spoke with.

After Neil reached them, he pointed his chin toward the far-right corner. "Look who's hanging out at the back of the room."

When Caprice looked that way, she recognized the man immediately. It was Detective Jones.

"I was called in for questioning again," Neil said, sounding bitter about it. "He was the one who interviewed me."

"Was there a specific reason they called you in?" Caprice asked.

"Sure was. The detective wanted to know who might want to sabotage our wines. I told him about our main competitor and suggested Jarrett might want to do it too. They told me about the teenager who tried to pour something into the wine vat. I hadn't known about that because I'd been on the road talking to distributors. When I returned to the winery, Travis told me there'd been some trouble, but that he was taking care of it. That detective acted as if he didn't believe me."

"That's his way," Grant said. "He often goads a witness, hoping for honest reactions."

"All I had to give him was an honest reaction."

As Caprice thought about what Fred had told her, that he'd heard a conversation with Travis and Neil and blackmail had been mentioned, there was a commotion in the foyer of the funeral home— a loud voice, people murmuring, the funeral director following a woman into the room. She was waving her hands as she spoke to him. A black pillbox hat with a veil sat atop her very dark-brown hair styled in an upscale-looking blunt cut. She was wearing a black dress with an accompanying cape that was decorated with white embroidery. The outfit looked expensive. The shoes were Christian Louboutin. Caprice recognized them because Roz had shelves of pricey shoes. These were particularly noticeable with their red soles and very high heels.

Before Caprice could even form the question in her mind about the woman's identity, Jarrett rushed forward to greet her.

Michelle looked frozen and astonished.

"Who is she?" Caprice asked her.

"That's Travis and Jarrett's mother, Vivian Granville. I recognize her from photographs I've seen. She remarried after her divorce from William."

As Jarrett escorted his mother to the casket, Vivian began crying. She picked up the photo of Travis and her tears made streaks in her makeup.

"I'd better go over there," Michelle said. "It would only be polite. Come with me?" Michelle asked Caprice.

"But I'm not family."

"That doesn't matter. I just need backup support."

Since Caprice's first meeting with Grant's mom hadn't gone all that well, she could understand how disapproval emanating from someone important could damage self-confidence.

Grant patted Caprice's arm. "Go ahead." He leaned close. "If Michelle depends on you, maybe she won't depend on Vince."

Grant could be right. She nodded to Michelle and they both crossed the room to Jarrett and his mother.

Michelle said to Vivian, "It's horrible meeting

you under these circumstances. I'm Michelle, Travis's wife. This is my friend, Caprice De Luca. She's been a great support."

Jarrett said to his mother, "Caprice is trying to find out who would hurt Travis."

Vivian extended her hand to Michelle and then to Caprice in a graceful movement that told Caprice she was practiced in meeting people.

"Mom and I have been in touch. I e-mailed her the details about the funeral," Jarrett explained.

"I wish you would have told me she was coming," Michelle said to Jarrett.

He shrugged. "I wasn't sure she was."

Vivian inserted herself into the conversation. "I was overcome with grief. I didn't know if I'd be able to travel."

"I should have picked you up at the airport," Jarrett said.

"I used one of those car services and he brought me right here."

"You have your suitcases with you?"

"I do. He said he'd wait until I come out, and then take me where I need to go."

"I can drive you to the house," Jarrett said. Apparently realizing that maybe he didn't have a say in that, he asked Michelle, "Is it all right if my mother stays with us at the house?"

Put on the spot, what could Michelle say?

With a smile that was definitely forced, Michelle told Vivian, "Of course, you can stay. But I have to warn you—I had to let my housekeeper go. We'll have to cook our own meals or bring in takeout."

"Or we can go out for dinner," Vivian suggested as if that were a normal occurrence.

Caprice had the feeling that Vivian's visit to Rambling Vines Winery was going to be an uncomfortable one.

Two and a half hours later Grant and Caprice mingled with others who were paying respects to Travis or Michelle at the house at the winery. Michelle was absent a good amount of the time and Caprice wondered where she was. But after the food was laid out on the long dining room table, Caprice knew. Michelle had been in the kitchen, readying the platters.

Along with meatballs in a silver urn, there were platters of deli meats and cheeses, several different kinds of salads, and sheet cakes for dessert—one vanilla and one chocolate.

As Caprice went to the head of the table to pick up a plate—a paper plate—Michelle placed a bowl of fruit salad on the table. "There," she said. "I think I got it all. Isn't Grant getting something to eat?"

"He's talking to people he knows. They might be clients. I don't know. He doesn't tell me."

"The way it should be," Michelle said. "I would have liked to have asked Nikki to cater this, but I didn't want the expense."

"I'm sure she would have given you a discount."

"That wouldn't have been fair to her. Besides, this wasn't so much trouble. I picked up everything at the downtown deli early this morning. I would have preferred someone here to ready it before we got back from graveside, but this works."

"It does," Caprice said, knowing traditions were

going to be broken in this house if it wasn't sold
first.

"Walk with me a few minutes, will you?" Michelle
asked.

Caprice set down the paper plate. "Sure."

Passing through the dining room, they came to
another parlor. Sliding glass screened doors led
out to the sunporch but Michelle stopped in the
parlor. "I just want you to know I didn't intend to
make trouble for Vince."

"Trouble?" Caprice asked innocently.

"Yes. Apparently, Roz doesn't like him counsel-
ing me. But I just want you to know he's keeping
his emotional distance. We're not talking about
anything but business and the police when they
question me."

"Did he tell you Roz wasn't happy with this arrangement?"

"He didn't have to. I know he tells her when he
calls me. Or if I call him. And like today, he was in
and out of the funeral home after an 'I'm sorry'
and a hug. I understand. And the truth is—I can't
pay some expensive lawyer right now."

Caprice nodded her understanding but she
heard a male and female voice close by. Apparently, someone had come into the sunporch from
the outside.

Michelle caught on immediately and whispered,
"That's Vivian and Jarrett."

Neither woman moved but Caprice knew they
should.

They stayed put when Vivian said, "I tried to
reach Travis over the past few years but he would
never return my phone calls or e-mails. Why couldn't

he understand that I'd changed and was no longer drinking?"

Jarrett's tone was gentle as he answered. "You have to stop thinking about it. There's nothing you can do now."

Before Caprice knew what Michelle was going to do, she opened the screen and stepped into the sunporch. "Caprice and I were in the parlor and I overheard you. Vivian, when did you last try to contact Travis?"

Since Michelle had made their presence known, Caprice joined her.

Vivian glanced at Jarrett. "Over the holidays I sent him an e-mail."

"I saw pictures of you that Jarrett had set on his dresser when he lived here. I'm sorry we never met formally. Travis would never talk about your divorce from his father or why you left."

"I slunk away," Vivian admitted. "I went home to New Hampshire. My mother was still alive then and she grounded me. When I couldn't hold a job, I got sober."

"Good for you," Michelle said with sincerity. "Were you happy in your work?"

"I began working at a cloth mill and soon became executive secretary to the owner. After all, I did manage this house and a housekeeper, butler, and maid. I planned cocktail parties. I definitely knew how to organize. But that wasn't what made my life happy. I spent a lot of time with the owner of the mill. We fell in love and married. When Lawrence died, I inherited everything. I sold the mill a year ago and have been at loose ends since."

Michelle volunteered, "We no longer have a

maid, butler, or housekeeper. I'm sorry about that. I might have to sell the winery and the house. But, for now, you're welcome to stay. I'd like to get to know you. Maybe we can find out more about the Dodd family. I imagine you want to know about the years you lost with Travis and I'd like to know about those years before you divorced William Dodd."

"That could be painful for you both," Jarrett suggested, frowning.

"Sometimes you have to get through the pain to get to the other side," Vivian advised. She reached out and gave Michelle's hand a squeeze. "I like your idea and I'll be glad to spend time getting to know you, as well as having discussions with my son."

Because Caprice knew Michelle, she sensed her sincerity in the proposal. But Vivian? Was she being sincere or did she want something? And Jarrett . . . She could ask the same about him.

Yet she knew from experience the truth would out, one way or another. The only question was— would the police find it first, or would she?

When Grant put his SUV in reverse as they were leaving, Caprice had an idea. "While we're out here, don't you think we should visit the neighbor who Michelle suggested could have murdered Travis?"

Grant gave her an *are-you-sure-you-want-to-do-this* look.

"I'm sure we should do this," she told him without him asking the question. And the good thing is, you're with me. I'll be safe."

"Tell me again why Michelle thinks he could have killed Travis."

"Because he has a temper. He shouts. He raises his fists. Ever since they built the reception hall, he's against the activities they have there because they create more traffic. He also hates music and dances. Michelle told me he even threatened Travis with slicing everyone's tires the last time they had an outdoor band playing."

"It's a far cry from slicing tires to murder," Grant offered.

"I agree, but I'd like to talk to him myself . . . to get a feel for him."

"All right. Which direction should I go off the lane, east or west?"

"West," she told him with a slight smile.

He gave her a slanted glance. "Do you think you're going to get your way all the time when we're married?"

"I can only hope," she said brightly.

Grant laughed. "At least you're honest."

She hoped they would always be honest with each other.

Since Andrei Moldavan was Michelle's closest neighbor, Grant didn't have to drive far. The lane to Moldavan's house, however, was more dirt than gravel, more potholes than smooth road. As they approached the house, they could see it was shabbily maintained. It was more like a cabin with wood siding that had once been painted white. It needed to be repainted. There was a chicken wire

fence around the yard and hung on it was a sign
that said BEWARE OF DOG.

The front porch seemed to sag a little at one
end. The one saving grace for the house was the
forsythia bushes in the front yard. There were two
on either side of the walk just inside the fence, and
two more on either side of the walk at the steps
that went up to a small porch at the front door.
Parked close to the house, a tan-and-white Silver-
ado stood on the grass. A rusted-out car was raised
on blocks a ways from the house.

"Why do I feel that I should be packing a re-
volver for this visit?" Grant asked.

"I'll bet the BEWARE OF DOG sign is a bluff,"
Caprice decided.

Grant grimaced. "I don't want to find out the
hard way."

"See? Isn't it good you're with me? You wouldn't
have liked it if I had come out here alone."

Grant parked right in front of the fence so that
Moldavan could see his vehicle and know they
were there. "I wouldn't want to sneak up on a guy
like this. And if he tells us to leave, we leave," he
warned her.

"Got it," Caprice said cheerfully as she unfastened her seatbelt and opened the door of the
SUV.

Grant came around to her side. The gate was
rickety. When Grant opened it, it gave a loud
squeak.

"That's probably his security alarm," Grant muttered.

A few seconds later they found out that Grant

was right. A man with long, flowing gray hair and a gray beard to match came out on the porch with a scowl. He was wearing workpants with suspenders and a brown T-shirt. Caprice guessed he might be around fifty.

"Ain't you seen the sign?" the man grumbled.

"Do you have a dog?" Caprice asked. "I love dogs. I have a cocker spaniel and so does my fiancé, Grant Weatherford. I'm Caprice De Luca."

Her introductions didn't coax any from him. "I got a Doberman inside, and if I let him out, you'll be sorry."

A Doberman wouldn't have much room to roam in a house that size. It was probably a thousand square feet. She doubted if the man had a Doberman that he'd keep him inside.

"Who are you again?" the man demanded.

Grant stepped forward. "Are you Andrei Moldavan?"

"Who wants to know?" he asked belligerently.

"Mr. Moldavan, I'm going to be honest with you," Caprice said.

"I'll bet," he mumbled.

She looked him straight in the eyes. He had an alert hazel gaze that seemed more curious and intelligent than he let on. "My name's Caprice and, as I said, this is my fiancé Grant Weatherford. We're having our wedding reception at the winery. I'm trying to gather information to clear Michelle of the suspicion of murder. That's why I wanted to talk to you."

Now the man's expression seemed to soften a bit. "Michelle ain't so bad," he admitted. "But her husband got what he deserved."

"Do you mind if I ask if you know anything about the murder?"

Moldavan crossed his arms over his chest and was silent until he said, "I didn't tell the police nothin' and I'm not telling *you* nothin'."

"Why won't you give the police information to help capture the killer?" Caprice asked.

Uncrossing his arms, Moldavan glared at the two of them. "I want you to leave."

"If you *sort of like* Michelle, you should help her. If she sells the winery, there's no telling what the next owners could do."

Now the man took a step toward them, and when he did, Grant caught Caprice's elbow. He gave it a squeeze. "Come on," he urged her.

They both turned their backs on Moldavan and hurried down the walk. Grant closed the gate behind him.

"If he thinks about what I said, he might open up," Caprice suggested hopefully.

"And he might not," Grant insisted. "Don't ever come out here alone."

Usually Caprice became defensive when Grant tried to protect her or give her orders. But this time, she knew he was right.

Chapter Twelve

Caprice expected the high-end buyers who had seen the photos from the "Bohemian Rhapsody" house online or in newsletters would love it. The quirkiness of the six-thousand-square-foot stone-and-brick home had drawn them here. From that turquoise curio cabinet in the foyer to the beautiful unique mosaic fireplace along with the macramé chair in the sunroom, this house would be hard to forget. Dustin and Althea might not get a contract today, but she expected they would soon.

Nikki had put together a variety of foods from *kolaches*, which were sweet yeast buns filled with a raspberry-almond filling, to shrimp ceviche to a cabbage dish with caraway seeds and sour cream to pork chops and dumplings. The food was as unique as the house. The piece-de-resistance was a *babovka*, a bohemian cake with lemon rind, ground nuts, and coconut, topped with powdered sugar. Caprice had had a taste of the food. Like all of Nikki's dishes, it was exceptional. The dining room table with its dark wood and curlicue legs was already full from couples who had gone through the buffet line and settled there. The valance-like wooden feature around the tabletop added to its unique nature. The tall luxuriously tufted but armless chairs made seating as many guests as possible around the table comfortable.

A couple came down the staircase, commenting on the photos on the wall. When they reached the bottom, they saw Caprice. Today she was wearing a long Bohemian-style empire-waisted maxi-dress that was patterned with a colorful print in turquoise and fuchsia. With it, she'd worn the pink sapphire earrings Grant had given her for Christmas. They matched her heart-shaped pink diamond engagement ring. She wore turquoise shoes with leather straps that crisscrossed her ankles. The waitstaff who assisted Nikki wore colorful Bohemian-print tops over black leggings. Nikki and Caprice had tried to coordinate every aspect of the open house.

When the couple reached the first floor, they crossed over to Caprice. "You staged the house, didn't you? Someone pointed you out to us."

Caprice extended her hand and introduced herself. The couple did the same. "Are you interested in the house?" Caprice asked. If they were, she'd show them to the real estate agent in charge today, Denise Langford.

"We might be," the husband said. "Can you tell us if the furniture would go along with the sale?"

"That might be negotiable," Caprice told them. "The owner told me they couldn't take everything with them when they move. So it would be quite possible."

Caprice spotted Denise exiting the dining room. She beckoned to her. "You might want to talk to these folks. They have some questions about the sale of the house."

"Why don't you come to the library with me," Denise said. "We'll get acquainted and I can answer any questions you might have."

Denise gave a nod to Caprice in thank you. She and Denise had sold many houses together. Though Denise could be a little brash at times, Caprice liked her forthrightness, if not always her attitude. Nevertheless, she sold houses and Caprice's reputation as a home stager was spread a little farther.

Caprice stopped in the kitchen to see Nikki who stood at the butcher-block counter going over a list. Caprice tapped her on the shoulder. "We have a nice showing today."

"The real estate agents involved have done a good job of spreading the word and screening clients. I heard a couple from New York say they were thinking about making an offer," Nikki revealed.

"I just spoke to a couple who are interested too. Maybe there will be a bidding war."

"That's better for Denise's pocket than yours," Nikki joked.

Her sister knew she charged a flat fee for her stagings, depending on what changes she had to make with the house and how much time was involved.

Suddenly there was a commotion in the foyer.

Caprice heard a dog barking. She thought she recognized that bark. Was that Dylan?

Although Roz had adopted Dylan, Caprice had
found him as a stray and given him a home. But
then Roz had had a crisis in her life and she and
the little black-and-white fluffy-furred dog, part
Pomeranian and part Shih Tzu, just seemed to
connect.

"I'll see what's going on," Caprice told Nikki as
she hurried through the house and out to the
foyer. Roz was standing there with Dylan dancing
around her feet. When Roz saw Caprice, she picked
up Dylan and murmured, "I hope this isn't a problem."

Caprice wasn't sure what "this" was, but she
knew Roz looked as if she had been crying. She
hooked her arm around Roz's shoulders and
guided her to a side parlor. Once inside, she
turned toward her friend. "What's going on?"

"I hated to barge in like this, but I just had to
talk to somebody, and I wanted to talk to you."

"How did you find me?"

"Grant. I know you keep your phone turned off
during these open houses, or at least keep it on vi-
brate, but sometimes you don't feel it."

"This dress doesn't have a pocket, so I left my
purse in the car. It has my phone in it. Why are you
so upset?"

"Michelle called Vince again. Afterward, we had
a terrible fight, so I packed a bag. Can Dylan and I
stay with you tonight . . . or maybe for a few nights?"

"Of course, you can."

"Did you and Grant have plans for tonight?"

She was always honest with Roz. "He'll probably

come over while you're there. I told him I'd put a pot roast in the slow cooker. But I can call him and tell him not to come."

"Oh, don't do that. Will he mind if I'm there?"

"He won't mind. He knows you have a key and you know the security system code. I'll text him and tell him you're going to be there."

"I hate to impose like this, but I couldn't go to a hotel because of Dylan." Roz's eyes were so troubled Caprice gave her a hug.

"We were housemates once before. We got through a difficult time then and we will now."

Roz backed away. "But you and Grant . . ."

"Grant knows I have friends, and I know he has friends. Besides, you're not just a friend, you're family. Are you going to let Vince know where you are?"

"No," Roz answered tersely while Dylan tried to lick her face.

"Roz," Caprice said in warning.

"Let him worry a little bit. That might not be very nice, but he's caused me so much worry—"

She glanced at Caprice's expression, and although Caprice didn't say anything, Roz acquiesced. "All right. I'll text him. Maybe in a couple of hours."

Caprice knew that was the best she was going to get for now. She scratched Dylan around the ears and gave him a pat on the head. The little dog got along with Lady and Patches so there wasn't a problem there.

"I took Lady over to Grant's before coming here today, so when Grant comes over he'll be bringing both dogs. Are you okay with that?"

"They'll get along. I don't know how Sophia and Mirabelle will feel about it."

"They'll adjust," Caprice said matter-of-factly. "They might sit on their top two shelves of the cat tree, but they'll be fine. And if Grant's there, he's pretty good at keeping them all calm. You go to my place, get comfortable, and relax. I'll be home as soon as I can and then we can talk."

Roz gave Caprice a hug with Dylan still in her arms. "Thank you."

"No thanks necessary. Come on, I'll walk you out."

After Roz got into her car and drove away, Caprice felt like calling her brother. But she wouldn't. She had to stay out of this to a certain extent. But only to a certain extent.

When Caprice walked into her house, she had to smile. Grant, Roz, and the three dogs were watching TV. She hung her sweater coat embroidered with flowers on the antique oak mirror stand in her foyer and laid her purse on the marble-top table. Grant had left the small Tiffany-style lamp burning to welcome her home.

The aroma of pot roast simmering in the slow cooker wafted through the house. She was glad she had started it this morning and made a salad to accompany it. Redskin potatoes and carrots were nestled around the roast, so supper would be ready when they were.

As soon as Grant heard and saw her, though, he was on his feet. Crossing to her, he gave her a hug and a short but thorough kiss. "I'll leave so you and Roz can talk."

"That's silly," Roz said from the sofa. "Caprice has supper ready and I'm sure you're hungry. I am too, but probably shouldn't be. Stress eating. Stay with us and tell me about the plans for the addition. Your perspective might be different than Caprice's."

Grant chuckled. "I don't know about that. We had to approve the plans together, and we did that. I think they're going to fill both of our needs and make the pets happy too."

Dylan, who was sitting on Roz's lap, roused, jumped off the sofa and ran over to Caprice. Patches and Lady, together on one side of the coffee table, stayed napping.

Caprice stooped to the little dog and picked him up. "I'm glad somebody's excited to see I'm home."

Grant tapped her on the shoulder. "I'm excited to see you're home."

She laughed.

"How did the open house go?" Roz asked. "I'm sorry I barged in like that. I never should have done that. I should have just had you meet me outside."

"No harm done. I think we had three couples who were seriously interested. We'll see what happens in the next few days if a contract comes in."

"Are you sure you want me to stay?" Grant asked Roz, expecting her to be honest.

"I do," she said. "We'll talk about additions and pets and have a nice meal."

Roz and Grant both helped set the table while Caprice dished out the main course. As they passed the meat platter and serving dishes, Grant described the office addition along with the attached powder room.

"That's a great idea," Roz said. "Not only for your office and your clients, but if you ever had a guest who needs to stay here."

"Exactly what we thought," Caprice said. "How about blueberry bread for dessert? Grocery Fresh had some beautiful organic blueberries. I couldn't help but pick them up."

"And coffee?" Roz asked.

"Of course. Decaf or caffeine?"

"I'd like caffeine," Roz said. "I'm sure we're going to be up late talking."

"That's fine with me," Grant agreed. "I have work to do after I get home."

Caprice studied him, hoping that in less than a month he would consider *this* his home. Wouldn't he? Or would it always feel like her house?

Grant shook his finger at her. "I know what I said and I know what you're thinking."

"There's that reading-minds talent again," Caprice teased, wondering if he really could.

"After we put the addition on here, this will be your home and my home, together. It will be the same yet different. I'll have my space if I feel I need it, and we'll have that new sunroom too, though I imagine you're probably going to fill it with cat condos and dog beds."

"How did you guess?" Caprice joked.

He shook his head while trying to hide a smile.

They kept conversation light over dessert and

coffee. But then Grant stood. "Do you want to see me and Patches out?"

"I'll start cleaning up," Roz offered.

Caprice was about to say, *You don't have to do that*, but she knew Roz would anyway. It was her way of repaying Caprice for her hospitality.

As Caprice walked Grant and Patches into the foyer, he said, "I did want to talk to you in private."

"Is something wrong?"

"No, nothing's wrong. My parents called this afternoon and said that they *will* stay with your parents."

"Victory," Caprice said with some excitement.

"Maybe. Maybe not." Grant ran his fingers through his thick black hair. "I just hope they'll all get along."

Caprice could see Grant was worried about his parents and hers. "I'll warn my parents to be on their best behavior," she assured him. "But Nana is another story. She can be blunt and tactful but sometimes she's just blunt."

"My parents got a taste of that when they had dinner with your parents and Nana. They'll respect her even if they don't like what she says."

He blew out a breath and Caprice knew he wasn't finished relaying "news." He went on, "My parents also said they were unaware that the groom's parents should pay for the rehearsal dinner and plan it. I thought it was best to be honest with them, and I told them Roz had offered to have it for us. My father was on the upstairs phone and my mom on the downstairs phone. That's when Dad broke in and said he insisted on paying Roz at least half the cost."

"Should we let them duke it out?" Caprice asked. "Roz can be pretty insistent."

"And my dad can be stubborn. Maybe that would be best. They can figure it out *after* the wedding."

Caprice hoped nothing would cause discord, but she also knew something might. When families got together, anything could happen. "Do your parents know about the murder at the winery?"

"I didn't tell them. If it comes up, we'll deal with it. We'll explain that the events room where the reception is held had nothing to do with it."

Grant wrapped his arms around Caprice, and she was so glad he did. She felt safe in that circle. She felt right. She knew she was independent enough and smart enough to live a contented life on her own. She didn't want to. Somehow Grant *did* make her life feel complete. She loved everything about him even when they didn't agree. They might have bumpy times in the future as well as joyful ones. But they'd get through them . . . together.

After Grant left and the kitchen was cleaned up, Caprice pulled a bottle of wine from her refrigerator. She and Roz sat in the living room. Lady had awakened when Patches left and now she played chase with Sophia around Caprice's downstairs. Dylan joined in and the three made a racket as their paws pounded on the hardwood floor and upended the edge of throw rugs.

Roz clinked her glass against Caprice's. "Thank goodness for pets."

"Thank goodness," Caprice agreed.

After a few sips of wine, Roz reached up to the back of the sofa to pet Mirabelle who was napping there. "I don't know what to do about Vince or Michelle or the way he thinks about his house."

"If you ignore any of it, it's not going to go away. I mean, even if he stops calling Michelle or if she stops calling him, you're going to have resentment there because of it. You need to come to an agreement about it."

Roz set her wine glass on the coffee table. "What kind of agreement? It's okay if he has Michelle as a client?"

Calmly, Caprice responded, "If that's all she is. Let me ask you something and don't get upset, okay?"

"Everything upsets me these days." She picked up her wine glass once more. "Go ahead."

"Are your insecurities in your relationship with Vince causing you to see more than there is between him and Michelle?"

Roz was quiet for several seconds. "I suppose that's possible. I'd like to think I'm not that close-minded. There's just a familiarity when he talks to her that really bothers me."

"They dated for a few months, Roz. They know each other to a certain extent, at least their backgrounds. Familiarity just comes naturally if they're amicable."

"Oh, they're amicable."

Caprice just gave her a steady stare.

Roz sighed. "I see what you mean."

Caprice pulled her leg under her. "What bothers you the most about the whole situation?"

"Not having my name on the title of the house," Roz answered without thinking about it. "Vince lets me pay utilities but that's not the same thing."

"Then you have to tell him how much that upsets you. Make him understand, Roz. Talk and talk
and talk until he does."

"That's harder than it sounds."

"He's my brother. Don't I know it?"

Roz gave her a half-hearted smile. "All right. I'll
do what you suggest. But for tonight, how about
another glass of wine and just girl talk."

"Sounds good to me."

And it did. She missed the time she once spent
with Roz. Still, they managed to reconnect even
when it wasn't a serious occasion such as this. Roz
would talk to Vince—*if* she wanted to have a future
with him.

On Monday morning, Roz—who said she was
letting her manager run her shop this week—slept
in late while Caprice worked on her computer.
She was perusing her list for the next house staging. The theme would be Floral Fantasy. After she
finished the list for what she might lease from a
local rental company, she decided what she could
need from an online company. She also went over
the list of her inventory in her two storage com-
partments.

As she checked off items, she realized what was
missing. She could use glassware. She knew Mikasa
had made pretty bowls and vases with floral ac-
cents. Chances were good Isaac Hobbs's shop
Older and Better might just have a few at a good
price. And while she was out, she just might stop at
the Black Horse Winery and nose around.

There wasn't a question of taking Lady along,

not with Dylan at the house. The two dogs got along well. If they made too much of a ruckus, Roz would get up.

Caprice called to both dogs and they ran into the kitchen, still having plenty of morning energy even though they'd already been out once.

"How about a play session outside before I leave?" she asked them. "Then you'll be good and tired and maybe take a nap. What do you say?"

Dylan did a little dance and yipped. Lady just cocked her head as if to ask, *Why aren't you opening the door already?*

Caprice laughed. "Come on, pooches. I'll even throw a ball for you." She said to Lady, "The yard's not going to be quite as big once we put on the addition."

Lady glanced over the yard as if she was inspecting it.

"But you're going to like the sunroom. I'm sure of that."

Dylan gave another yip and ran down the steps from the porch as if to say, *Come on, let's play.* Lady followed happily behind him.

Caprice picked up two balls—one larger and one smaller—that sat on top of the robin's-egg-blue metal glider. She played with the dogs for a half hour, even going over basic commands. They passed with flying colors. After she'd settled them inside with chew toys, she wrote Roz a note with the time the dogs had been out, picked up her purse and left.

Since her retro-style boxy jacket and Katharine Hepburn-style slacks didn't require a coat or sweater, she was comfortable driving toward Isaac's shop which was located on the outskirts of Kismet. When she reached his parking lot, she noticed only one other car. That was good because that meant she and Isaac could chat.

The door to the antique shop opened and an older woman stepped out. Caprice greeted her and then went inside. Isaac was pushing a dry sink back into place against the wall.

"Rearranging furniture?" Caprice asked, teasingly.

Isaac stood, straightened and gave her a scowl. "I'm not sure I appreciate your humor this early in the morning."

"It's ten o'clock."

"That means it's past time for coffee. That woman who just left wanted me to pull out the dry sink so she could look at it—all sides of it. After spending fifteen minutes doing just that, she decided she didn't want it."

"I'm sorry. But you know how picky some people can be. They want an antique with no marks on it."

He grunted. "Come on. Caffeine makes everything better."

Isaac's coffee used to taste like sludge. Then he'd bought a coffee maker that brewed one cup at a time from little pods. Each cup was delicious. He even had flavors.

"What kind do you want today?" he asked.

"How about Chocolate Dream?"

He grimaced. "So you're going to have *that* kind of day. You have to start out in a decadent mood."

She laughed. "Maybe. While I'm sipping on my coffee, I'd like to look around at your glassware.

I'm looking for pieces with floral themes, and I was thinking about Mikasa. They had a few pieces with rose patterns. Some of them were even pale pink."

"I know exactly what you're talking about—Mikasa's *Bella Rosa Pink*. I think I have a bowl in that Shaker hutch." He pointed across the room while he began brewing Caprice's coffee. She went to look and saw that the bowl was exactly what she wanted. She brought it up to the counter.

"We'll haggle after I look around some more," she joked.

"You're one of the best hagglers around." He set the mug of coffee on the counter for her. "Half and half and sugar?"

"A little of both. After all, I'm in the mood to be decadent this morning."

That brought a smile to his lips. "Where's Lady?"

"Roz is staying with me and Dylan is there with her, so I knew Lady wouldn't want to leave."

"Uh, oh. Trouble in paradise? Vince isn't thinking about serial dating again, is he?"

Lots of people in town knew about her brother's history. He had definitely changed after he met Roz. "No, not serial dating."

"So it *does* have something to do with the murder."

"Not the murder per se. But he dated Michelle before he met Roz, and Michelle is depending on him for advice."

"A past girlfriend. That will lead to trouble," Isaac assured her. "*You* had experience with that."

"Naomi wasn't an ex-girlfriend. She was an ex-wife. If I had just trusted Grant more, that wouldn't have been a problem at all."

Shrugging, Isaac added cream and sugar to her mug of coffee. "You two figured it out."

Yes, they had, because they'd kept communication open. Roz and Vince weren't doing that yet.

Changing the direction of their conversation, Caprice asked, "Do you know anything about Vivian Dodd Granville?"

Isaac thought about it. "Not so much. Everything that could be hush-hush about the Dodd family was . . . unless someone who worked for them leaked gossip. One thing was obvious, though."

"What was that?"

Isaac inserted another coffee pod in the brewer. "There were plenty of rumors that Vivian drank too much and neglected her children. Her drinking was definitely true. People saw her when she was sloshed. But neglecting her children? I'm not sure about that. That could have been something that William Dodd cooked up to get her to leave."

"He retained full custody."

"Yes, he did. From what I understand, he wouldn't let the boys see her. But that didn't stop Jarrett. It was true he couldn't visit her. Yet word on the street was that the two of them exchanged letters through a friend of his so his father or brother couldn't intercept them."

"That's terrible that he even had to think of it that way!"

"Maybe so. You know how it is. Probably no one knew the real story."

The real story. Just how could she discover the real story?

Only by nosing around more. Something told her that the Black Horse Winery could be one place to glean more information, maybe not about Vivian, but about Travis and his father and the winery business. Passion led to murder. So did greed. So could failure.

Yep, the Black Horse Winery would be her next stop.

Chapter Thirteen

The Black Horse Winery's estate was very different from Rambling Vines. The building where the wines were created had a stone base. The same stone had been used for the gables, as well as the front portico that had been added. It wasn't a portico as much as a very wide covered walkway. It had been designed with several arches. There wasn't an events building but Caprice knew weddings had been held somewhere on the twenty-acre vineyard. When she'd studied the winery's website, the first thing she'd noticed was the fenced-in area behind the building where three black horses ran. They were beautiful.

She'd booked a tour online so she could actually meet the owner, Earl Hoff. After she parked on the gravel expanse for that purpose, she saw a man emerge from the winery. He stood under one of the stone arches and raised a hand to her in a wave.

She went that way. The winery owner looked to

be in his late forties, with gray hair that parted high on his hairline. He looked fit and she wondered if he did some of the vineyard work himself.

"Hello," he said amiably. "Are you Miss De Luca?"

She extended her hand to him. "Just call me Caprice."

"And just call me Earl. As I told you in my e-mail, part of our tour takes place outside this area and you can actually see the grapevines. Inside the winery, I can tell you about the wine making process. Right now, in the springtime, we're bottling so you can actually see that happening."

"Sounds good," Caprice assured him. "I'm ready to learn everything about the operation."

"Are you thinking about opening a winery?" he asked jokingly. "The Susquehanna Valley is an up-and-coming area. More wineries open each year."

As they walked, he showed her into the tasting room. Again, it was nothing like Rambling Vines. It was a narrow room behind the walkway with a brick floor and stone walls. There was a counter with oyster crackers and a few shelves with simple wine glasses lined up in a row.

"A tasting first?" he asked.

"Sure."

"What's your pleasure? Semi-dry, dry, semi-sweet, sweet?"

"Actually, I love fruit wines. I know they're more for dessert than drinking with a meal, but I prefer the lower alcohol content."

"Fruit wines are great for friendly visits too. We call them sipping wines. But, as you said, they're also good with chocolate desserts and cheesecake.

You might think of them as aperitifs too. Then again, it tends to depend on how heavy the flavor is."

"Tell me about your fruit wines."

"I want you to keep in mind that our fruit wines are actually fruit wines. They are not grape wines with extract."

"Is this a specialty for you?"

"Few wineries put the care and expertise into their fruit wines that we do," he said with a most serious expression.

She knew a sales pitch when she heard one, but on the other hand, maybe he was being honest about it.

"One thing I remember about my grandfather," Caprice told him, "was that he liked black raspberry wine. He would pour it over vanilla ice cream and even fruits."

Earl chuckled. "Do you have an Italian background?"

"I do," she said with a smile. "Both sides."

He nodded. "Does your grandfather ever make wine?"

"My Nana tells stories about the few years that he tried. I'm not sure how successful he was."

"It's an art form in some ways, although science principles have to be applied."

He pulled a bottle of black raspberry wine from under the counter. Using a corkscrew, he opened it. "Would you like this in a cordial glass or should I spoon it over ice chips?"

"A cordial glass would be fine."

After Earl set the glass in front of her, she picked it up and swirled it a little. Then she took in the aroma. Sweet raspberries. As she took a sip, she savored it. What she liked most about black raspberry, even the one she remembered from way back when, was that it was satiny in flavor.

"Mmmm," she said. "I don't think we'll find one to beat this."

Again, Earl laughed. "This is definitely our sweet wine. Even our apple wine is semi-sweet. Would you like to try that? We also have a spiced apple that's particularly popular in the fall."

"I'd be glad to try the apple wine."

"Cordial again?"

She nodded.

He poured it and set it in front of her. She swirled it, smelled it, and took a taste. She waved her hand back and forth. "It's good. But as you said, it's a semi-sweet. I'd like two bottles of the black raspberry, please."

"You don't want to try anything else?"

"Not today. I'm going to keep one and give one to my brother. He likes to tour all the different wineries."

"As I said, there are enough of us in the area now that it would be easy to do a wine tour in a day."

"I'm having my wedding reception at Rambling Vines Winery."

Earl narrowed his brown eyes. "Did you come to compare?"

"Not exactly. I really did want to taste your fruit wines and see your winery. But I'm also trying to help solve Travis Dodd's murder."

He studied her for a few moments, then he snapped his fingers. "Caprice De Luca. I thought that name sounded familiar. You've been written up in the local papers. Something about helping the police and finding homes for animals."

"I've done both," she admitted.

"And why aren't you buying Rambling Vines' wines?"

Her purpose for being here was simple. "Because I want to know if what I've heard about the business is true."

He frowned. "What have you heard?"

"You said more wineries are opening up in this area."

"Throughout the state, really."

She nodded. "I imagine you're all competing for the same customers."

"We are."

"Can you tell me if the rivalries are friendly?"

Now Earl poured himself a cordial of the apple wine. He raised his glass and she raised hers and they clinked. "You want the dirt, not the PR we give everybody else, right?"

"Murder usually has something to do with dirt."

After he studied her for a few moments, he revealed, "For the most part the rivalries are friendly. We all want to do well. As you said, we're competing for the same customers across the state. In our local areas, customers can shift from one winery to another. For instance, some of us have wine subscription services. Many wineries call them clubs."

"Can you explain them?"

"Sure. We have e-mail lists, of course, to go out to our customers for events, new wines, specials. That's just like any other business does these days. But the clubs have definitely added revenue. They run for a year. Some clubs are miscellaneous. That means each quarter you would receive three bottles of wine to be selected by the winery. You might join the fruit club. Each quarter you would receive however many bottles of wine that you choose for that year. Then there's a specials club. Each month we run a special on a different wine. So every quarter you would receive the three bottles that ran as a special in that quarter. Do you see what I mean?"

"I do. Because customers have signed up for a year, I imagine they receive a discount for signing up for the whole year and paying at the start of the year. That way, you have customers committed to buying your wines."

"You *are* a business woman. That's exactly how it works. Those who pay quarter by quarter don't get a discount. First quarter payment is up front, of course."

"Of course. Gossip runs around the wine business as much as any other business, I imagine."

Earl took another sip of wine, set the glass down with a thump, and asked, "So what have you heard about Black Horse Winery?"

"I heard that Travis Dodd paid off a reviewer so his new wine got a good review and your new wine received a bad review."

"That's not a rumor. That's true."

"Can you prove it?"

"You aren't a professional undercover cop, are you?"

"No way. My sister Nikki is dating a detective. I give him information, but he rarely gives me any."

Earl set his elbow on the counter. "All right. Consider this off the record."

"I don't know if I can do that if it has something to do with Travis's murder."

"I doubt that it does. Let's just say I have a friend who's very good with a computer. He managed to get a copy of the reviewer's e-mails. He has a copy of the message that says Travis would pay the guy five hundred dollars to give a bad review to Black Horse Winery."

Wow! The tech age at work. "Did the review affect business?"

"Of course, it did. As I said, each area has its customers. If they don't buy my new wine, they might buy the wine from Rambling Vines or Adams County or anywhere else."

"How badly did this affect you?"

"Not nearly as much as it would have affected Dodd. I don't overspend like he did."

Her instincts perked up. "Overspend?"

"Just look at that events building where you're probably having your reception. Imagine what that cost, not to mention redecorating, redoing the tasting room, putting in gardens. Above all, the money he spent on the promotion."

"Promotion other than subscription lists?"

"Exactly. If somebody said they could sell his wines for him, he paid. That's so foolish. Research has to go into it. It's necessary to find out from other wineries and winemakers if ads at those particular venues pay off. It does no good to place an ad and then only break even."

"I can see that would be true."

Earl straightened, ready to wrap up their conversation. "So you only want the two bottles of black raspberry?"

"That would be great for now. But I'll tell my brother he should stop in. I'm sure he will."

"Do you want the tour or did you learn enough?"

"I'd love a tour of the vineyards. It's a beautiful day and I'd like to learn about your grapes."

He cut a glance to her. "Even though you like black raspberries better?"

She laughed. Then she grew serious. Earl Hoff could be a personable guy. However, could he have committed murder? That was hard to say. After her tour of the vineyard, maybe it was time to meet with Brett and just see how far his investigation had progressed. She could lay out her suspect list. He might not tell her anything, but his attitude and his expression sometimes gave her hints.

One good hint might be all she needed.

Caprice met Brett at the Sunflower Diner that afternoon. He was already sitting in a booth in the back when she arrived, staring into his cup of coffee. There was an empty dish in front of him that Caprice suspected had held a slice of cherry pie. A dab of filling dotted the side of the dish. At one time, Grant had thought Brett was interested in her. But whatever had been true back then, now Brett only had eyes for her sister.

A waitress had followed Caprice to the table. Caprice smiled and said, "What he had."

As the waitress scurried away, Brett reminded Caprice, "I don't have a lot of time. I'm going over witness statements and bank records."

"Travis's bank records?"

Brett kept his mouth closed tight.

"Right. I'm not supposed to ask that. Will you be bringing in more people who knew Travis for questioning?"

He looked as if he thought about that question before answering. "Yes, and some we'll be bringing in for a second or third time."

"You mean Michelle?"

Again, he kept his mouth closed.

"You know the phrase tight-lipped doesn't do itself justice when it's applied to you."

This time he gave her a shrug.

"You're taunting me on purpose, aren't you?" she demanded to know.

His mouth twitched in a bit of a smile. "How am I doing?"

She shook her head. "Men."

"You're putting Grant in my category?"

"No, I'm putting Vince in your category."

"Oh, no," Brett said, holding his hand up in front of her like a stop sign. "I'm not getting mixed up in that. He knows he should cut his ties with Michelle Dodd, but I imagine you've told him that more than once. Or haven't you?" Brett asked with a raised brow.

"Of course, I have. He's not doing his relationship with Roz any favors. She's staying with me right now."

Brett couldn't keep a look of surprise from crossing his face. "Nikki didn't tell me that."

"You don't tell her everything, so I'm sure once in a while *she* doesn't tell *you* everything."

He scowled. "Before you ask, we're getting along fine."

"Really? Even through this murder investigation?"

His eyes narrowed. "Have you spoken to her?"

"No," Caprice said honestly. "If she wants to talk about you, she'll do it on her own terms. But I can bug *you.* Are you communicating with her through this?"

He shook his head. "You never quit."

"Not when I have my sister's back."

His stoic expression gentled. "I know you do. We really are fine. She knows I can't predict when I'll get home when I'm working a murder, and she's busy with spring engagement parties and weddings. Mostly we're texting, but I'm going to meet her for coffee at the Koffee Klatch at seven a.m. tomorrow morning. Both of us can at least carve out a half hour for each other."

The waitress brought Caprice her order. Caprice added cream and sugar to her coffee. "I hope you'll be finished with this murder investigation before my wedding. I know that sounds selfish but I don't want you to have to worry about that too."

"Too?" He actually laughed. "Do you think it's going to tax me to be a groomsman?"

Caprice smiled back. "No, but it will take up a chunk of your time."

He nodded. "So tell me what information you have for me that maybe I didn't find out on my own."

Caprice considered everything she'd learned. "Did you know that Travis's mother is now staying at the house with Jarrett and Michelle?"

"Yes, I did know that."

"Did you know why she and William Dodd divorced?"

Brett shrugged. "I've heard rumors. I was going to ask that of her myself if I bring her in for questioning."

"If?"

"She wasn't in Kismet when the murder happened. We checked her whereabouts and she was still in New Hampshire. We have verified proof of that. But I think she could provide us with welcome history."

"Isaac Hobbs told me some of that history," Caprice said.

Brett took a few swallows of his coffee. "Fill me in."

So she did, relating exactly what Isaac had told her.

He looked thoughtful. "So she and Jarrett have been in constant communication?"

"It seems that way. Travis and his father cut her loose but Jarrett didn't. My guess is that Jarrett would have rather lived with her but William wouldn't let him."

Rubbing his jaw thoughtfully, Brett said, "From what I understand, William was a hard man even with Travis."

"Maybe that's why Travis wanted to prove he could make the winery a success on his own."

Brett leaned forward, all of his attention focused on her. "What do you mean?"

For the next few minutes she told him about her visit to Black Horse Winery and what Earl Hoff had told her about Travis.

"Essentially what Mr. Hoff told you was that Travis Dodd didn't know how to spend his business money in an expedient way, that he was wasting it, and that's why the winery is in tough shape now."

"That seemed to be the gist of it. I mean, if Travis caused Earl Hoff's sales to decline, and he found himself in a not-so-solid situation, I suppose Earl would have been angry enough to commit murder. It's hard to tell how much rage people keep inside."

"Yes, it is," Brett agreed. "It's true a violent past can predict a violent future. But many times the murder is committed by the person you'd least expect."

She'd also found that to be true.

Checking his watch, Brett took out bills to pay for their coffee, pie, and a tip.

"I'll take care of it," Caprice said. "I asked you here."

"Nope. I still believe that the man does the paying."

"Nikki hasn't torn down your misconceptions about that yet?"

"We've agreed to disagree on that one, so she humors me."

After Brett stood, he leaned down to Caprice, his hands on the table. "I can't tell you much but I can tell you this. We're looking at other suspects besides Michelle."

"Does Vince know that?"

Brett just gave her one of his I-don't-know shrugs. Still leaning toward her, he said, "I want you to promise me if you see a hint of trouble, you'll call me immediately."

"I'm not looking for trouble."

"No, you're doing worse than that. You're looking for murder suspects. I know I can't stop you, not unless I want to toss you into jail. I really don't want to do that because you do gather good information from time to time. But I want to keep you safe and I know Grant does too. If you get tempted to get into trouble, just remember, you have a wedding date on May 12. "

"Believe me, I'm not going to forget."

Brett straightened, gave her an encouraging smile, and then added like a big brother, "Maybe once you're married, you won't have enough time to interfere in our investigations."

Before she could comment, he left the diner.

Sitting in Fred and Agnes's living room the next morning, Caprice couldn't keep the smile from her face. The Schnoodle who they'd named Grayson didn't leave Agnes's side. When she dropped her kerchief on the floor, the Schnoodle had whisked it up in his jaws and set it in her lap. They were obviously a good match.

Agnes lifted her cup of coffee and took a sip. She glanced at Fred. "Good coffee, honey."

"It's decaffeinated like your doctor ordered," Fred told her.

"But with a bit of real cream."

"You could use about twenty pounds."

She wrinkled her nose at him. "If you keep buy-ing pastries for breakfast, I'll certainly gain them."

"So you're feeling stronger?" Caprice asked Agnes.

"I am. I've even gone for walks with Grayson. We don't walk on the road, of course, just around the yard. I use my walker and he stays right by my side. I already love him to death."

"He's not bad," Fred grumbled.

This time Caprice hid her smile. "I'm glad it's working out."

"More than working out," Agnes said. "Fred doesn't feel so guilty when he leaves me now to go on errands. I never feel lonely."

"No, not lonely," Fred said, with a frown. "Grayson climbs up between us on the bed."

This time Caprice did laugh out loud, and Agnes and Fred joined her. "That's what pets who bond with their parents do," she told them.

"I used the search engine on my phone to find out more about you," Fred confessed.

Caprice wasn't insulted. After all, she'd brought him a dog without asking. "And what did you find out?"

"I found out that you rescue lots of animals and try to find them homes. Besides that . . . you've solved a few murders."

"I've *helped* solve a few murders," she corrected.

"Nonsense. You've put yourself in danger more than once. There was that fire, and a chase through woods, and something about you using self-defense techniques."

"I had taken a self-defense course years ago and then I took a refresher. It seemed like the prudent thing to do if I was going to nose around in murder investigations."

"You first did it because of your best friend."

"That's right, I did. And this one . . . It's not just my wedding reception at stake, or Michelle's winery. My brother Vince knew Michelle before, and he's advising her when the police call her in. Roz, who is my best friend, is living with Vince. His involvement is causing tension between them."

"Living together, not married?" Fred asked, with a bit of judgment in his voice.

Caprice shrugged. "Vince had the same parochial school training that I did. I figure he has his base values and I have mine. So I don't interfere in his life."

"But you are now."

"Not directly," she hedged. "But if this murder gets solved, that will help everyone who's involved in any way."

"Have you made any progress? Do you have any idea who did it?" Agnes asked.

"There are a lot of suspects."

"I was at that convenience store that's not too far from the winery. I heard that Vivian's back. Is that true?"

Gossip zoomed around Kismet as fast as the electricity over the wires on the poles. "Yes, she's returned. She's staying in the house with Michelle and Jarrett."

"At least Michelle and Jarrett have a chaperone," Fred grumbled. "That is they do if Vivian's sober. Is she?"

"I've only seen her briefly, but from what I could tell, yes, she was sober."

"William drove her to drink," Agnes said sadly.

"Why do you say that?" Caprice asked, ready to soak in new information.

"He wanted her involved in charity work and the hospital board," Agnes maintained.

"But she didn't have the personality for that," Fred added. "She wasn't cut out for it. Agnes and I went to cocktail parties now and then when William was introducing a new wine or having a seasonal promotional event. Vivian would just stand in a corner. She had trouble making conversation with strangers. Travis and his dad saw that weakness and they hated her for it. They judged her because of it. Their judgment led to her drinking."

"So it's true that Vivian's drinking is the reason William divorced her?"

"I think she became a bother and a nuisance to him," Fred explained. "William didn't want to come home and find her drunk. He didn't want her embarrassing him anywhere they went together. The more he yelled and scolded, the worse her drinking got."

"A lonely woman with too much time and money on her hands turns to something that will give her a little peace," Agnes noted perceptively.

Caprice supposed that was true. She asked Fred, "Have you put in applications for a job at other wineries around here?"

"I don't want a long commute. Most of the local wineries are small. They don't need me. But, yes, I put applications in. I even looked up how to do a résumé and submitted those with my letter. But I haven't heard anything from anyone. They probably put it in their circular file."

The waste can. Caprice hoped that wasn't true. She had a feeling that Fred had loved making wine. Yes, he was older but she imagined he still enjoyed working in a field he had a passion for.

She liked talking to this couple and making friends with them. She just might have to invite them to her wedding.

Chapter Fourteen

That afternoon, Caprice tried the door to the events room at Rambling Vines Winery and it opened. She said to Nikki, "Michelle told me she'd keep it open for us. She had errands to run."

Following Caprice inside, Nikki's gaze canvased the room. "I think I remembered correctly, but I want to make a diagram so I can decide where to set up the servers' station."

As they walked through the large hall, Caprice suggested, "Probably over near the bar, don't you think?"

"What will you have at the bar? Beer, cocktails, wine?"

"Just wine. Several different kinds. But just wine. Grant and I discussed it and that seems to be the best idea."

Over at the bar area, Nikki made notes and drew something with her finger on the screen of her tablet. Off-handedly she commented, "I'm seriously considering renting space for Catered Ca-

pers. I think it's time to move my cooking base out
of the condo. I think I found a storefront that will
work. It used to be a French café. It won't take too
much modification, and the rent is right."

"Where is it?"

"It's behind Country Fields Shopping Center
next to a donut shop. I really don't need to be in a
high traffic area since everything I do will be behind the scenes. I can cook at a greater volume,
maybe hire more assistants. I should be able to in-
crease the money I bring in that way."

As they strolled over toward the bar area, Caprice asked, "Have you talked about your business
plan with anyone?"

"I've talked about it with Brett."

"Is he good with figures?"

"He's good with just about everything except . . ."

Caprice focused on her sister rather than wedding incidentals. "Except?"

Nikki looked up from her tablet. "Believing I'll
stick around. So I guess I'll just have to prove it to
him and stick. Anyway, can we look at the space on
the way home?"

"Sure. Will it be open?"

"I can text the manager of the property. I have
his cell number." Nikki took one last look around.
"I think I have everything I need here."

"Let's leave by the back door," Caprice suggested. "It's locked from outside in, but the alarm
is turned off so we should be able to get out that
way. Michelle said just to make sure the door was
closed solidly behind us."

"Why do you want to go out that way?"

"If the doors are up on the garage, I wouldn't mind taking another peek at those classic cars."

"I know Dad would like to take a look," Nikki said.

"Probably."

Gardens had been planted at the rear side of the property and the grass was manicured. Knockout roses along the building would soon be blooming. There wasn't a weed in sight.

The doors to two garages were open and Caprice broke into a wide smile. Then she saw someone moving around in the garage.

As they approached, Caprice told Nikki, "That's Leon Wysocki. He's the mechanic who restores the cars."

Leon must have heard their feet crunching on the gravel. He was wearing gray denim overalls, an Orioles ball cap with a large bill, and a white T-shirt. In his hands he held a cloth that was grease streaked.

"Hi, there," he said, recognizing Caprice.

"Hi, Leon. This is my sister Nikki. I told her about these cars. I was hoping we could catch another glimpse."

He motioned toward both open garages. "Take a good look. I just waxed them all before I started tuning up the engine on this Thunderbird. I want them in tip-top shape so Michelle can sell them."

"Is she planning on doing that?"

"She's not sure yet. What about you? I've taken a fancy to that yellow Camaro."

Caprice laughed. "Nope. It's not for sale. Not now and I hope not ever. I'd like to pass it down to my kids."

Nikki bumped her elbow and whispered, "So we're thinking about that, are we?"

In the same whisper, Caprice returned, "Yes, we are."

Leon had turned back toward the garage and hadn't heard their interchange. He said, "If you like that classic Camaro so much, then you might be interested in a Dodge Challenger I'm restoring. It's cobalt blue with a black vinyl top."

Caprice shook her head. "I don't think so. One classic car is enough for me."

Motioning to all the cars again, he claimed, "Travis always insisted that they were a good investment. And they are. But Travis needed to pour his energy into something other than cars and wine."

Before she could stop herself, Caprice blurted out, "He could have poured it into his marriage."

As Leon stood by the Coronet, he nodded. "I agree with that. But what not many people know is that when Travis married Michelle, he thought she'd be malleable like his mother was. She wasn't. After all, Michelle had been a nurse. She saved people's lives. Just because she was a little quiet didn't mean she'd do whatever he wanted. He often got angry because she wouldn't do things his way."

Anger and a failing marriage could be a lethal combination. "What did he do with his anger?"

"He wasn't violent or anything like that," Leon said, though Caprice wondered if anyone knew exactly what went on in a marriage. "But he kept a lot from her."

"Can you give us an example?" Nikki asked.

Leon closed his eyes for a moment as he thought

about it. It didn't take him long to come up with something. "Travis had a way of doing business that Michelle didn't approve of. Much of that was Neil's fault. Neil started giving kickbacks to a distributer or two so Rambling Vines wines would get a push and other local wineries wouldn't."

Caprice wondered if underhanded tactics were actually common in the wine business despite what Earl Hoff had told her. Maybe that was another question she'd have to ask Neil sometime and see if he looked guilty.

As Nikki and Caprice walked along the garage with Leon, someone called to them.

Caprice walked farther along the gravel lane and saw that the person calling to them was Vivian.

Vivian was a beautiful older woman. She had a confidence and vitality about her now that made it hard for Caprice to imagine she'd been a wallflower during her husband's cocktail parties. But people could change according to their circumstances. Apparently Vivian had.

As Leon walked back to the garage, Caprice and Nikki met Vivian half way. Caprice introduced Nikki.

"Why don't you come to the house with me and have a glass of iced tea? Michelle is away on errands and I'm a bit lonely."

Caprice exchanged a look with her sister, and Nikki gave a small nod that meant she had time. Caprice did too. She had left time in her schedule today for wedding details.

Caprice and Nikki followed Vivian to the house. Instead of going to the parlor, Vivian took them to the kitchen. Caprice had redecorated this room too, suggesting marble counters and a wooden hood above the chef-quality stove. Its stainless steel matched the refrigerator and dishwasher, both which were built-in. There was a copper rack in the ceiling above the kitchen's island that held saucepans. A chandelier with copper and wrought iron hung above the kitchen table.

The kitchen had been decorated in cream and taupe as Michelle had wanted. There was a framed photograph of poppies on the wall and poppy placemats on the table. Other than that, now the room looked barren and unused.

Going to the refrigerator, Vivian produced a pitcher of iced tea. "I made this myself this morning. It's country peach, sweetened a little."

"That sounds good," Nikki said. "Our sixty-degree days will soon turn into seventy and eighty."

"As a caterer, I imagine you spend a lot of time over a hot stove," Vivian noted.

"A good amount," Nikki confirmed. "My assistants do too. Caprice and I are going to stop at a space I might want to rent for a commercial kitchen."

"You're expanding?" Vivian asked.

"I want to expand. The problem is—I can't handle more from my condo. It would be nice to have my condo back as a refuge rather than a place I work."

Vivian addressed Caprice, "But you work at home, correct?"

"I do, but that's very different. I'm mostly at my computer, taking client appointments, going to rental furniture warehouses, meeting with my assistant at client's houses for staging. So all of my work isn't accomplished at home."

Vivian took a tray of cupcakes from the counter and brought it along with the iced tea to the table. "They are not home-made," she warned them. "I bought them at The Cupcake House.

"Her red velvet cupcakes are the best," Caprice said. "They're a favorite of my friend Roz."

"Roz is the one who's dating your brother Vince who's helping Michelle," Vivian said, as if she'd gotten a complicated math problem correct.

Caprice smiled. "You're learning fast."

She shook her head. "It gives me something to do so I don't think about Travis. I can't help but wonder if I hadn't left, would he'd be dead."

"Did you have a choice whether or not you wanted to leave?" Caprice asked, remembering the gossip she'd heard.

"If I'd had a stiffer spine and less alcohol in my system, I might have at least gotten a place in Pennsylvania so I could see my sons. On the other hand, if William wouldn't let me see them, it would have been that much more heartbreaking to stay here. I think that's why I ran home to New Hampshire. He won full custody so there wasn't much I could do."

"That must have been so difficult for you," Nikki sympathized.

"It was. William met me when I was young and impressionable. He was on vacation in Connecticut as was my family. We met at a yacht club. Back then I was proficient in sailing. I took him out on our boat, but then he rented one twice as big and took me out on his. He was handsome and I wanted to impress him. Apparently I did, but I was smitten with him too. He was ten years older but I didn't think that would make a difference. Young people never do. Are you and your fiancé close to the same age?"

"Grant's four years older than I am."

"That's about right," Vivian decided. "My second husband Jeffrey was a year younger than I was, and still he died before me. One can never predict what life's going to hand out. But I have learned to control what I can. I try not to look back or too much forward. Living in the present is better for everyone."

Vivian patted Caprice's hand. "Though I imagine when you're younger, you want to look forward as much as you can."

"That's why Caprice and Grant are building an addition onto her house," Nikki said. "Then they won't have to worry about growing pains in the future."

"The addition will make the house *ours*," Caprice explained.

Vivian nodded. "Is it an extra bedroom?"

"Actually, no," Caprice said. "It's an office for Grant with a powder room. He can work from there, see clients, but also use it as his man-cave."

"Whoever devised that term *man-cave?*" Vivian wanted to know. "I've never heard my female friends say they needed a woman cave."

Both Nikki and Caprice laughed.

Becoming serious again, Vivian said, "If I had been older, closer to William's age, he probably wouldn't have looked at me. On the other hand, if I had been, maybe I would have been better with people. I don't have a problem now meeting new people, one on one, but in a crowd, I still freeze. So I avoid crowds. That's the freedom I've had in getting older. My second husband understood that."

"Michelle said you worked for your husband?" Caprice asked.

"That's how I met Jeffrey. When I went back to New Hampshire, I had to find a job. I'd managed William's house before I started drinking so much. I'd organized the staff. So I applied as Jeffrey's secretary. Back then every female knew how to type. Eventually I began handling his books and inventory too."

"That's a lot of responsibility," Caprice noted.

"It was, and I was good at it. After a few years, we became romantically involved. He was such a gentleman. He hadn't wanted to start anything before that because he knew something in me was broken. Back in New Hampshire, I began to heal, stand up for myself, and have confidence in my own abilities. After Jeffrey died, I handled running the mill on my own for a few years."

"Then it's possible you could help Michelle with the business aspect of the winery," Caprice suggested.

Vivian took a cupcake and ate it. Then she took a few sips of her iced tea. Caprice and Nikki did the same thing, but Caprice realized Vivian was thinking about something. Whether she should confide in them any more than she already had?

Finally, after she'd turned her sweating glass around twice, Vivian admitted, "I not only returned here for Travis's funeral but to convince Jarrett to run the winery with Michelle. I thought maybe that would give his life purpose. But he doesn't want to do it. He has his heart set on working at that crab shack. Can you imagine?"

"I guess the question is whether he wants to work at the crab shack because he enjoys it or because he's running from something," Nikki said.

Vivian pointed her finger at Nikki. "You're a very wise young woman. Maybe I'll ask Jarrett just that."

Caprice hoped Nikki hadn't given Vivian ammunition to start a family argument. On the other hand, it would be a good question for Jarrett to answer.

As Caprice pulled up to a parking space in front of the address Nikki had given her, Nikki asked, "Is Lady alone?"

"Not exactly alone. Sophia and Mirabelle are with her."

"You know what I mean. You said you have three appointments this evening. Is Dulcina going to watch her?"

"No, Mom and Dad are. Dad said Blitz needs play time, so leaving Lady with them will work out well."

Her father had adopted the Malamute that had belonged to a friend who had died. Her dad and Blitz had bonded, and were practically inseparable.

"Once you and Grant are married, Lady and Patches will be together all the time," Nikki commented.

"Maybe, maybe not. We'll have to work that out. When Grant goes downtown to his office, he often takes Patches along. It will do Lady and Patches good to have a change of scene."

"Just like humans," Nikki said. "Let's go look at the space."

As soon as Caprice walked in to the empty building, she knew why Nikki liked it. It had plenty of windows, both in the front and in the back. It was the last store space in the row so it even had high windows on the outside wall.

"I like the amount of light," Caprice told her as she walked around. "But it's not much to look at." All of the appliances had been torn out.

Caprice said, "I can imagine a French café wouldn't do well in Kismet. I doubt if we have many French food connoisseurs here."

"Isn't that stereotyping?" Nikki asked, trying to hide a smile.

"We like Italian food, so of course I think there's a market for that, and there's definitely a market for Chinese. But the other restaurants in Kismet? We're talking subs, burgers, and pizza."

"Put pizza in your Italian category," Nikki reminded her.

"You know what I mean." Caprice glanced around the space again. "It's going to cost you to put appliances in here. I know what kind of appliances you're going to want."

"It's not a matter of wanting, it's matter of needing. I have to have the right equipment to cook as I want to."

"I suppose that's true. You're just going to cook here, correct? You're not going to have tables."

"No tables. We're not opening a restaurant. We're a catering company, just like our title Catered

Capers says. I think I will wall off a portion of this to use as an employee lounge."

"Do you have the funds to invest in this?"

"I've been saving. Why do you think I've been cooking out of my condo for so long? The past year, business has really picked up. You know I don't spend money on anything frivolous."

No, she didn't. Nikki had always been the economical one.

"Plus, I'm going to get a loan," Nikki went on. "Brett said if the bank won't approve as much as I want, he'll lend me some. I don't really want to take him up on that offer. But if I have to, I will."

"Have you shown Brett the space?"

"Do you think I should?"

At first Caprice thought Nikki was joking, but when she looked into her sister's eyes, she realized she wasn't. "Just how serious are you and Brett?"

Nikki walked a few feet away and paced back and forth. "I'm not sure."

"If I ask *him* that question, will I get the same answer?"

"Don't you dare ask him that," Nikki protested.

"It was a hypothetical question."

"Then hypothetically speaking, he'd probably give you the same answer I did," Nikki commented.

"You know, sometimes I think the two of you should go away for a weekend and talk, day and night."

"I don't know if he'd do that."

"You can ask him."

Nikki fidgeted with the shoulder strap on her purse. "Yes, I guess I could. But if I have to ask—

don't you think that says something about our relationship?"

"What if *he* asked *you?*"

"I'd go."

"So why is it so different if *you* ask *him?*"

"Because I think I've made it more clear how I feel."

"Really?" Caprice asked doubtfully. "I don't think either of you are taking steps forward."

"He's had murder investigations to deal with. That limits our time together."

"You make time for what's important to you."

"Yeah, I guess so, and so does he."

Impasse. "Maybe my wedding will put some ideas in his head," Caprice suggested.

"Or make him run for the hills."

Caprice shrugged. "Then at least you'd know."

Nikki spun around. "I guess you're right. The thing is I don't believe Brett is swayed by weddings or romantic movies or anything like that. And if there's something in his past he's not telling me . . ."

"Do you think that's what keeps him guarded and keeps him believing that you won't stick around because he's a cop?"

"I know that's what I need to explore," Nikki said with some exasperation. "But I don't want to push him too hard. He might just . . . walk away."

Caprice's cell phone played. She pulled it from her pocket. "It's Mom. She should be in class, shouldn't she?" Their mom was an English teacher at the local high school.

"Unless she's on a break between classes," Nikki reminded Caprice.

Caprice swiped her finger across her phone and accepted the call. "Hi, Mom. Are you calling me to tell me tonight's not convenient to keep Lady?"

"No, tonight's just fine. But when I checked my phone at lunch, I had a message from Grant's mother. So I called her back."

A little *uh-oh* went off in Caprice's head, but she stayed silent. As she expected, her mom continued, "I hope we didn't make a mistake asking the Weatherfords to stay with us."

"Why do you think it's a mistake?"

"Grant's parents learned that a murder had taken place at the winery. I got an earful about how they're not sure the reception should be there."

She heard her mother sigh. "His parents are very opinionated."

Amused by that conclusion, Caprice returned, "And you and Dad aren't?"

Again there was silence until her mother chuckled. "I suppose everybody has strong opinions at some point or another. And you're right, we do say what we think. So does Nana. And that's one reason why I don't know if this is going to work out."

"Grant's brother is going to stay at Grant's townhouse. It's a nice thing you're doing, asking the Weatherfords to stay with you. You and Dad and Nana just do your best. Grant and I will deal with the fallout."

"Do you think there will be fallout, even if your dad and I are as tactful as we can possibly be?"

"I truly don't know, Mom. Grant's dad has a habit of being critical. My advice would be don't rise to any bait."

"In-law advice from my daughter. What is the world coming to?"

Caprice laughed at the sarcasm in her mom's voice. "It will all be fine. Grant and I are determined not to get ruffled by anything. You and Dad and Nana should make that vow too. We'll take everything about the wedding and the reception an hour at a time. We'll all enjoy it."

"Do you have your playlist finished yet?" her mom asked.

"I've added *For Sentimental Reasons* by Nat King Cole. It's coming along."

"You might have to put your playlist on my phone," her mother joked.

"I'd be glad to do that for you."

"All right. I'd better get going before my class arrives. I'll see you and Lady tonight."

"I love you, Mom."

"I love you too, honey."

After Caprice ended the call, Nikki asked, "Trouble?"

"That depends. Do you think Mom or Dad or Nana can hold their temper if Grant's father criticizes something about the house or the way they run it?"

"I think for your sake and Grant's, they'll be on their best behavior. They'll treat his parents like valued guests."

But Caprice was still worried whether or not she'd ever have a good relationship with her in-laws.

Chapter Fifteen

When Grant arrived for dinner that evening, Caprice wasn't sure what to tell him about her mom's phone call. In the kitchen, as she spooned beef teriyaki over wild rice, she glanced at Grant who was now sitting at the table. Patches led Lady in a run around the circle of her downstairs. At least Mirabelle and Sophia weren't following them.

When the two cockers didn't return to the kitchen, she supposed they'd found a toy to play with . . . or a feline to bother. They were all getting used to each other and that was a good thing. Why couldn't humans adjust as well as animals?

She brought the plates with the stir-fry to the table. Grant had poured tall glasses of iced tea. He picked his up and took a few swallows. "Sweetener is just right," he said. "I like that bit of lemon too."

"Good." She was still thinking about what she should tell him.

As they ate, Grant told her about his day. He'd taken Patches to the office with him, so he related how his clients had reacted to him. Most of it was good. Patches had to stay with Giselle at her desk during one client interview because the man was allergic to dogs.

"Patches did pretty well, but I think that was because Giselle gave him treats every five to ten minutes," Grant related in a wry tone.

Caprice laughed. "That's one way to keep a friend close."

Grant grinned at her as he pushed his plate away. That grin always melted her insides. She didn't want to hurt his feelings or seem critical of his parents. On the other hand, they'd always been honest with each other, even when it wasn't easy.

"I've told you all about my day, now why don't you tell me about yours?" he prompted.

"Do you want coffee?" she asked.

"No, I still have iced tea. I'm good."

"Chocolate mousse?"

"No, not right now. I think you're stalling. What happened today?"

She took a deep breath and started with something easy. "I learned more about Vivian. Just personal stuff about why William divorced her and why she didn't stay around Kismet."

"Anything Brett needs to know?"

Caprice shook her head. "I doubt it."

"Nikki was with you?"

"She was. After we went to the winery, we looked at space for Catered Capers. I think she found something she likes."

Grant was still studying her with a steadfast look that she knew well. He was trying to read her mind. "Is that all you want to tell me?"

"No. But what I have to say is sticky."

"Sticky . . . as in I probably won't like it?"

"You probably won't, and I don't want to say the wrong thing." Her voice caught. Talking about their parents simply wasn't easy.

"Since when did we worry about saying the wrong thing?" His brows arched and his face registered surprise.

When he reached across the table and took her hand, Caprice began with, "My mother called me."

Grant cocked his head as if that could make him listen better. "Is she still trying to coax you to change the wedding reception to someplace other than Rambling Vines?"

"She's not the only one," Caprice murmured.

"I don't understand." He was perplexed by her rambling explanation. She'd better just say what she had to say. "Mom had a message from your mother. She called her back over her lunch break."

As if Grant could see where this was headed, he pulled back his hand. "And?"

Caprice kept her gaze on his. "My mom thinks your parents accepting my parents' invitation to stay with them could be a mistake."

"Because?" Grant pressed, his face expressionless.

Instead of answering him directly, she asked, "Did you tell your parents that the murder was in the tasting room at Rambling Vines?"

"No. But my dad keeps up with the goings on in Kismet ever since I told him I was engaged to you. Maybe he thought I'd come back to Vermont to practice law. I don't know. Now he realizes we're going to make a life here. So he subscribed to the

Kismet Crier. He possibly read about the murder in the newspaper."

"I see," she said, not really wanting to say more.

"Why does your mom think asking my parents to stay with them is a mistake? I can still reserve a room for them somewhere."

"No, don't do that. My mom wants them there. It's just that she's a little concerned. She mentioned that they seemed very opinionated."

As Grant was about to say something, she cut in. "And I said something to Mom to the effect that she and Dad and Nana are too."

He nodded as if he approved.

"But, Grant, she said your mom went on and on about why we should change our reception from Rambling Vines to somewhere else."

"Would that be so awful if we changed it to somewhere else?" Grant asked her.

She was tired of everyone second-guessing her . . . second-guessing them. "The reception is all planned down to the color of the tablecloths and the type of flowers. Nikki knows where she's going to set up, and I like the events room. Don't you?"

"Sure I do," he said patiently. "Or I never would have agreed to have it there. But with the murder and the publicity—what if we end up with reporters there?"

"They can report on our wedding." She knew her voice had gone up in volume because Lady came barreling in, stopped at her chair, and looked up at her.

"We don't want our reception ruined," Grant protested.

"How will it be ruined if friends and family and

relatives are all in that room with us? It's bad enough Roz and Vince are on the outs. The murder was in the tasting room. That has nothing to do with the events room. They're in separate buildings." She knew her temper had just flared but she didn't know what to do about it. Maybe all the planning was getting to her. She just hated to think about starting over somewhere else.

Grant rose to his feet. "You think my mom's opinionated, but you are too."

"I'm the bride. I have a right to be opinionated."

As if it was taking all of his self-control not to say what he really thought, Grant said, "I think I'd better leave. When you calm down, maybe we can talk about this more rationally."

Nothing else he said could have been more incendiary. "Rationally? That's *not* what you mean. You mean unemotionally. Just say what you want to say, Grant. Don't keep it in or we'll end up like Vince and Roz." She felt close to tears and that wouldn't do at all.

He crossed his arms over his chest. "You want me to say what I think? Fine, I will. I don't think your parents really want my parents to stay with them. They're just doing it to look good."

That assessment added more fuel to her temper's fire. "My parents don't do things to look good. They asked your parents to stay there because they felt it was the right thing to do."

"So the wrong thing would be for our parents to spend their time separately so there isn't tension between them?" he shot back.

"We have to do something about that tension,"

Caprice said. "Avoiding each other isn't going to end it."

"Our parents confronting each other isn't going to do it either." His voice had risen now too, and Patches was looking to him and then Caprice as if he didn't understand what was going on at all.

"When we're married," Caprice insisted, "they'll be related in a way. It would be good if they start understanding each other."

"My father will never understand your love for animals or my penchant for taking Patches to work with me. All the talk in the world isn't going to change that."

Grant's vehemence about that conclusion stoked worry that had begun winding inside of her at the start of this argument. "What *else* aren't they going to understand?" she demanded.

His answer was quick in coming. "Why I didn't stay with Naomi. Why I chose to seek an annulment."

"Why you chose to marry me?" she added. "Maybe they would have liked to pick out the right woman for you. Maybe your mother thinks the right woman for you this time is Sharon Stillman. When we went to visit your parents after Christmas, your mother couldn't say enough good things about her."

"I knew Sharon in high school. My mother knows her parents. They've had a long relationship. You're not jealous, are you?"

"Jealous? No. I was hurt and disappointed. Why can't your mother see *my* good qualities? She asked me more than once why I wear retro clothes. She also doesn't understand why anyone would want to stage a house."

Grant uncrossed his arms and ran his hand across his forehead as if a headache had started there. "They've always lived in a small town, Caprice."

"So have I."

"You've been to college," he countered. "You have a career. You know what big city life is like. You visited New York and D.C. and Baltimore. You're well-spoken and you expect others to think like you do."

That last part jabbed at her heart and hurt. "Oh, really. Then why are you marrying me? I believed you and I thought about most things in the same way. Am I wrong about that?"

Grant raked his fingers through his hair, went toward the dining room and snapped his fingers at Patches. "Come on, boy. We're going home."

"That's just great, Grant. Walk out so we can't resolve this."

"I don't think we can resolve anything tonight."

Caprice couldn't help but think, *Maybe we won't resolve it ever.* She felt like bursting into tears. She didn't walk with Grant to the living room to get his jacket. As she blinked really fast, she didn't even say good-bye. If she did, she'd cry, and she was not going to break down and cry in front of him. He'd think she was being irrational. Maybe he needed to learn the difference between emotional and irrational.

As she heard the front door close on Grant and Patches, she realized they'd never had an argument like this before. Would he always walk away when something was too difficult to discuss?

That question made her heartsick.

* * *

Caprice couldn't stop thinking about her argument with Grant, and it kept her up most of the night. She reached for her phone to text him so many times, but texting just didn't seem to be a solution. She thought about calling him, but she was afraid she'd hear the anger in his voice that she'd heard last night. She could confront his anger. That wasn't the problem. It was just that he'd never used that tone with her before. Then again, when she'd blurted out everything she'd been thinking and feeling, she realized she'd never used that tone with him before, either.

She'd always felt a connection to Grant, a real communion with him. It had started when he was her brother's roommate at college. She'd been seventeen. He'd been twenty-one. She'd had a major crush. He hadn't paid her much notice, just treated her like a kid sister whenever he came home with Vince.

She did remember, however, the day Grant and Vince had graduated from law school. She and her parents had traveled to Carlisle and they all had gone out for a celebration dinner. At that dinner, her gaze had kept connecting with Grant's. When she'd hugged him at the end of their evening together, she'd known he was taking a job in Pittsburgh. That hug had seemed powerful in a way, like a current she'd never felt before had run through her. But, afterward, she told herself she was just being foolish. Two years after that, her

brother had told her Grant had married. She'd
tried to close the book on the two of them, but
after the death of Grant's child, after his divorce,
after he'd moved back to Kismet to be Vince's law
partner, she'd realized that book had never been
really closed.

They hadn't had an easy path to where they
were now, but she'd believed . . .

She almost drove past the entrance to the property she was looking for. Ace had asked her to
meet him and Marsha and Trista here. Marsha was
thinking about buying the house. Although the
driveway was a short one, it led through blue
spruce that gave the lot an aura of privacy. Caprice
emerged from the trees to follow the asphalt along
the side of the house. It continued to the back.
Caprice parked behind a black Lexus that was
Ace's vehicle of choice when he wasn't being
chauffeured somewhere. Since only that one car
sat in the drive, Caprice surmised Ace, Marsha,
and Trista had all come together.

Exiting her car, Caprice followed the walkway to
the front of the house. It was a Craftsman-style but
a modernized one. Marsha had looked at houses
before and they weren't this small. From Caprice's
experience with this type of home, she figured it
was about two thousand square feet. But it was particularly attractive. There was a covered porch with
large stone pillars and white trim. White trim also
outlined the windows and paneled door. The roof
was stiffly peaked with a large front gable with four
multi-paned windows. Caprice guessed that front
area might be a loft. The siding and the gable were

cedar. The siding on the rest of the house looked like shiplap.

Ace opened the door and met her with a wide smile. "Marsha bought it," he said proudly.

Caprice supposed that meant that Ace bought the house for Marsha and Trista. As far as she knew, Marsha didn't work. Before she'd met Ace, she'd run a small boutique in Alexandria.

"How about we take a tour?" Ace said. "Do you have sample books in your car? I'm sure Marsha and Trista will want to look at them."

"Is Brindle here too?" Caprice asked jokingly.

"No, she's back at my place with Mrs. Wanamaker who is probably feeding her too much people food."

Trista came running to the door. Ace's daughter was a striking girl. Tall and lanky, she had more confidence now than when Caprice had first met her. Caprice could see that confidence in the way Trista stood straight and squared her shoulders. Her long face, her beautiful chestnut hair, and her very green eyes had come from Ace.

She gave Caprice a huge hug. "I can't wait to decorate the house with you."

Caprice looked over Trista's head to Ace. He just arched his brows.

"I think your mom might have some say in it too," Caprice offered.

Trista ended the hug. "I guess we'll let her. But you and I are going to do my room all by ourselves."

When Caprice had first decorated Trista's room

at Ace's estate, she'd done it according to his instructions. Lots of pink and ruffles. Trista had protested loudly when she'd seen it. Being an absent father too much of the time, Ace had been willing to do anything to please his daughter. He'd let her and Caprice come up with a new plan and a new style for the room.

While Marsha and Trista showed Caprice the house, Ace said he'd retrieve the sample books from Caprice's car.

The house was completely empty, devoid of furniture, draperies, or anything to make it livable. Because of that, Caprice had a good sense of space. From the foyer, Trista showed her to the left where there was a small office and a powder room with a cute bowl sink.

Marsha was standing inside the office looking pleased. "Hi, Caprice. Isn't the house terrific?" Without waiting for an answer, she rushed on. "This will be a perfect place for me to put my computer and file cabinets for important papers. I can't wait to show you the rest."

As they left the office, Marsha gestured toward a staircase that led upstairs. "Shall we go upstairs or continue with the first floor?" she asked Caprice.

"Let's finish the first floor."

They did, walking through a nice-sized living room, the dining room, and a kitchen with high-end appliances and a marble-topped island. There was a laundry/mud room to the rear of the kitchen. The mud room had an outside entrance. Lastly, they toured the master suite with its en-suite bath and shower.

"Now let's go upstairs," Caprice said.

She'd been right about the loft to the front of the house. "Is this going to be your reading nook?" Caprice asked Trista.

"That's a good idea," Ace's daughter said.

There were two bedrooms with a shared bath on the second floor. Trista motioned to the one on the left. "That room's mine. It's bigger than the other one."

Caprice studied the room, the closet space, the windows that let in a nice amount of light. "Do you have a theme yet?"

When she'd redecorated Trista's room at Ace's, they'd gone with a country horse theme.

"Instead of a theme, can I just go with colors?"

"Sure, you can. Except we'll have to decide on the style of furniture."

"I'd like color blocking on the walls, blue and lime green. And the furniture?" She paused and thought about it. "I'd like a bookshelf bed, maybe in knotty pine or light oak."

Just as before, Trista knew what she wanted.

"Are you sure you want a bookshelf bed instead of a fabric headboard?"

Again, Ace's daughter thought about it. "I want to go with the bookshelf bed and maybe a desk to match. I just have a laptop so it doesn't take much space."

"Maybe floating shelves above it would be good," Caprice suggested.

"Yeah, they would be. I have a lot I could put on those."

"I hope decorating the rest of the house is as easy," Marsha teased.

After they went downstairs, Marsha said, "The detached garage out back has a space above it that could be an apartment. I don't know what I want to do with that yet. So we might just not do anything for the time being."

Downstairs in the kitchen, they found Ace who pointed to the sample books he'd set on the island. "Why don't you and Trista go through those," he suggested to Marsha. "I want to talk to Caprice for a moment."

"That's fine," Marsha commented, meaning it. At one time, she'd thought Caprice and Ace were romantically involved. She'd found out differently fairly quickly.

While Trista and Marsha went to the kitchen island to page through the sample books, Ace motioned Caprice into the office at the front of the house. "I suppose you're wondering why Marsha bought this house instead of just moving in with me."

"That's none of my business."

"Maybe not," Ace agreed. "But she wants to take everything between us slow, not only for her sake but for Trista's. She had to put up with a lot from me. We got our divorce for good reasons. She wants to make sure those reasons don't still apply."

Caprice knew groupies and drugs had been involved. But since then, Ace had cleaned up his act and made a comeback. "I imagine it's a hard life to be married to someone who's always out on the road."

"It is," he confirmed. "But I'm determined to

make a relationship between us work this time. The tours are absolutely necessary in today's climate to sell a new CD. Sure, a lot of music is digital now. But the concerts still rev up the fans."

"I hope it works out for you this time, Ace."

"I know you do. So I wanted to tell you that if you want to change your venue for your reception, you can have it at my place."

A troubled look must have crossed her face because Ace asked, "What's wrong?"

"A lot. I thought Grant and I could wade through the wedding preparation without having stress. How stupid was that?"

"So the murder is a stress?" Ace asked.

"It's not just the murder. Grant's parents are in the mix, his whole family really. We got into an argument about that, and about the wedding reception. I think he thinks we should change the venue too. But I don't want to bail on Michelle. His parents think we should change it, but they have their own opinion about a lot of things, including me."

"What about you?" Ace looked mystified.

"My fashion sense, my love of animals, my honesty, my family."

"Wow! That must have been some argument."

"We've never had an argument like that before," she said with her voice breaking.

Ace put his hand on her shoulder. "Anything that involves a major life decision is stressful. I'm sure it's not only the wedding. Grant's going to be moving into your house. You're going to be building on an addition. There will be lots of life changes. So don't be too hard on either of you."

"What am I supposed to do about his parents? They're going to stay with my parents while they're in Kismet and I'm not sure that's the right decision either. What if they fight? What if there's a wall between them? What if they never want to see each other again?"

"Whoa, girl. Where is this coming from? It's not like you."

"I just want everything to be . . . perfect," she confessed.

"Maybe you should elope."

"You know we can't do that. And I really don't want to. But I'm so afraid this argument that Grant and I had is really going to come between us. He just walked out without discussing the situation further." She felt absolutely sick at heart when she thought about it.

"You do know men and women are different, right?"

Caprice took a deep breath. "Of course, I know that."

"When women are upset, they like to talk. When men are upset, we just want to be alone somewhere. You gave Grant space once before. Give it to him again. It will work out. I know it will."

"I'm glad you're so positive," she said, still with a catch in her voice.

Changing the subject, Ace gave her a probing look. "Are you making any headway on the murder?"

He knew her too well. She'd helped him when he'd been a suspect in a murder investigation. "I think I'm missing something because the pieces just don't all fit together right. Do you know what I mean?"

"Tell me who your suspects are."

She went through the list, from Michelle and Jarrett and Vivian to Neil, the owner of Black Horse Winery and the neighbor.

"You know Michelle could be the big winner because of Travis's death," he pointed out.

"How do you figure? The winery's not doing well," Caprice argued.

"Maybe not. But if she could sell the place, she could more than pay off their debts. And doesn't Travis own classic cars? They're worth serious money too. Maybe you shouldn't give Michelle a pass simply because she used to be Vince's girlfriend."

As Caprice thought about what Ace said, she nodded. "I don't know nearly enough about Michelle. I think I have to find out more."

"How are you going to do that?"

"Michelle had a former assistant that Travis insisted she let go. You know how assistants are. They usually know the nitty-gritty on their boss. I think I'm going to have to talk with her."

"At least you have the murder to concentrate on while you and Grant work things out."

"We have to, Ace. I love him."

"I know you do. Because of that, the two of you will find your way. There aren't many couples like you and Grant. You fit together. You're honest with each other, and honesty is probably what has you both frazzled now. But remember one thing—in-laws can be the downfall of any marriage. Marsha's parents never approved of me, and that certainly didn't help anything."

"And Grant's parents don't approve of me."

"They don't know you. Just be yourself with them, Caprice. Really, in the end, that's all you can do."

Maybe it was. But for Grant, would that be enough?

Chapter Sixteen

Caprice fully intended to spend her morning at the computer, designing floor plans and searching her favorite suppliers for furniture and decorative items for Marsha's house. However, she couldn't stop thinking about Grant. They seemed to be at a standstill. He thought he was right. She thought she was right. In the past, it had been difficult for Grant to share his feelings. In the past six months or more, it had been much easier for him. But now . . . would he make the first move or should she?

She thought about their argument again when she took Lady for a long walk. Tulips were blooming in the gardens along her street. By the end of the month, roses would be budding too. She liked her street because this was an older neighborhood with mature trees and houses with character. Sure, the tree roots buckled some of the sidewalk and houses could be thought of as out-of-date. But she didn't see them that way. From ranchers to bi-levels, from brick and stone to siding, each one made a statement about the people who lived there. She was so grateful that at Christmas Grant had presented her with the plans to put on an addition . . . so grateful that he wanted to live in her house. It wouldn't be *her* house any longer. It would be *their* house. She truly felt that way.

The walk didn't give her any more insight than she'd had before she started. But Lady had enjoyed the exercise and it was good for her too. She wondered if Roz would be out of bed yet. She'd thought of taking Dylan along on their walk but she hadn't wanted to disturb Roz if she and Dylan were both sleeping. Even the days Roz opened her shop, Caprice doubted that she rose before eight a.m. Caprice was usually up at six.

Back inside, after she dished Lady's breakfast into her bowl and fed the felines, she grabbed a container of yogurt from the refrigerator. Since it was organic and plain, she sliced a peach on top. She didn't want to gain weight before her wedding and not fit into her gown. She'd always considered herself ten to fifteen pounds overweight, but Grant had always said her figure was perfect . . . rounded where it was supposed to be.

Grant.

Lost in thought, she found Lady, Mirabelle, and Sophia finished their breakfast before she did. They all followed her to her office as she switched on her computer and settled herself at the desk. Lady was right by her side as Sophia jumped up onto the printer. Mirabelle, like the princess she was, sat in the chair next to the desk. It was turquoise and Mirabelle's white fluffy coat looked beautiful against the color.

Caprice had drawn each room of Marsha's house on graph paper last night before she'd gone to bed. Marsha had told her she liked Swedish-style furniture. Caprice knew exactly what that meant and where to go to shop.

The first piece she found online was a Swedish dresser that came in many finishes, including a cashew color. Caprice decided to start with that for the bedroom. What she liked most about the dresser was that it was fashioned of alder wood and crafted in North America. The dovetail drawers meant quality.

Ace had told Caprice that price was no object. Apparently, he was covering the cost of furniture and decorating the house. After taking a screenshot of the dresser and e-mailing it to herself so she'd have access to it on her tablet, Caprice went to the same supplier of the dresser and found a Swedish two-door bookcase. The company handcrafted in small quantities. Solid brass hardware spoke of the quality. The bookcase would be a nice addition to either the bedroom or the living room depending on what else she found. It wasn't long before she spotted a Swedish cottage bed headboard inspired by late-nineteenth-century furniture. Like the dresser, it came in a multitude of colors. She took screenshots of each. She'd show them to Marsha. After all, she might want to put a pop of color in the bedroom with the bed in robin's-egg blue, burnt caramel, or even red hot. She also needed to know if Marsha wanted a full or queen-sized bed. She imagined she'd want the queen for nights when Ace stayed over. A king would be too large for the bedroom.

Caprice was about to start looking into living room furniture when her computer screen suddenly went blank.

Had the electricity gone out?

She turned on the lamp on her desk and that was just fine. She had power. But other than that, she had nothing.

Roz was used to dealing with her computer system at her dress shop. Maybe she could take a look and find out what was going on.

Caprice thought she'd heard Roz come downstairs while she was working. She'd heard the kitchen storm door close and figured Roz had let Dylan outside for his first run of the day. Caprice smelled coffee.

She called into the kitchen. "Roz, can you come here?"

A few moments later, Dylan came running into her office with Roz not far behind. He went to Lady immediately and they sniffed each other. Then Dylan danced around and barked at Mirabelle. The Persian stood, squinted down at the little dog, and then sat back down again, winding her tail around her.

"Is something wrong?" Roz asked. "Usually I try to let you alone so you can work."

"Yes, something's wrong. Look at my computer screen."

The screen color was a dull gray. No screen saver. No icons. Nothing.

"Do you have it turned on?"

"Yes, I have it turned on. I was in the middle of finding furniture for Marsha's house and it suddenly went blank."

"Uh, oh. That doesn't sound good," Roz decided.

"What do you mean?"

"It sounds like it might have a virus. Let's see what happens when we turn it off and then back on again."

Caprice turned the machine and the monitor off, gave it a few moments to settle, and then switched both back on.

Roz gasped when she saw what was on the screen. "This isn't any ordinary virus," she said in a whisper.

On the screen in bold print and large letters flashed a warning—STAY AWAY FROM RAMBLING VINES WINERY . . . OR ELSE.

There had only been one thing to do with the threatening message. She knew better than to keep it to herself. She called Brett Carstead.

Roz left to check in at her shop, taking Dylan along as she usually did. About an hour after Caprice called Brett, he showed up in her video monitor at her front door. He had somebody with him. When she opened the door, Lady ran to him. After all, she knew him.

He reached down and ruffled her ears and ran his hand down her flank. "Hi there, girl. Keeping your mistress safe?"

The man beside him said, "The way she greeted you, I don't think she'd make a good guard dog."

Brett smiled. "You're probably right. This is Matt Leighton. He's a tech expert, and I thought we could use him. He's going to take a cursory look at your computer, but my guess is he's going to have to take it with him."

"Thank goodness I took screen shots of the furniture and e-mailed them to myself."

"Furniture?" Matt asked. He had red hair and blue eyes, and a smile that maybe could charm a virus from a computer. He was wearing jeans and a T-shirt rather than a uniform. There were tattoos on his arms, one of an anchor and something else she didn't recognize. The way he stood straight and tall, she wondered if he'd been in the military.

"I'm a home stager," she explained, "and a house decorator. This morning I was sorting through furniture to show one of my clients for her new house."

"I imagine it takes more time than one thinks to do that," he offered. "Since I know my way around a computer, I realize that."

"Are you part of the Kismet police force?" she asked.

"Let's just say I'm a consultant," he commented.

"She asks a lot of questions," Brett told Matt in a warning tone. "But you don't have to answer them."

After Caprice wrinkled her nose at Brett, she took the men back to her office. Matt took one look at the message, sat at her desk, and pressed a few keys. He turned the computer off and then booted it up again and shook his head. "This is going to have to go back to the station with me. I have equipment there that could help me figure out what's going on."

"My guess is he already knows but he wants to make sure," Brett told Caprice. "While he unplugs and collects everything," Brett said, "let's go to your living room and talk."

"Do I need a lawyer?" she asked, half joking, half serious.

"You know you don't . . . *this* time."

After they were both seated in the sixties-chic living room decorated with bright colors in geometric shapes, Brett gave her a steady look. He laid his hand on the arm of the sofa that was striped in purple and lime and fuchsia to compliment the sixties décor of the room that included a lava lamp. His gaze fell on the seventies, pop-art, psychedelic framed print on one wall.

"Is this lecture time?" she asked Brett.

"No, because I know a lecture won't do any good with you. What I want you to do is to take that threat seriously. Back away from this."

Her answer was immediate. "I can't. My wedding reception is at the winery, and don't tell me to change venues. If I was supposed to, I'd feel it in my gut."

"Maybe your gut's too excited about getting married to have a sixth sense about anything else."

Brett's tone was gentle and she realized he was probably right. Still . . .

"Michelle has become a friend, and if I got a threat on my computer, then apparently I'm getting close to something."

Shaking his head, Brett insisted, "I can't understand you or Vince."

"We're nothing alike."

"Oh, yes, you are. You're both De Lucas, both

intent on getting your own way. You should be concentrating on your wedding, and Vince should realize he could lose Roz if he doesn't wake up."

Apparently, Nikki had been talking to Brett about the couple. "You're welcome to talk to Vince."

Brett waved her words away. "I know how much good that would do."

"It might. He respects you."

"Grant could talk to him."

"Grant feels it's better to stay out of people's private lives."

"Good thing. He can balance you out." Brett's tone was wry and a bit teasing.

But he'd struck a nerve. "Maybe I don't need to be balanced out. Maybe we just need to listen to each other."

Brett gave her a questioning look. "Uh, oh. Problems before walking down the aisle?" He wasn't teasing this time. He was asking as if he wanted to know.

"I don't know," she said honestly. "We need to talk but both of us are being stubborn . . . or something."

"As I said, you're just like Vince," Brett reminded her. "You know what to do if you're both being stubborn. Give in."

Caprice sighed. "Why is that so hard to do?"

Shrugging, Brett explained, "For guys, it's a matter of pride. I don't know about women. Maybe if they feel they've gotten a raw deal at times, they want to stand up for themselves."

"Aren't you perceptive."

"It comes with the territory. I *do* have to be able to read suspects, you know."

"I know." Enough about her. She decided to turn this around. "Since you're giving advice, maybe I can ask a few questions and give some to you?"

He made a point of looking at his watch.

Just then Matt came out of her office carrying her computer tower. "I'll be back in for the monitor."

"I have to go," Brett said.

"Are you and Nikki having more than half-hour coffee dates early in the morning?"

"With this murder investigation, we're not even having many coffee dates. And don't ask me anything else." He shook his finger at her. "You are *way* too nosy."

"One of my best qualities," she joked, hoping Grant could accept that about her as well as everything else.

After Brett and his tech friend had left, Caprice was deciding how she could work without her computer. She could work on her tablet but that wasn't the same thing. There were necessary programs on her desktop. Still, she'd settled on the sofa to choose more furniture for Marsha. Shopping she could do on her tablet.

When her cell phone rang, or rather played, Bella's face popped up on her phone's screen.

"Hi, Bella, what's up?"

"I'm at All About You with Roz. I came in to work a few hours for her. Don't you think it's time you find a dress for the rehearsal dinner?"

"Do you think Roz has dresses that would work?" She'd found a couple of outfits at Secrets of the Past to take along for the honeymoon.

"I do. I have a few picked out. This is important

enough that you really should take some time for it, don't you think?"

"Brett was just telling me the same thing."

"Brett? Does this have something to do with your computer? Roz said you were having problems."

"Long story. I'll tell you when I see you. But, yes, I'll be there in about ten minutes."

"Terrific. We'll be waiting."

Bella had a lilt in her voice. That meant she was going to try to talk Caprice into something. If she did, that was okay as long as the dress was pretty and looked good.

Two hours later, still worried about Grant because she hadn't heard from him, Caprice carefully laid the dress she'd chosen in the back seat of her Camaro. It was reminiscent of the 1920's style in a beautiful shade of turquoise and it would be just right . . . if everything between her and Grant was just right.

Knowing if she went home, she'd fidget and think, and deciding her pets could wait another half hour for lunch, she drove to the nearby community center. She was going to have a talk with Leanne, Michelle's former assistant.

The community center was located just outside of the downtown area. It wasn't far from Restoration Row where Roz's shop was located and was within walking distance of the stores, restaurants, and professional buildings. The community center had once been a warehouse that had been renovated more than twenty years ago. Since it needed renovations again, the board had been fund-raising.

A chain link fence surrounded the outside basketball court. Inside were a game room, an arts-and-crafts room, a couple of offices, and a meeting room. She entered through the game room entrance. That room had been given a fresh coat of beige paint not so long ago. There were finished murals on three of the walls. One depicted teenagers standing in a group. The other two were similar—one with boys playing basketball and the other with girls kicking a soccer ball. Kids from the center had painted the murals with particular help from Danny Flannery, a teen Caprice had come to know well during a previous murder investigation. He was a true artist and Ace was helping fund his dream by sending him to art school.

Caprice checked in at a desk and asked Reena, the receptionist, if Leanne was there.

Using the phone system on her desk, Reena called one of the offices. She held her hand over the phone and asked Caprice, "What's this about?"

"It's about Rambling Vines Winery."

Reena just arched her brows and conveyed to Leanne what Caprice had said. When she hung up the phone, she told Caprice, "She'll be right out."

Because Leanne was coming out to the game room, Caprice suspected she wanted to have a short conversation. But that wasn't entirely what Caprice had in mind. When she saw Leanne, she thought how pretty the woman was with her short blond hair, pretty green eyes, and pale-blue sheath dress.

"Caprice, how are you? Reena tells me you'd like to talk to me."

Caprice leaned in a little closer as if what she had to say was confidential. "Since I'm having my wedding reception at the winery, I'm helping gather information for the investigation into Travis's murder. As Michelle's assistant, I thought you could help with a few things. Is there somewhere we could go to talk?"

Leanne studied Caprice with a piercing look but then she nodded. "Let's step outside. There are too many listening ears in here."

Caprice understood how people liked to gossip.

They exited through the entrance Caprice had come in. Leanne motioned to the walk that wrapped around the building. "Let's step over here in the shade of the building."

Caprice followed her and they stopped.

"What is it you'd like to know?" Leanne asked bluntly.

Remembering what Ace had said about Michelle and that maybe Caprice should dig deeper, Caprice was blunt too. "Since you were Michelle's assistant, you must have become friends working so closely together."

Looking across the street to the apartment building there, Leanne took a moment to answer. "We were friends but Michelle didn't tell me everything."

Leanne's comment alerted Caprice that there was more to learn. She'd have to be tactful about it. "I assure you, I don't want you to break any confidences. But the police are trying to find Travis's murderer."

"How is Michelle really?" Leanne asked.

"I don't know how to tell exactly. I guess upset would be the closest word. I've learned some things about Travis, and maybe now that he's not in her life, she's relieved. But I'm not sure about that, either."

Leanne again let silence settle between them. Finally she revealed, "Michelle loved Travis, and as the years passed, I think she still wanted to love him but was having trouble doing it."

"Because of his attitude?"

"From what I understand, before they were married, he treated her like a princess. After they were married, he had expectations of her but was so wrapped up in winery business he didn't spend much time with her."

"And?" Caprice prompted.

Leanne looked left and then she looked right. Satisfied no one was in earshot, she admitted, "I'm not breaking any confidence because I figured it out by myself."

"Figured what out?"

"Michelle became lonelier and lonelier. I'd often see her fighting tears. Then suddenly she wasn't."

"Travis's attitude changed?" Caprice asked, knowing that probably wasn't the case.

"Oh, no. His attitude didn't change. If anything, it became worse. But Michelle's attitude *did* change. Suddenly she was smiling again and even humming when she was working. I accidentally found out why. She and Dion Genet from Oak Grove Winery were having an affair."

"How do you know this?"

"Michelle and I had gone to Oak Grove Winery to talk to Dion about a joint promotional venture for the York County Fair. Michelle thought I was in the office picking up brochures, but I wasn't. I went into the winery area and I saw the two of them kissing. I backed out quickly and Michelle didn't know that I knew."

"Did anything else give it away?" Caprice asked.

"Michelle received texts from Dion that came much more often than they should have for business. But I could tell without her confiding in me that Dion was making her happy. I had no idea what his intentions were or what hers were. She might have been planning to file for divorce. But if she was . . ."

If Michelle was planning to file for divorce, that would give the police even more reason to suspect her of Travis's murder.

Caprice was surprised by the news of Michelle's affair but she realized she shouldn't be. If someone is unhappy in a marriage, that kind of thing happened.

She considered going directly to Michelle, but Michelle hadn't told her the truth so far, and she could deny the affair. That left a couple of options. She could go to the source, Dion Genet, or she could talk to her brother Vince first. He was familiar with the local wineries. And while she talked to Vince about that, she could give him sisterly advice about Roz.

Chapter Seventeen

Vince was surprised when Caprice turned up on his doorstep in the late afternoon. She'd called the office and Giselle had told her he'd gone home for the day. That was unusual. Had Roz's exit from the house really challenged him?

He invited her inside the house with a wave of his hand. Before she even had a chance to sit, he asked accusingly, "How long is Roz going to stay with you?"

"You do realize I'm in the middle," Caprice said.

"In the middle of *what* is what I want to know. Roz is upset because I'm giving Michelle serious advice. I keep the calls short. Roz knows when Michelle calls because I tell her. I don't know what more she wants."

Caprice settled in on his sofa. "Will you accept advice from me?"

Vince rubbed the back of his neck and he looked tired. His shirt was rumpled again and his tie pulled down. She spotted a glass of wine sitting on an end table.

"What advice?" he asked tersely.

Caprice pulled one leg up onto the sofa. "You need to talk to Roz before she moves out of your house permanently and into an apartment."

"Is that what she told you she's going to do?"

"Vince, I'm really trying to stay impartial. I'm not going to be a messenger."

"But she *is* still staying with you?"

"Yes, she is."

"Did you come here just to give me advice?"

"That was one reason, but I have another too." She motioned to the glass of wine.

"If you're going to tell me to give up drinking wine"—he blew out a frustrated breath—"I'm not overindulging if that's what you're worried about."

"Since when did you become so defensive?"

He sighed and settled on a chair across from her. "Since I'm not getting enough sleep or eating right. Giselle told me today I was a grouch. It's why I left early to come home. But you know, it doesn't feel like home anymore."

"I didn't stop in to scold you about your wine habits. In fact, I need your knowledge on the subject."

"Does this have something to do with the murder investigation?"

"It does, and don't shake your finger at me or I'll shake it right back."

A bit of a smile twitched his lips. "All right. What do you want to know?"

"Do you know anything about Dion Genet from Oak Grove Winery?"

Vince looked surprised. "What does *he* have to do with anything?"

"Tell me what you know. What do you think of him?"

"From what I know, he's a standup guy. He's descended from a family of French vintners and his wine is superb."

"Is he married?"

"No. As far as I know he's never been married. As a child, he was brought up in France. Then his father moved here and opened the vineyard. He and his dad still run it together. I think he lost his mother a year or two ago. Why are you asking?"

"I don't want to start rumors, so I prefer not to tell you, at least right now. But I'm following up on a lead."

"That he might have murdered Travis?"

"I'm not ruling anybody out, but I'll know more after I talk to him. I just wasn't sure how to approach him. But if he's an honest standup guy, it should be easy, right?"

"Unless you ask personal questions he doesn't want to answer. You're well known for doing that."

"I only ask personal questions because I think I can help."

"I know," Vince admitted, leaning his head back against the sofa cushion. But then he sat upright again. "You know, Grant hasn't been in such a great mood either. I think Giselle was fed up with both of us. What's *his* problem?"

"You'll have to ask *him*."

"Honestly, Caprice. Does this have something to do with the wedding?"

"It's all about the wedding," she said with a nod.

"And family, and whether or not we're going to be able to meld our lives together."

Vince sat up straight now and his eyes were piercing as he asked, "Are you and Grant having problems too?"

"I'm not sure what's happening. Our emotions are ratcheting up because of the wedding, and we're dealing with two very different families."

"In-laws," Vince said. "The bane of every marriage."

"They shouldn't have to be."

"Sometimes you and Pollyanna have too much in common," Vince griped.

"Because I want us all to be happy? It *is* possible, you know."

Vince sat forward. "Only if you limit your expectations, and don't have an idea that anything is perfect."

"I think I prefer my attitude over yours."

"No surprise there. Do you want to have some dinner with me? We could go to the Blue Moon Grille."

She uncurled her leg, then stood. "Oh, Vince. I can't. I'm sorry. Roz is taking me to the Country Squire Golf and Recreation Club. We're going to check out a room for the rehearsal dinner. I have to make some decisions about what they can provide."

"Is Grant meeting you there?"

"Not this time. We're just going to look around and get a list of possibilities. He and I will go over the list together, I hope."

Vince must have seen the worry on her face because he stood too, crossed to her, and gave her a very tight hug. "Everything's going to be all right," he said, trying to give her comfort.

She leaned back and stared at him. "Do you really believe that's true?"

"Thinking about it, I do like your attitude better than mine . . . for now."

Caprice thought about attitudes and perceptions on her drive home. She wanted to change clothes before they went to the Country Squire. She suspected bell-bottom jeans, a Beatles T-shirt, and a fringed vest weren't exactly what she should wear there.

After she arrived home, Roz waved at her from the living room. Dylan was on her lap and Lady was at her feet. Mirabelle was spread out on the arm of Roz's armchair and Sophia sat on the top shelf of her cat tree looking bothered. Caprice guessed she and Dylan weren't getting along.

Roz was dressed in a camel-colored twin sweater set and cream slacks. Her tan pumps coordinated with the outfit. She always looked so put-together.

Setting her purse on the table in the foyer, Caprice smiled. "I'm just going to go up and change. I don't think this outfit would do at the Country Squire."

"Don't change for my benefit. That's up to you. You're going to be their client."

"Actually, *you're* their client since you're paying for it. Have you thought about Grant's parents paying for half?"

"They don't have to, and I'd like you or Grant to tell them that. But if they want to, I understand.

I'll take care of the extra touches like flowers if you want any, and any decorations. I already let Lady and Dylan out so I'm good to go when you are."

"Just give me ten minutes and I'll be back down."

Caprice ran up the stairs thinking about her conversation with Vince. It so preoccupied her that she hadn't even petted Lady or Dylan or Mirabelle or Sophia. She thought about attitudes and perceptions and expectations. Not everybody could be happy all of the time. Some people couldn't be happy any of the time. Was that the case with Grant's parents?

Lady came running up the stairs. Before Caprice entered her bedroom, she crouched down and gave her cocker a rubdown all over. Lady lay on her side in canine heaven.

Caprice told her, "I'm sorry I ignored you. I have a lot on my mind, but that's no excuse. I promise when I get back tonight, you can sit on the sofa beside me."

Lady gave a small *ruff* as if she understood.

Lady followed Caprice into her room and onto the swirled pastel hand-braided rug by the bed. Caprice's bedroom was colorful in a more muted way than downstairs. Each piece of furniture had been hand chosen, from the brass four-poster bed to the antique yellow armoire, hand-painted with hummingbirds and roses.

She went over to her dresser, stopped in front of it, and looked into the mirror. She didn't know what she was looking for. She didn't wear much makeup. Maybe she should. She didn't curl her hair. It was sleek, long and straight, and she liked it that way. But maybe she should think about a different hairstyle. She checked out her clothes. They were retro. It was the type of fashion she liked. Maybe she should change that.

Then she shook her finger at herself in the mirror. "Grant asked you to marry him because you're *you*."

Quickly Caprice changed into a violet boxy jacket and high-waisted tailored pants in the same color. Underneath the jacket she wore a cream blouse with a seventies-style bow. After she took a quick brush to her hair, she opened her jewelry box to look for her gold hoops. But her eyes didn't fall on the hoops. They fell on a charm bracelet. Seth Randolph, a doctor she'd dated, had given it to her.

She removed it from the jewelry box and studied it. There were several charms and glass beads. The beads were painted with colorful flowers. One of the charms was a peace sign and another was a kitten's profile. A small heart dangled from the center of the circle of charms. She and Seth had almost been serious. That had been the problem . . . *almost*.

Seth's career as a trauma physician would always come first. He hadn't been ready to settle down. And then there had been Grant in the shadows . . . in the wings . . . in her life. He'd been in her life since he was Vince's roommate at law school. She'd never forgotten him, even after he'd moved away and gotten married. She'd never expected their lives to intertwine again, but they had. And she didn't want to lose him.

Taking her phone from her dresser, she brought

up her messaging favorites and tapped Grant's name. Then she texted him three heart emojis. That should tell him what she was feeling . . . that should tell him she wanted to talk . . . that should tell him she was willing to make the first move.

Just what would his response be?

After taking a long walk with Lady in the morning, Caprice met with a prospective client in York. Since the woman was a dog lover, Caprice took Lady along. Mrs. Carter's dog, a cute dachshund named Heidi, made friends with Lady right away. The two dogs entertained each other while Caprice took a tour through the house and sat with Mrs. Carter to talk about staging. Caprice left Mary Carter's house with the optimism that the woman would sign on the dotted line once Caprice worked up the proposal. To do that, however, she needed a computer.

In her car with Lady, she said to the cocker, "You helped me sell my services that time. Thanks for making nice with Heidi."

Lady sat up proudly, cocked her head, and Caprice imagined her dog almost smiled. She reached into the little pouch she'd hung on her belt and pulled out a treat. When she gave it to Lady, she said, "Now don't you tell anyone we're in the Camaro instead of my van. You aren't in your kennel."

Lady took the treat and then looked expectantly out the side window.

Taking her phone from her purse, Caprice

brought up Roz's contact information. She texted her.

Can I use your laptop?

She knew Roz had left it on the kitchen counter. Her friend didn't need it when she was at the dress shop.

Caprice had just put her key in the ignition to start the car when her phone played the Beatles song "All You Need Is Love." Roz had messaged back.

No problem at all. You know the password.

Yes, she did. She kidded Roz all the time that she should change it, but Roz wanted to be able to remember it. The password was *allaboutyou* in small letters and *8*, Roz's lucky number, followed by an exclamation point.

Caprice texted back a thumbs-up.

"We're good to go," she told Lady. "But as soon as I write up the proposal, I need to go on another errand. It shouldn't take too long, so I'll leave you at home to entertain Mirabelle and Sophia." Lady swiveled toward her, her brown eyes sad.

"Don't give me that look. I'll leave your Kong ball with treats."

Lady gave a soft bark and turned to look out the window once more.

After Caprice finished the proposal and e-mailed it to her client, she gave Lady lunch and took her outside for a few games of fetch. When she returned inside, she poured kibble into the cats' dishes. She wasn't hungry. She hadn't been since her argument with Grant. This errand was just another way to keep her mind distracted.

Oak Grove Winery was located near Dallastown, a small town outside of York. Each winery she visited was unique. Oak Grove, like its name, featured a profusion of oak trees all over the property. The wine-tasting room looked as if it was an old barn that had been refurbished. From what she'd seen on the Internet, the first floor was a tasting room that led outside and overlooked a pond. The second floor, with the winery itself, had entrances at its ground level on the other side of the barn. Huge multi-paned windows, with at least twelve panes, lined the tasting room and the winery on the pond side.

This is where Caprice parked, knowing she was stopping by the tasting room. After locking her car, she went to the tasting room door.

When she walked in, a bell dinged. There were at least ten tables with four chairs at each and a counter in front of a wine shelf. The man behind the counter, who'd been checking wines, straightened. Caprice could see that he was a handsome man, probably in his mid-forties. He was well built and looked muscled.

She walked up to the counter and he smiled at her. "Welcome to Oak Grove Winery," he said.

His hair was brown, some strands bleached by the sun. There was also silver at his temples. He had a Patrician nose and a firm chin. "Hi, I'm Caprice De Luca. I'm looking for Dion Genet."

"You found him," he said with another smile, extending his hand.

She took it and shook.

"Would you like to taste a few of our wines?"

She decided to be blunt. Checking him over again, she knew he would have been more than able to wield a cheese knife to kill Travis. "I'm not here to taste wines. I'm here hoping I can help Michelle Dodd. The police are looking at her hard for Travis's murder."

Dion paled, but he asked, "And what do you think I have to do with that? Are you with the police?"

"No, I'm not. I'm a friend of Michelle's. She once dated my brother. My fiancé and I are having our wedding reception at Rambling Vines. I know a detective on the police force and I help him sometimes. If you want to check me out with Michelle, go ahead. I heard you were tight friends." She didn't think he would check on her. She was bluffing. But you never knew what would happen with a bluff.

He studied Caprice for a few long seconds. She caught him looking at her shoes. She'd worn flat ones.

"Maybe you don't want to taste my wines, but how about a walk. I need to check the vines."

"Are you concerned someone will overhear us?"

"There's staff all around, offices in the back of the tasting room, and of course, the winery up above. I never know when someone will barge in. Are you afraid to walk with me?"

She took another look at him, and especially studied his dark-brown eyes. She saw no malice there. What she did see was a bit of fear. For himself? For Michelle?

"It's a beautiful day. Sure, I'll walk with you. But

just remember, I have my cell phone at my finger-tips." That wasn't a bluff. She'd slid it into the pocket of her khaki gaucho pants.

"I'll remember that," he said with a nod. Then he came out from behind the counter and motioned her to go through the door ahead of him.

They walked in silence for a while about a quarter of the way around the pond. Then he motioned toward a hill. "Up this way. There's a path for us."

She saw that there was. She also saw the rows and rows of grapes. "What kind of grapes?" she asked.

"These are Catawba."

"How many acres do you have?"

"About thirty." After they walked up the hill, he veered to the right and so did she. He studied the vines hanging on the trellises. "But you don't want to know about my winery. What do you want to know?"

"As I said, I heard you and Michelle were tight friends. I'd like to know how tight."

He stopped and turned toward her. "Where did you hear this?"

"From Michelle's assistant, Leanne Colbert."

It was obvious that he recognized Leanne's name and he knew Caprice wasn't fishing aimlessly.

She went on, "You weren't at Travis's viewing or funeral. Aren't you supporting Michelle through this difficult time?"

At that, his face took on color. He looked as if he wanted to blurt out something, but instead he blew out a breath. "You do know that Michelle was disappointed in her husband."

"Just disappointed?" Caprice pressed.

"You said you have a fiancé and you're getting married. Then you know how a loved one can make you feel if he's critical, or if he says spiteful things that get you down."

"Grant doesn't do that."

"But if he did, imagine how you'd feel. Probably hurt, probably insecure. You'd probably feel as if you weren't attractive or maybe that your husband didn't love you anymore."

"Are you saying you took up the slack? That you helped Michelle feel better about herself?"

This time Dion didn't watch his response. "I helped her feel loved. By the time Travis died, she almost hated him."

"Why?"

"Because of all the things I just told you . . . because he wouldn't let her go."

"You mean a divorce?"

"He said he'd contest it."

"That doesn't tell me why you haven't been around to support Michelle."

He brushed his hair over his brow. "It just seemed better for now that I stay away."

"Because of the police investigation?"

He nodded. "If Leanne is talking to you, I imagine she'll talk to the police eventually, and they'll find out Michelle and I were having an affair. I'll deal with that when the time comes. But for now, I don't want to add to Michelle's troubles."

"Were you just having an affair? Or was your relationship more?"

This time he didn't raise his voice. "I love Michelle."

"You realize, don't you, that your feelings for her give you motive for murder? Did you kill Travis?"

Dion peered over the vineyard. "You know, sometimes I wish I had. But, no, I didn't because I knew that would only separate me from Michelle, not bring us closer."

Was Dion Genet telling the truth? If she was reading him correctly, he was.

However, she'd been mistaken about someone's character once before and had almost gotten killed because of it.

Chapter Eighteen

That evening Caprice didn't know what to think about first. On the top of her list—Grant had never answered her text. It wasn't much of a text, she knew, but she had been reaching out with it. Didn't he realize that?

Roz wasn't even at the house tonight. She was handling her own stress by going to the Green Tea Spa for a massage and facial. She'd left Dylan with Caprice and that was fine. He was company for Lady. Lady missed Patches.

Travis's murder, of course, was always swimming around in her head. There were lots of murder suspects and she didn't know which one might be fooling her—from Michelle and Neil, to the owner of Black Horse Winery and Dion Genet, to Jarrett and even his mother. Maybe Vivian could have fooled the police and she *had* been in the vicinity the night of the murder.

Caprice picked up Mirabelle's brush. The Persian was sitting on the back of the sofa on the afghan Nana had crocheted as a housewarming gift. She showed the brush to the beautiful cat and Mirabelle jumped down onto the sofa and stretched out on her side. She was affectionate, smart, and listened well. Caprice had to laugh when people said that cats were antisocial. A pet owner just needed to know how to communicate with them. Mirabelle was vocal and that helped. But she also knew what she liked and Caprice played on that.

Now as she used the brush on the cotton-soft white fur, she tried to relieve her own stress with the simple motion. After she finished one side of Mirabelle, the cat turned over so she could do the other side.

"You are such a princess. If there was a Green Tea Spa for cats, I'm sure you'd make an appointment."

Mirabelle meowed and that brought a smile to Caprice's face. She looked up at Sophia. "Are you next?"

On her cat tree, Sophia opened her eyes, stood, and turned her back on Caprice. Caprice knew what that meant. She wasn't interested in being brushed.

The doorbell chimed and Caprice wondered if Roz had forgotten her key. Or maybe Vince had arrived for more advice. Or possibly her neighbor Dulcina had run over to catch up. They hadn't visited for a while. She knew she should check her monitor before she went to the door but it was in her office. So she looked out the peephole instead.

It was Grant. Had he texted and she didn't hear

her phone play? No, that couldn't be. It was laying on the coffee table where she could hear it, and she wouldn't have been able to miss the Beatles song.

She was almost afraid to open the door. But she saw that he had Patches with him, and he was carrying a bag. What was he bringing her? Something she'd left at his place? Was he going to call off the wedding? She couldn't let a thought like that even enter her head. She trusted Grant. She'd told him that and she'd meant it.

Then why was her stomach doing somersaults and her heart beating as fast as a kitten's?

Taking a deep breath, she wished she was wearing something other than her lounge pants in pink and black with paw prints all over them. The white tunic top had pink and black paws all over it too. No time to change. She was who she was, pink fluffy slippers and all.

When she opened the door, Grant looked so somber that fear grabbed her all over again.

They just stared at each other for what seemed like forever. She couldn't seem to find her voice.

His tone was gruff when he asked, "Are you going to invite us in?"

Not only did she look foolish, but she felt foolish. "Did you text me and I missed it? I would have changed if I'd known you were coming over."

There was a hint of a smile as he glanced down at Patches and asked, "We like what Caprice is wearing, don't we?"

The dog seemed to check her out too. Then he took a step forward as if they expected to go inside. But Grant said to him, "Wait. We have to be invited." Patches sat looking up at Caprice with soulful brown eyes.

Caprice could read Patches' mind right now, but not Grant's. She stepped back. "Come on in. Dylan and Lady are watching *Animal Planet.*"

Once Grant and Patches were inside, Grant released his dog from his leash. Patches ran over to the other two dogs and they greeted each other, sniffing to make sure they knew these friends. Patches looked up at Mirabelle on the back of the sofa. She looked down at him as if trying to give him a warning—don't come up here.

He must have gotten the message because he followed Lady and Dylan into the kitchen. They were probably going to wait there for a snack.

Grant looked uncomfortable. He hadn't bothered with a jacket but was wearing a black Henley shirt and jeans. Docksiders were on his feet, but he didn't have any socks on. That wasn't like Grant.

When he saw her looking down at his feet, he blew out a breath and squared his shoulders. "I was in a hurry to get here. When I first saw your text last night, I wasn't sure how to respond. This morning—I got an idea and executed it. But then I was in court all afternoon. By the time I got home, I realized you might be disappointed because you hadn't heard from me. So I thought the best thing to do was just to come right over. I don't like this distance between us, Caprice. I wouldn't like it even if we weren't getting married."

"You don't want to get married?" She jumped to that conclusion because it was her worst fear.

"I didn't say that," he responded, frowning. "What about you? What have you been thinking?"

With her heart beating way too fast, with Grant standing before her, she could hardly think. But she could feel. "I'm afraid. I don't want anything to come between us. I shouldn't have been so emotional. I've come to the conclusion that our parents might never get along and I'm asking myself if it matters. But mostly I'm just holding onto the fact that I love you, and I hope you still love me."

Grant dropped the bag he was carrying onto the sofa. He put his arms around her, brought her close and held her against his chest. "Count on *you* to be able to put it all into words," he murmured.

"You'd rather I didn't?" she asked, leaning back.

"That's not what I meant, either." He seemed frustrated with himself. "I'd better spruce up on my communication skills. I have trouble with words that come with feelings. You know that. But *you* don't have trouble. Everything you just said I've been thinking about since I left here. Maybe we should take them one by one." Lowering himself to the couch, he pulled her down beside him. "Because I'm not so eloquent with words, I brought a few gifts that I'm hoping will tell you exactly how I feel."

The words that almost came out of her mouth were—*I don't want any gifts. I just want you.* But that would sound like rejection and she certainly didn't want to reject him. He was handing her the blue bag that had blue tissue paper peeking out.

He suggested, "Just reach in and pull out the first thing."

She felt inside the bag without looking. Her fingers closed over a package, something in cellophane. She pulled it out. She had to laugh. It was catnip.

"I brought that for Sophia and Mirabelle. I have to stay in their good graces. I was hoping they'd put in a good word for me with you because I was stupid to leave like I did the other night."

"Not stupid," she was quick to say. "My guess is you were hurt and disappointed too."

He brought his hand up to her cheek and caressed it. "Sometimes you know my feelings better than I do."

"I just knew what I felt and that you might be feeling it too."

After a long look into each other's eyes, Grant suggested, "Open the next packet."

When she reached in this time, her fingers closed on a bulkier package. Pulling it out, she saw that it was one of Perky Paws' special bags filled with dog treats.

"They're for Lady," Grant said. "It's up to her if she wants to share them with Patches."

"I'm sure she will. Sharing is the best part of being together."

Tenderly taking her hand in his, he squeezed it. "The final gift in the bag is for you."

Caprice slowly pulled out a yellow box like any gift shop might use. She just stared at it for a while.

"Open it," Grant encouraged her.

After she took off the lid and pushed back tissue paper, she felt tears rush into her eyes. Inside the box was a wooden heart with their names burned into the wood.

When her gaze met his, he said, "I thought about giving you flowers or jewelry, but that wouldn't tell you what I was really feeling. I found the heart and a wood-burning iron at a craft store. My dad once did woodwork with engraving on it. It was just a side hobby, and he always said his pieces weren't good enough to give away. But I thought he was wrong. I inscribed our names on there and stained it because I wanted you to have something . . . for you . . . something that I meant just for you . . . something that would tell you I was sorry."

"Oh, Grant." She wrapped her arms around his neck. "It's perfect. I'm so sorry too. I never should have said what I did."

"You were speaking the truth that night and so was I. And the fact that it *is* the truth means we have to deal with it. But I think we'll be a lot better dealing with it together than separately, don't you think?"

"Oh, yes, I think that's true. I was so worried you didn't want to marry me anymore . . . marry me and my family."

He cupped her face in his hands. "Not anything will keep me from marrying you. You can't still be insecure about how I feel, can you?"

"When something like this happens, I think about how much easier it would have been for you to marry someone else, not to have to go through the whole annulment process, not to have to deal with the expectations from my family."

"But don't you realize what you're saying is true for me too? We've gone through it together. We've gone through everything together—my grief over losing Sally, my letting go of enough of it to move forward. You trusted me during the time I needed to find closure with Naomi, and I did. I am who I am because of you. Something my mother said when we visited them hit home as the truth." He dropped his hands from her face.

Her heart was still beating rapidly. "What?"

"She said all those times I came home with Vince when we were in law school, I started to have feelings for you then but denied them. I was four years older. You were seventeen and I was twenty-one. And you were my best friend's sister. I absolutely denied anything I felt. But my mother said it could have been one of the reasons why my marriage with Naomi didn't work out."

"Is that true?" Caprice asked in almost a whisper.

He took her hand in his once more. "I don't think it's true, per se. I think when we met, I liked you a lot. By the time Vince and I graduated from law school, you and I had gotten to know each other better, and I think there were feelings there. But you were ready to embark on your adult life and so was I. After I moved to Pittsburgh, took a job with a big firm and met Naomi, I headed in another direction."

Now he stared at their clasped hands a few moments before he went on. "I didn't know Naomi had stopped taking birth control on purpose so she could trap me into marriage. That's what I always felt—trapped. I still have no doubt marrying her because of our baby was the right thing to do. I told myself that over and over. But Naomi and I . . . We never had the closeness you and I have. We never laughed the way you and I do. You and I began a friendship base way back then that grew. When Naomi and I lost Sally, we blamed each other. Our marriage, not the best to begin with, began tearing apart. When I found out Naomi had an affair while we were both grieving, that was the end of it. We didn't fit together."

He blew out a breath. "I didn't mean to talk about my marriage. I just want you to remember that I *chose* you. I chose to be your friend when Vince was in law school with me. When I came back to Kismet, I told myself I wasn't interested in anyone. But when we had those De Luca family dinners, I couldn't keep denying that I enjoyed being with you. Letting go of the past was hard. Loving you was easy."

She was openly crying now instead of trying to blink the tears away. She didn't know how she was going to stop crying. Of course, her tears were joyful because Grant had given her an even better understanding of him than she'd had before.

Once she had caught her breath and he was holding her close against him on the sofa, she asked, "Do you want to change the venue for the reception?"

He shook his head. "No. Not after all the plans we've made. As you said, the tasting room is in another building. Our parents will just have to accept that. For all we know, it will give them common ground to get along."

Caprice smiled, but then she became serious again. "What are we going to do so they *do* get along? Under my parents' roof, they probably won't be able to avoid controversy."

"We'll let *them* hash it out. We'll be on our honeymoon. When we get back, your parents will be in Pennsylvania and mine will be back in Vermont."

"But if we want to have a holiday together—"

"My parents love me and your parents love you. They'll work it out, Caprice. I know you're worried that they won't. If we have to, we'll celebrate every other holiday with the two families. We'll do that. But they are not going to come between us."

Caprice's cell phone played. "I'll let it go to voicemail."

"You're in the middle of a murder investigation. Maybe you should at least see who's calling."

She kissed Grant lightly on the lips. "More of that later," she assured him with a smile and picked up her phone. "It's Brett," she said. "I'd better take it. But there's no reason why you can't listen in."

She swiped the screen to accept the call. "Hi, Brett. I'm going to put you on speaker phone because Grant's here."

"That sounds good. Then I don't have to explain this to both of you separately. Grant, do you know about the virus on Caprice's computer?"

"No, I don't." He turned questioning eyes to her.

"Someone got to her hard drive, either by phishing or a Trojan horse. Anyway, the virus originated from a burner phone. There's no way to really trace it. We're investigating the point of sale and then we'll see if we can get video footage. It's a long shot but I think it's worth a try. I just wanted to keep you informed."

"Do I need to buy a new computer?" Caprice asked.

"It might be a good idea. We're going to hold onto this one for a while longer."

"Maybe I'll just look into a laptop for the time being. It would be good to have a backup."

"That would suit us just fine," Brett said. "My techs can put excellent security on it for you. After all, I owe you for the leads you've come up with for me."

"I'd appreciate that, Brett. I really would. I'll give you a call when I get one."

"Sounds good. You and Grant have a nice evening."

After she ended the call and laid her phone on the coffee table, Grant took her into his arms again. "You didn't tell me about the virus."

"I didn't think you wanted to talk to me," she said.

"And I didn't think *you* wanted to talk to *me*. Never again, right?"

"Never again," she vowed.

He bent his head closer to hers. "And we *are* going to have a very nice evening."

"At least until Roz comes home."

"Then we better get started." He bent his head and kissed her.

The following Tuesday, Caprice drove to Baltimore-Washington International Airport, also known as Thurgood Marshall Airport, to pick up her Aunt Marie. She admired her aunt and was eager to see her. She pulled off the road in the area for communicating with a cell phone. As soon as she tapped her phone open, the message signal popped up. Her aunt had texted.

**I'll wait for you outside at Southwest Airlines,
door number 4.**

Caprice quickly texted back with a thumbs-up
emoji then pulled back into the stream of traffic
ready to pick up her aunt.

Her aunt was unique and didn't quite fit in with
the rest of the family. An artist, she created sterling
silver jewelry in her studio in Taos.

Aunt Marie was easy to spot at the curb where
she'd crossed the traffic lanes at door four. She
wore a gauzy maxi-dress in shades of green and
blue in an ombré effect. On her feet, she'd slipped
on Birkenstocks and she wore a yellow shawl
draped around her shoulders. Her hair was black
like Caprice's dad's. It was as straight as Caprice's
and even longer. Every time she'd seen her aunt
over the years and in pictures, Marie was usually
wearing her hair in a long braid. Today was no ex-
ception.

They'd spoken on the phone over the weekend
so Caprice could catch up her aunt on what was
happening and the fact that Roz would be staying
with them too, at least for now.

"You didn't bring Lady along," Aunt Marie said,
sounding disappointed. "I was hoping you would
so I could meet her."

"She's at my house with Roz and Dylan. Roz
needs a distraction right now, and the dogs will
help with that. You'll meet Lady as soon as we get
home."

Her aunt buckled her seatbelt and Caprice pulled
away from the curb.

Aunt Marie sighed and leaned her head against
the seatback. "I'm definitely not a world traveler.

Flying messes up my body rhythm. My yoga teacher once said the human body is created for a horse and buggy, not for breaking the sound barrier."

"You'll have a couple of days to rest. At the rehearsal dinner Friday night, you'll meet Grant's family."

She was so glad she and Grant had talked about everything. It was like a weight had been lifted from around her heart. She supposed that each time they argued and made up—and there *would* be arguments—their relationship would grow stronger.

"Are you sure you don't want me to stay somewhere else if Roz is there with you?"

"Roz asked me the same thing before I left. I have two spare bedrooms. I'm sure you met Roz when we were in high school and you were still around Kismet. And I'm even more sure you'll like the adult version. She's my best friend, other than Bella and Nikki, of course."

"Of course," Aunt Marie said with a smile, sitting up straight again. "I'm going to love taking care of your animals while you and Grant are on your honeymoon. I can't wait to meet him as well as Lady."

Caprice laughed. "I'll tell him that. I bet your two cats are going to miss you."

"Maybe. My next-door neighbor will take good care of Midnight and Bianca. She'll check on them a few times a day and feed them, and maybe stay overnight at my place a couple of nights."

"It's good you have someone you can trust."

Her aunt often e-mailed Caprice photos of her cats. Midnight was an ebony black cat and Bianca was white with blue eyes. Yin and yang. Her aunt had moved to New Mexico, and Taos in particular, because she wanted to be in a more spiritual atmosphere. Spiritual, not religious. Her aunt had a different take on the world than her traditional family did. She was the one who'd convinced Caprice to do affirmations each day. As far as Caprice was concerned, those affirmations worked, or at least kept her thinking in a positive mode.

Caprice concentrated on driving on the Beltway, and her aunt rested until they veered onto I-83.

Her aunt asked, "Has anything changed about the murder investigation since we spoke?"

"Not exactly. Brett could use a little more information about a rival winery." She told her aunt about Black Horse Winery.

"Anything else?"

Caprice hesitated.

"A confidential matter?"

"Possibly. But I know *you* know how to keep secrets." Her aunt had been around during her school years and Caprice had often confided in her. "I also visited another winery, Oak Grove Vineyard. I'd heard from someone that Michelle had been having an affair, so I went to the source."

"The man himself?"

"Yes."

"Wasn't that dangerous?"

"I didn't feel it was. And from what he said, I think he truly cares for Michelle, and she for him. Unless she was just trying to escape the loneliness of her marriage and using Dion. If so . . ."

"Are you thinking *if so*, maybe he resented it and killed her husband?"

"I really don't know. Like Brett, I need more information."

"I doubt if you should talk to Michelle directly. Is there anyone else you can discuss it with?"

"Travis's brother lived at the winery for a year. It's possible he might know something about it."

"Is it safe to talk to him?"

"I don't know who's safe and who isn't anymore. The plans for the wedding have been swirling around me like a cloud, and maybe that's tilting my reasoning. But I think it would be safe enough to ask Jarrett. He seems to be pretty straightforward. Maybe I can get back to the winery tomorrow."

"I could always go with you," Marie suggested. "A little adventure is good for the soul. Besides . . . Resting is overrated."

Caprice laughed. "Tell you what, I'll think about that."

Her aunt patted her hand.

Caprice felt it might be a kind of insurance to have her aunt along. Insurance in the middle of a murder investigation could be a very good thing.

Chapter Nineteen

Since Roz wasn't going into her shop until later in the day, she stayed with the animals while Caprice and Marie drove to the Rambling Vines Winery on Wednesday. After they parked, Caprice took a look around from the house to the tasting room to the events room. She pointed out each to Marie.

Glancing toward the garage, she spotted Jarrett at an open garage door studying the MG.

"Jarrett's at the garage," Caprice said. "Do you want to come with me to talk to him?"

"You might get more out of him if I'm not with you. Why don't I take a look at the tasting room and events room if they're open?"

"If they aren't, maybe Jarrett can open them for us."

"If you don't make an enemy of him first." There was amusement in her aunt's voice.

"I'll try not to do that."

"I know, but it's hard to keep doubts about

someone from showing on your face. Like your dad, you really can't lie well."

"Speaking about showing emotion on your face, are you nervous about seeing Uncle Dom again after all these years?"

Marie's expression sobered. "Not nervous, exactly. He and I haven't been in touch at all. I know your dad called and visited him over those years, but Dom wouldn't talk to Nana. After I moved away, I thought about him, but I didn't know if he'd want to hear from me. So we'll see if tonight's dinner at your mom's is a reunion or a clash of hurt feelings. I know how Mama was hurt when he married Ronnie, and then when she kept him from his family. Mama thought a man should stand up for what he believed in and so did I."

Marie was right about how Nana had felt. Caprice said, "Uncle Dom believed in keeping his wife happy, but I do think he regrets that now."

They were at the tasting room and Caprice left Marie there when they saw that the door was open. Her aunt said to her, "You text me or call me if there's a problem. Or do you want to keep the line open?"

"I don't think there's a need for that. I have my phone in my pocket and I'll keep it open to my contacts screen."

Her aunt said, "Good luck," and opened the door to the tasting room.

Caprice walked around the tasting room to the gardens. As she passed the bubbling fountain, she saw Jarrett running his hand over the MG. Maybe he was thinking about the amount of money Michelle could collect from the sale of the cars. Or maybe he was just admiring them. It was hard to know.

Jarrett noticed her approaching and gave a wave. He didn't look as if he were doing anything he shouldn't, but then that just might be his surface charm.

"Are you thinking of driving one?" she teased.

He studied the cars in the garage. "No. I'm just wondering why Travis had to buy so many, or have so many restored. He was collecting them as if he was collecting Hummels." Jarrett shook his head. "I just don't get it. There are so many things about my brother I didn't understand. But that was true of my father too."

Jarrett's openness always surprised Caprice. As he did seem to be open, she asked, "When are you going back to Maryland?"

"My mother wants me to stay another week. She's trying to convince me to take over the winery with Michelle."

"Have you talked to Michelle about it?"

With a shrug, he explained, "I don't know if I'd even think about doing it. So there doesn't seem much point in discussing it. On the other hand, I'm not sure Michelle wants to keep the winery. So much of it probably reminds her of Travis, good and bad memories. She's worried about getting a job to pay basic expenses. If you're here to see her, she's on an interview this morning about a nursing position. But there's no way she can run the winery and work too. She's looking at all options, I suppose."

Caprice wanted information from Jarrett that

he might not want to give. The best way she knew
to get it was just blurt out the question. She might
take him off guard. "Did you know what was going
on between Michelle and Dion Genet?"

Jarrett's eyes widened for a moment and he hesitated. "I knew. I wonder if the police know."

This time Caprice shrugged. "If I could find out
about it, they can too."

Jarrett muttered, "Travis was such a bastard to
her. That day he accused me of making a pass at
Michelle, it just tore her apart that he'd even think
that. I was just comforting her after a trying day.
She had a lot of them with him. She began to hate
her life with Travis."

"Because he wasn't the man she thought she
married?"

"That was a huge part of it." Jarrett's voice had
gone deep and somber.

Caprice felt there was something Jarrett wasn't
telling her. Did he know Michelle well enough to
believe whether she would or wouldn't kill her
husband? But she decided information gathering
was an art. You had to know when to push and
when not to push. If she wanted Jarrett to give her
or anyone else information later, she should stop
now.

"The reason why I'm here is that I brought my
aunt along to see the tasting room and the events
room. She's in the tasting room now. Is it all right
if we take a little tour?"

"Neil's probably in the tasting room. Sure, you
can take a tour. If he's not there and you need me
to open the events room, just come get me. I'm in-

ventorying the cars and exactly what Travis had here. Michelle needs to get some resell prices."

"Sounds good," Caprice responded.

Jarrett nodded and picked up a clipboard that he had laid on the roof of the car. She supposed he really was taking inventory.

For Michelle's sake? Or for his own?

That evening Grant picked up Caprice and her aunt. Caprice had thought that was the better way to go so Marie could meet Grant and Patches before they set foot in the De Luca family boisterousness. The three of them had had coffee and spent about an hour talking. Grant and her aunt seemed to get along right away, and Caprice was glad of that. No, it wasn't a given that everybody on Caprice's side of the aisle would like Grant. She had no illusions about that. But her aunt seemed to connect with Grant on a deeper level than the surface.

When they walked into her mom's house, everyone but Nana and her mom were in the living room. When Uncle Dom saw Marie, Caprice noticed that Dulcina patted his arm. Caprice supposed that was a signal of some kind or else just a touch of support.

Caprice's gaze met Vince's. She was so annoyed with him. Roz had refused to come tonight and had actually gone out of town to visit a friend. The truth was—Caprice didn't know if she could keep her annoyance in check.

As Grant unleashed Patches and Lady and the

cockers went to say hello to Blitz who lay in the sunroom off the living room, Marie stood frozen in the doorway. She took in everyone gathered there from Bella and Joe, Megan, Timmy, and Benny, to Vince, to Dom and Dulcina, to Nikki and Brett. The first thing she did was go to Brett. "Since I know most of these other people, I'll talk to the people I don't know first. I suppose you're Nikki's Brett?"

Caprice noticed Nikki flush. "Aunt Marie," Nikki said, "This is Brett Carstead."

"I surmised as much," Marie said. "He's a detective with the Kismet PD who Caprice helps once in a while."

Brett's lips quirked up in a smile and he extended his hand. "It's good to meet you. Sometimes I'm not sure if Caprice helps me or I help her."

Next Aunt Marie headed for Dulcina but Dom stood. Then he closed the gap between them and gave his sister a huge hug. "It's good to see you, Marie. I'm sorry for all the years I stayed quiet."

Caprice could see that Marie had tears in her eyes when she leaned away so she could study him. "You're looking good, Dom. Life must agree with you."

"It does since I moved to Kismet."

"Caprice tells me you're pet sitting now."

"I am. I like it better than I ever did financial work. How about you? Are you making jewelry?"

"I am. A few shops in Santa Fe and Taos sell it."

"There's someone I want you to meet," Dom said, taking a step back and motioning to Dulcina. "This is Dulcina."

Standing, Dulcina extended her hand. "It's good to meet you. Dom has told me stories about your growing-up years."

"You mean how he got into trouble much too easily."

Dulcina laughed and any tension that might have been there dissipated.

Just then her mom and Nana came into the room. There was more hugging and chatter and De Luca chaos.

Caprice leaned close to Grant. "I'm going to pull Vince aside."

After remaining silent for a beat, he asked, "Are you sure you want to do that now?"

He was giving her the chance to reconsider. "I do, because the conversation will be over with and won't get lost in the shuffle. We'll be able to enjoy dinner."

"I don't think Vince is enjoying much these days," Grant muttered.

When Caprice angled toward Vince and caught his elbow to lead him into the sunroom, she saw that Grant was right. Her brother looked pale and tired.

"You look awful," Caprice told him.

"Gee, thanks, Sis."

"I can see you're just as miserable as Roz."

"Don't start on me again. I know I have to make her a real part of my life if I want to keep her, and I do want to keep her if it's not too late. But there are a few things I have to do before I can talk to Roz. Believe me, I'll make this right as soon as I can."

Caprice wondered about those few things he had to do but decided not to question him. Nevertheless, she did have something to tell him. "I suppose some of those things you have to do concern Michelle."

His jaw jutted forward. "She's my client."

"Did you know she's having an affair with Dion Genet?"

Vince looked totally surprised. "No, I didn't. Are you sure about that?"

"I confirmed it with Jarrett and with Dion himself. It's possible she murdered Travis so they wouldn't fight over everything in a divorce."

"That's not Michelle," Vince protested.

"All right, but I thought you should know. If you ask her about it, maybe she'll come clean with you. Have you talked with Jarrett much?"

"I had one interview session with him. Why?"

"Because I think there's something he's not telling us or the police. I want to see him again and poke a little more."

"He could be your killer just as easy as Michelle. Be careful."

"I will."

Vince was silent for a few moments and they both just listened to the conversations and chatter in the living room. Finally, he said, "I want Roz to be here meeting Aunt Marie. I want her beside me at your wedding. I'll tell you the first thing I have to do. I have to convince Michelle to call the defense attorney I recommended for her. I'm not going to give her a choice."

Caprice wasn't sure how that would go. But sometimes her brother had more tact than she gave him credit for. Maybe she'd say a rosary tonight that Vince could untangle this mess.

* * *

Caprice took her Aunt Marie out for lunch the next day to the Sunflower Diner in order to show her a favorite Kismet watering hole. They walked inside and the hostess greeted Caprice by name. After she'd shown them to one of the front booths, her Aunt Marie asked, "Do you come in often?"

"Often enough. We brought Grant's parents here for dinner when they first visited Kismet."

"How did they like it?"

"To tell you the truth, I'm not sure. I do know they don't like anything pretentious so that's why Grant suggested here."

The waitress, a redhead in her twenties with a pixie cut, whose nametag read SUSAN, brought them menus and asked about drink orders. After they ordered drinks, they studied the menus. "I'm still full from the meal last night," Marie said. "I think I'll just have their corn chowder and a salad."

"That sounds good," Caprice agreed. "I do want to be able to fit into my wedding gown."

Marie smiled. "I can't wait to see you in it."

"Now that our wedding is getting closer, I just want it to happen. It seems that Grant and I have been waiting forever, even though we just got engaged last fall."

"Nikki told me you're being very traditional about this wedding. It's not as if the two of you are living together. Your wedding is going to change both your lives." Marie winked. "And because you're traditional, I know how much that wedding night is going to mean."

"I guess Nikki doesn't believe my business is private."

"Not with family," Marie reminded her. "Everybody knows you two haven't slept together yet. I think it's admirable."

Caprice felt herself blushing. Even though she was a modern woman and considered herself able to talk about anything, it still embarrassed her to talk about it with her aunt.

Caprice studied her aunt for a moment and then asked, "Why haven't you ever gotten married?"

"I was in love once a long time ago when I first moved to New Mexico. That was a big change for me. It was almost like starting my life over again. I met someone at a flea market where I was first selling my necklaces and bracelets. He had a spirit of adventure and his passion was his motorcycle. You should have seen me riding on the back of it. The only thing I could compare it to would be riding a horse at a full gallop."

"What was his name?"

"His name was Jorge."

Caprice unrolled her silverware from the white paper napkin and placed the napkin on her lap. "I don't remember the family ever discussing this."

"That's because they didn't know. They still don't."

"Why not?"

"Because Jorge was killed on that motorcycle two years after I met him."

Caprice reached out to her aunt and took her hand. "I'm so sorry. Why didn't you tell anyone?"

"Believe it or not, Dom and I were the closest growing up. I felt betrayed when he married and then didn't keep in touch. I was very hurt. The truth was, as you said, I didn't want anybody in my business. The fact that I was in New Mexico kept me separate. I didn't need all the De Lucas descending on me to give me condolences. You know I'm not like that. I know you enjoy your family gatherings once a month, but they always made me feel claustrophobic."

"I suppose I can see that, especially if you're a very private person."

"From what you've told me about Grant, I'm surprised he's comfortable there."

"He started enjoying De Luca gatherings when he and Vince were in law school. I think because he wasn't close to his own family, he liked being part of the De Lucas."

"I hope he continues to like it because it's going to be a way of life for the two of you."

Caprice fingered her fork, thinking about the future. "He was really cut off emotionally from everyone for a long time because of his daughter drowning and his marriage breaking up. But then, little by little, it was as if he came alive again. I think one of the turning points was when he adopted Patches."

"You e-mailed me about that situation. I'm glad you found the owner of that cocker and homes for all of her babies."

The waitress returned for their orders and they gave them. After the waitress had gone, Caprice told her aunt, "The pie here is really good . . . just in case you're interested."

"I bet it's not as good as Mama's."

"Probably not," Caprice agreed.

Customers had been coming and going as Caprice and her aunt talked. Suddenly, however, a shadow fell over Caprice. At first, she thought the waitress had come back with a question. But when she looked up, she couldn't have been more shocked. A man was standing at their table and one she recognized—Andrei Moldavan.

"Hello, Mr. Moldavan," she said to let him know she recognized him.

"Your name is De Luca, isn't it?" he asked in an almost belligerent attitude.

"Caprice De Luca. And this is my aunt, Marie De Luca."

"I'm not making no social call. I just happened to see you here and I thought you should know something."

The hairs at Caprice's neck prickled when she talked to this man, but she was in a public place with her aunt and nothing bad was going to happen. "Just what do you think I should know? Something about Travis's murder?"

Her aunt's dark-brown eyes went wide at Caprice's question to Moldavan. Maybe she shouldn't have asked it, but she couldn't understand why he was stopping to talk to her.

"This don't have nothing to do with the murder. I just want to tell you that your reception will be the last one at Rambling Vines. I'm going to put in an offer to buy the place so I can shut it down."

Caprice's astonishment must have shown on her face. She'd never expected that he had that kind of money.

He must have translated her expression accurately because he wagged his finger at her. "Don't you underestimate me. I made my money in the stock market during the tech boom. I had a plumbing business in Baltimore and I moved here for peace and quiet. That's what I'm going to get again. You can tell Michelle Dodd my offer will be coming in and she'd better take it because she won't get another one like it." His face redder than it should be, he turned away from the table and stalked out of the restaurant.

"You know that man?" her aunt asked her.

"He's a neighbor to the winery. He has both religious concerns—he doesn't like the dancing and the music—and personal concerns. He hates the traffic that the winery causes."

"He certainly seems mean enough to commit murder," Marie said.

Caprice was thinking that same thing when her cell phone played. When she took it out of her pocket and studied the screen, she told Marie, "It's Grant."

Her aunt waved for her to take it.

"Hi," she said a bit breathless. The thought of him always made her breathless.

"Can you talk?" he asked.

"I'm at lunch with Aunt Marie at the Sunflower Diner, but yes, I can talk. What do you need?"

"I picked up Holden at the airport. Can you come to dinner tonight at my place? I'm cooking."

She supposed Holden was in the car with Grant. Just why did Grant want her to come to dinner on Holden's first night here?

"Just me?" she asked.

"Just you."

"Do you want me to bring dessert?"

"That would be great."

"I'll make that coconut cake you like so much."

"Do you have time?"

"I'll make time. What time do you want me there?"

"How about six?"

"Six o'clock it is. Tell Holden I said hi. I'm looking forward to meeting him."

"And he's looking forward to meeting you. I'll see you at six."

After Caprice arrived at Grant's townhouse, she'd find out what was really going on . . . besides dinner.

Caprice walked in on *something* at Grant's townhouse that evening and she wasn't sure what.

Patches ran over to greet her and Lady. After she took off her color-blocked poncho, she noticed the tension both in Grant's stance and on Holden's face.

Grant introduced them. "Caprice, this is Holden, my brother. Holden, this is Caprice, my fiancée."

She held out her hand to Holden and he took it, but his expression looked wary. She'd hoped tonight would be a fun night, a get-to-know-you-dinner. She'd worn a white full-sleeved blouse, a large flower-print vest with fringes, and pants with flutter bell-bottoms. Now she wondered if she should have dressed more conservatively as Holden looked her over. "Mom said you dressed like an escapee from the seventies," Holden said.

"Holden," Grant chastised.

Holden was about an inch shorter than Grant. His hair was dark-brown and his eyes green. He had Grant's well-defined jaw though, high cheekbones, and thicker brows. He was handsome and she supposed he could be charming if he smiled. He was wearing chinos, a beige polo shirt, and loafers.

Caprice could make a snappy sarcastic comment as a comeback, but that wouldn't advance any relationship. Instead, she said, "Thank you, I think. You should see my Beatles military jacket."

Holden gave her a disbelieving look, then smiled. "Mom said you had a sense of humor."

"Don't confuse a sense of humor with being tactful," Caprice responded with a smile.

Apparently Grant could see where this conversation was headed. He said, "Let me take your poncho, Caprice. I'll hang it in the foyer closet. Dinner's almost ready. If you want to settle in the kitchen, feel free."

Caprice followed Holden into the kitchen where the table was already set. After she set the cake on the counter, she took a seat across from Holden, leaving the head of the table open. "What are we having?" she asked.

"Steak, salad, baked potatoes. A manly man meal."

"Do you consider yourself a manly man?" she asked, half joking. Something had to lighten the atmosphere.

"Sometimes I do, but Grant always is. He's the perfect man. At least he was until he got engaged to you."

Choosing not to feel hurt, trying to swim past what she felt was a personal attack, she wanted to get to the bottom of Holden's problem. Or maybe it was Holden and Grant's problem.

"First of all," she said, "I don't think Grant would consider himself a perfect man. And I'm really interested in why you think marrying me would change somebody's opinion of him."

Holden frowned and shrugged. "My parents don't approve."

"Really? When we visited them after Christmas, they were welcoming to us, even to Patches."

"He brought the dog with him?"

"*We* brought the dog with *us.* I have a cocker spaniel too, Patches' sister. We thought two dogs might be a little much, so I left Lady with my parents. Your dad doesn't think of pets the same way we do."

"You use that 'we' pretty loosely."

"I know what Grant feels about animals. Do you?"

Holden's frown deepened. "Are you asking me if I know my brother?"

Just then Grant returned to the kitchen.

Caprice was glad for his presence. She was afraid she was delving into water that was much too deep for her alone. This serious conversation wasn't at all what she'd expected tonight. Holden definitely seemed to have a chip on his shoulder.

Grant looked from one of them to the other. Then he picked up two potholders and went to the oven, opening it to check the steaks. He pulled them out and cut one. "Medium well for everyone," he said.

Grant collected their plates and one by one forked the steaks onto them. Then he pulled the salad from the refrigerator and set the wooden bowl on the table. The baked potatoes wrapped in foil were next and he put one on each plate. Butter was already on the table, but he pulled the container of sour cream from the refrigerator.

"You thought of everything," Caprice said with a smile, wanting to give him encouragement.

"He always does," Holden said.

When Grant shot him a sharp look, Caprice had the feeling this was an old battle . . . or an old war.

They all began carving their steaks. Grant had prepared the salad with a vinaigrette dressing that Caprice had given him the recipe for.

Using a tongs, she served herself salad from the bowl and asked, "Anybody else?"

"Sure," Grant said, passing her his dish. After she served Grant, her gaze met Holden's. "How about you?"

"Why not?" Holden said. "I'll add something healthy to this cholesterol-lover's dream."

"I thought you liked steak," Grant said with a quizzical look at his brother.

"I usually don't buy Porterhouse. Way too expensive. Especially grass-fed. I saw the label on the steak package."

Caprice could continue the conversation about food or she could change the direction of it. "Grant told me you're the manager of a division in a medical supply company. Do you enjoy your job?"

"Is there anyone who really enjoys work?" Holden asked.

"I do," she answered him quickly.

"Right. You stage houses for high-end clients. Even rock stars. I've heard all about that. Must be really hard work."

Grant stopped eating and eyed his brother. Caprice knew that look. Grant was at the end of his rope and he was going to say so. Maybe she could stop him. She laid her hand on his arm, but he just patted her hand as if he understood what he was doing. He seemed determined.

"Caprice had an interior design degree and a decorating business. It started tanking because of the bad economy. Intelligent and savvy woman that she is, she recreated her business into home staging," Grant explained.

After he laid down the knife and fork he'd been holding, he continued, "Fairly quickly, she earned a good reputation and more and more clients. She spends hours with a client, decluttering their house. She pulls furniture from her storage shed. She works with her assistant to arrange the furniture they bring into the houses. She coordinates with her sister Nikki who's a caterer to put out a unique spread at open houses for each client if they choose to have one. She often works seven days a week with long hours, many of them on the computer. But she loves what she does. That's why it works. That's why she's successful. I like being a lawyer. That's why I can make a living at it. Why don't you tell Caprice what you're thinking about doing?"

Holden's face turned a shade of red as if he was embarrassed. "All right, I'll tell her what I want to do. I'd like to quit my job, drive out to California, maybe Venice Beach. I'd like to own one of those stores on a pier and sell T-shirts. I'd like to experience a little bit of paradise before it's too late."

"My parents don't approve," Grant told Caprice.

Holden bristled. "That's because there's only ever support for what *you* do, not what *I* want to do. Except in this latest stunt of you and Naomi going through an annulment. Mom and Dad don't understand canceling out a marriage. They also don't understand why you picked *her*." He pointed to Caprice.

"Holden, that's enough," Grant scolded, loud enough for Patches to come running to him.

Holden pushed back his chair with such force it almost fell over. "It's not nearly enough. I'm going to take a walk. You two enjoy dinner."

As he walked out of the kitchen, Grant called, "Holden. Wait."

But his brother acted as if he didn't hear him, and soon they heard the front door open and close.

"What was that about?" Caprice asked, turning toward Grant, reaching for his hand.

He interlaced their fingers. "It's about resentment that he's been harboring for a long time. I really don't know what to do about it."

"Why don't I help you clean up, then I'll leave. I have an early appointment tomorrow with Jarrett at the Koffee Klatch. When Holden comes back, the two of you can talk."

Grant shook his head. "I don't want you to leave this way."

"What way? I love you and you love me, and

we're getting married on Saturday. That's what I care about most. But I care about you and your brother too."

Grant leaned forward and kissed Caprice. Then he murmured, "That's exactly why I'm marrying you," and he kissed her again.

Chapter Twenty

It was seven thirty on Friday morning, the day of the wedding rehearsal and dinner, when Caprice met Jarrett at the Koffee Klatch. He'd told her he was meeting with distributers later in the day and this was the only time he'd had open. But he hadn't arrived yet as Caprice ordered a latté and then chose a table, thinking about her family and Grant's having dinner tonight.

Her mind had plenty of places to go. Grant had texted her last night to tell her Holden was back and they would talk. He'd said everything was okay. She didn't push for more because she knew he had a lot on his mind. He'd be picking up his parents at the airport today.

Not only was she worried about Holden and Grant, but when she'd gotten home last night, Vince was in her living room talking to Roz! She'd gone to bed and fallen asleep before Roz came upstairs. This morning Roz hadn't been up but she'd left a note—I WAS UP UNTIL 3 A.M. SLEEPING IN. I'M

PACKING UP MY THINGS AND GOING HOME TO VINCE
THIS MORNING. WE'LL TALK LATER.

While Caprice waited for Jarrett, she sipped her
latté and checked her phone. No messages. Was
he going to stand her up? It wouldn't surprise her.
He knew she was probably going to ask questions
he didn't want to answer.

How long should she wait? Until eight?

At seven forty-five, Jarrett came in the door,
looking harried instead of his usual casual self.
When he saw her, he waved and went to the coffee
bar. A few minutes later he was sitting across from
her. "I'm sorry I'm late," he said, "With my mother
in the house, a simple conversation can lead to a
situation that needs multiple answers."

"About the winery?" Caprice asked.

"Yes. My mother is tossing a few ideas around.
Michelle is considering them all. Michelle has to
think of her life different and separate from Travis's
now. She couldn't do that while they were married."

"Even though she was having an affair with
Dion Genet?"

"Even though. At heart, Michelle is a loyal person. She meant her vows. Oh, by the way, she got a
call from Vince yesterday. He cut ties with her. She
called a defense attorney he recommended."

After a look at Caprice, Jarrett said, "You can say
what you're thinking."

"I'm thinking I'm happy for Roz and Vince if
this fixes what their arguments were about."

"I know what you mean. You think you're arguing about what someone made for breakfast when
it's really about finances."

"So you *have* been involved in serious relationships."

"I have," Jarrett admitted. "But none were serious enough." He took a few swallows of his coffee and checked his watch.

Caprice got the message. "I know your time is limited today and mine is too. So I'll get to the point. I want to know what you're not telling me about Michelle or Travis. I can tell you're holding something back. Any tidbit could make a difference in solving the murder. Don't you want to do that for your brother?"

Jarrett drank more coffee as if bracing himself. But then he gave Caprice a shrug. "What I know has nothing to do with the murder. It just shows how despicable my brother was."

She was surprised at that answer. After all, they had been brothers. "Don't you want to know who murdered him?"

"You know, I really don't care." He frowned, stared into his coffee, and admitted, "That's not true. I care because I don't want Michelle to be blamed."

"And you think what you know will put Michelle in more jeopardy?" Caprice guessed.

"Possibly. If I tell you, you'll tell that detective . . ."

"Jarrett, it all has to come out. Don't you understand that? It's the secrets and lies that hurt people, not the truth."

"The truth," he scoffed. "Everyone sees the truth differently."

"I like Michelle. And, yes, there are two sides to every story, maybe even three. But facts are facts. What are the facts that you know?"

Jarrett glanced around as if he thought about escaping. Then he seemed to deflate. With resignation, he revealed, "My brother married Michelle, knowing full well he couldn't have children. But she didn't know that until a year into their marriage when she wanted to start a family. He told her then and she felt betrayed. That's when their marriage fell apart."

Whoa! Jarrett was right about *this* truth. This revelation gave Michelle even more motive for murder.

That evening after the rehearsal at St. Francis, when Caprice and Grant walked into the room at the Country Squire where their dinner was being held, Caprice stopped cold. Roz had said she'd take care of the decorations and she had . . . wonderfully.

Caprice murmured to Grant, "It looks like a fairy tale."

Grant confided, "Roz told me she was going to use a Cinderella theme. I told her just not to go too heavy on Prince Charming."

"That's not true at all," Caprice protested. "You *are* my Prince Charming, but a very human one. It just took me a while to figure out that I deserved one."

"And *you* are my quirky Cinderella, though I haven't seen you in the glass slippers yet."

Caprice laughed. The theme could have gone very much awry but Roz had excellent taste. She'd used lots of crystal with the vases and the decorations. The Cinderella coach atop the mascarpone and strawberry cake was spun glass and absolutely beautiful. Twinkle lights blinked everywhere.

Grant suddenly turned Caprice toward him and stared into her eyes. "You look beautiful tonight. I can only imagine you in a wedding gown."

Tonight, the dress she had chosen could have been worn in the Gatsby years. The lace inset bodice fell into three scalloped tiers. It was her favorite color—turquoise.

"You look pretty spiffy yourself." Grant was wearing a pale gray suit, a white shirt, and a geometrically designed gray tie.

"I'd kiss you but I'll mess up your lipstick."

"I don't care about the lipstick," she murmured.

Grant had just circled her with his arms when Vince and Roz came in behind them. Caprice immediately went to Roz and gave her a huge hug. "This is absolutely beautiful."

"I'm glad you like it," Roz said, beaming.

Vince encircled Roz's waist. He was grinning and Caprice could see the couple looked happy.

"Did you two come together?" Caprice asked.

"We certainly did," Vince said. "And we're going to be doing a lot more things together, including owning my house—our house. I have all the paperwork ready for Roz's name to go on the deed."

Caprice hugged her brother, realizing that his situation with Roz had been similar to when Grant's ex-wife came to town. The two of them had finally found closure to their relationship. Caprice hadn't been happy about it, but it had been necessary.

A short time later they were all seated at the table, everyone, that was, except Holden. The waitresses had just served the salads when Holden rushed in, carrying a large shopping bag. After he handed it off to his dad, he gave Grant and Caprice an apologetic smile. "Sorry," he mumbled, as he took a seat beside Grant. "But I bought a new tie. I'm glad I did. This place is grand."

Caprice had almost been ready to become defensive but she realized there wasn't any sarcasm in Holden's tone. When he seemed engaged in conversation with Aunt Marie who was beside him, Grant leaned close to Caprice. "I think it helped that I saw a parallel between Travis and Jarrett's relationship, and me and Holden. I have to let him find his own way."

"I'm glad your argument cleared the air. Maybe the two of you can find real bonds."

"I have a feeling there are a few more arguments in our future before that can happen. But at least we started." Leaning closer to her ear, Grant asked, "Are you off-the-wall excited about tomorrow?"

She turned her face toward his so their lips were almost touching. "Off the wall about describes it. I doubt if I'm going to sleep tonight."

"You and your aunt might be up late talking anyway."

"Maybe. But I don't want circles under my eyes for the wedding."

Grant gave her an understanding smile. "I can't wait to see you walking down the aisle toward me, ready to start our future."

Tears were burning in Caprice's eyes when Grant's dad did the unexpected and interrupted the conversation. He stood and clanked his spoon on his glass to capture everyone's attention. He glanced at his wife and she gave him a nod.

Addressing Caprice and Grant, he said, "I know you've probably gotten a couple of roomfuls of presents, but we wanted to give you something special. Holden brought it in his car for us. We didn't want anything to happen to it on the plane."

Suddenly Grant's dad stooped over and pulled a box out from under the table. It was about the size of a breadbox, wrapped in white shiny paper with a huge white bow. He brought it over to Caprice and Grant and set it on the table between them. He touched Grant on the shoulder and returned to his chair.

"Do you want to open it, or should I?" Grant asked her.

"Why don't you unwrap it and I'll take off the lid."

Grant didn't prolong the suspense. He slipped off the bow and set it on the table, then he tore off the wrapping. The box was a carton as if whatever the present was wouldn't fit into an ordinary gift box.

Caprice told herself she was going to be delighted whatever it was. But when she lifted the lid and laid back the tissue paper, she gasped. It was a beautiful wooden box with her name and Grant's burned into the lid.

"Your father made it," Diane Weatherford said proudly.

"Dad, it's beautiful," Grant said, his voice tight.

Caprice seconded his sentiment. "I love it."

"Now you'll definitely have a big enough box for your affirmations every day," Grant said, recovering, though he still had a world of emotion in his eyes.

"There's something inside," Grant's mother said.

Caprice's look told Grant's mom the box itself would have been enough. What made it even more special was the gift that Grant had given her when he'd wood-burned their names into a heart. The gifts were tradition passed down from father to son.

She motioned for Grant to lift the lid on the box. He did that, the scent of recent stain and wood emanating from inside. Tucked into the box were two velvet pouches. Grant handed one to Caprice and he took one. They unveiled what was inside at the same time. It was a beautiful pair of silver candlesticks.

Diane said, "These were handed down to me from my mother and her mother before her. When Sam and I were at Caprice's for dinner, I noticed the beautiful glassware and dishes that her Nana had handed down to her. That's how I knew she'd like these for her table whenever family gets together."

Caprice responded, "We'll treasure these, as well as the box."

And they would. She exchanged a look with Diane, her mother-in-law-to-be, that said they both knew now that they had common ground—their love for Grant . . . and tradition.

*   *   *

"You're still thinking about Grant's good-night kiss, aren't you?" her Aunt Marie asked with a sly smile.

Caprice had taken Lady out for the last time for the night and now they were in the kitchen having mugs of tea before they went to bed.

"I am," Caprice answered. "And I'm thinking about tomorrow. Grant said the temperature is supposed to be warmer and it's going to be sunny."

Marie stirred honey into her tea. "What are you going to do with the dogs during the Mass and the reception?"

"Grant will bring Patches over early in the morning without seeing me, of course, and we'll leave them here during Mass. But then Uncle Dom's going to pick them up and bring them to the reception. They can't be around the guests and the food, but Michelle said we can put them in her screened-in porch at the house."

"Now isn't that inventive. In a way, they'll be at your reception."

Caprice sat down at the table with her aunt. "I'm so pleased tonight went well with Grant's family."

"Your mother said they've been polite and not at all demanding since they've been there."

"Mom, Dad, and Nana are on their best behavior," Caprice joked.

Lady came over to Caprice's aunt's chair and sat under it.

"It's as if she knows you're going to be taking care of her," Caprice noted.

"Mirabelle and Sophia both let me pet them now. I'm sure we'll all get along fine. I'm looking forward to a few days of reading and sketching new jewelry pieces and spending some time with the family."

Caprice's cell phone played. She stood and took it from the counter where it was charging.

Marie suggested, "Maybe it's Grant wanting to say a last good-night."

Caprice studied the screen. "Nope. It's Michelle." She answered the call, worried their reception could still be in jeopardy.

Michelle began, "I know it's the night before your wedding and you're leaving on your honeymoon tomorrow. I really need to talk to somebody and I know I can't call Vince."

Michelle sounded panicked and Caprice didn't know why. "What's going on?"

"Jarrett's mother wants to invest in the winery and help me run it, but Andrei Moldavan wants to buy it. I need to talk this out with someone, someone who doesn't have an interest in what happens."

Caprice knew she wasn't going to be able to sleep. She covered the phone with her hand and asked her aunt, "Do you mind if I go to the winery? Michelle needs to talk over some business stuff, and she doesn't have anybody else to do it with."

"Do you want me to go with you?"

"No, you stay here with the animals. After I talk with Michelle, I'll make sure the events room is perfectly ready for tomorrow. Everything should be set up."

Returning to Michelle, Caprice said, "I have to change and then I'll drive out. But I can't stay too long. I do need my beauty sleep."

"I know you do. And I promise, I won't keep you long."

"Are Vivian and Jarrett there?"

"Yes, they are, but they've turned in for the night."

"All right, I'll be there in about twenty minutes."

Marie studied Caprice over her cup of tea. "Are you sure this is a good idea?"

"No, I'm not. But I really don't expect there's going to be a problem. After all, Vivian and Jarrett are at the house."

Her aunt still looked worried. Caprice would make this a quick visit and be back home before her aunt missed her.

Chapter Twenty-one

As Caprice walked up to the front door of the house at Rambling Vines Winery, Michelle called to her from the sunporch door. Lights ran along the sidewalk and across the roof of the porch so it was easy for Caprice to see where she was going. As she approached the sunporch, she noticed that Michelle was dressed in an emerald green short-sleeved sweat suit.

She asked Caprice, "Is it okay if we sit on the porch? We'll have more privacy out here. Even though Vivian and Jarrett went upstairs . . ." She stopped then explained, "I don't want to be over-heard, and they seem to hear everything."

Michelle had poured glasses of iced tea. One sat on the round wicker table next to the wicker arm-chair, and one sat next to the settee. When Caprice settled on the flowered cushion, she realized this was the type of wicker look that could with-stand weather. So many things weren't exactly nat-ural anymore. Was Michelle still dressed up because

Jarrett was in the house? Did she hope she could snare Jarrett and Dion Genet was just a stopgap?

When did you become so suspicious? she asked herself.

Caprice had changed into a tie-dyed T-shirt and embroidered jeans. She'd simply worn her jeweled flip-flops. She had to remember to pack them in her suitcase for her honeymoon.

A half moon glowed up above, and she wished she was sitting on the porch with Grant. "It *is* a beautiful night," she murmured.

"I had Neil open the events room for us so you can take a peek. I won't keep you very long. I promise. I know you want to be rested for tomorrow."

"It may take a quart of chamomile tea to do that," Caprice joked wryly.

Staring out into the dark, Michelle said, "I remember the night before my wedding. I was so excited. I had such plans for me and Travis . . . romantic plans. He'd been romantic when we were dating, but then it just stopped. Lots of things stopped."

Caprice decided not to let Michelle know that Jarrett had told her Travis couldn't have children. Michelle would realize what that meant for the investigation as well as Caprice did. After Caprice and Grant were on their honeymoon, she'd call Brett and give him the information. That way her conscience would be clear.

Michelle took a few swallows of her iced tea and so did Caprice. It was sweetened and tasted refreshing. Something from dinner, probably the crab cakes, had made her thirsty.

Michelle took in a long breath and exhaled. "As I told you, Vivian wants to invest money to get the winery back on its feet."

Caprice asked, "What about Vivian and her alcoholism?"

Michelle looked pensive for a moment and then said, "I brought that up with her. She insists she has no desire to take a drink. But she could work out of an office in the house, rather than at the winery. Or . . . if the wine does become a temptation, she'll be a silent partner, keep her investment in Rambling Vines and go back to New Hampshire. I know I need to consider the offer for lots of reasons. First of all, I don't want to declare bankruptcy. I don't like failing."

"If you want me to play devil's advocate . . ." Caprice suggested.

"Go right ahead," Michelle encouraged her.

"There are times when it's better to cut your losses and consider other options."

Michelle turned her glass around and around on the small wicker table. "I know. But the thing is, I really like planning the events here, and I'm not stupid. I could take over some of the business workings despite what Travis and his father thought."

"He didn't want you doing bookwork, inventory, that type of thing?"

"Travis wouldn't let me near his computer. He told me just to keep my mind on the events and running the house and he'd take care of everything else. But obviously he didn't."

"Who would you hire to help you?"

"I would fire Neil. He and I just don't think alike. Vivian has a good head for figures. After all, she ran the mill without a husband for a while. She and I could take over the finances. We wouldn't need Neil."

"It sounds as if you have this worked out."

Michelle shook her head. "The main problem is that I need someone to make the wine. I really know nothing about that. I could get involved in promotion for it, promotion that works. But I need a vintner."

Caprice decided to take a chance and plunge into delicate territory. "You could ask Dion to recommend a vintner."

Michelle's mouth opened in surprise. "You know about Dion Genet?"

"I know that you're close. I know that you and Dion possibly are having an affair. If you are, you should tell the police before they find out on their own," she advised, knowing from experience that the truth always came out.

"I love Dion. I want to have a future with him. He's helped me dream again. Because of him, I realize I do have self-worth. If I would decide to sell the winery, I wouldn't sell it to my neighbor. I could go back to nursing, and in some ways, that would be the easiest thing to do."

"There is another option if you don't want Dion involved."

"What?"

"You could hire Fred back. He's been making wine here for years. My guess is he was the creative force behind it." Caprice was about to add that he needed work when—

A boom pierced the night silence. The sound was sharp and slicing. Caprice knew exactly what it was because she'd heard the sound before. It was a gunshot.

Standing and getting her bearings, she realized the sound had come from near the garage. When another shot sounded, she doubted it was a backfire or someone shooting a groundhog at this time of night.

Michelle ran into the house and called up the stairway. "Jarrett."

Vivian called back downstairs. "He went out for a walk."

Before Caprice could stop Michelle, Michelle had run out the front door toward the tasting room and the garage.

Caprice jogged to catch up with her. "Michelle, wait. You could be in the line of fire."

But Michelle didn't wait. She kept running.

Caprice ran too but slipped her phone out of her pocket. She tapped in 911 and ran around the tasting room and winery to the garage. One of the garage doors was open. Halogen lamps lit them all.

Instantly she focused on Michelle kneeling on the berm of the garage, leaning over someone's body inside. Bloodstains registered before the man's identity. As she hurried closer, she realized the man was Neil Allen and he had been shot in the shoulder. Glass from the Dodge Coronet's window sprinkled the ground around him.

Her phone to her ear, Caprice told the dispatcher, "Rambling Vines Winery. A man's been shot. This is Caprice De Luca. Notify Brett Carstead."

The woman asked her to stay on the line. Michelle was already caring for Neil, checking his breathing and his pulse. She took off her jacket, folded it, and placed it over Neil's shoulder wound, putting pressure on it to stop the bleeding.

Caprice had just answered the dispatcher with, "Yes, I'm still here. The woman with me is a nurse. She's putting pressure on the wound."

The next second, however, she heard the loud rumble of an engine . . . a powerful engine.

A black quad-cab truck screeched around the far corner of the garage and paused. Its headlights glared. They were all caught in the spotlight gleam. Frozen, Caprice felt like prey.

Neil pushed Michelle away from him and yelled, "Run. Leon is going crazy."

Next, everything passed in a frightening blur.

Somehow Michelle ended up on the lane in front of the garage. Neil pulled himself up to his feet, using the frame of the garage door. Taking a step back, he hit a button and the garage door began to lower.

He shouted to them both, "Go to the events room and put the alarm on."

Panic gripped Caprice's chest and her heart raced as she tried to unfreeze her brain and absorb Neil's words.

The truck had braked when it had come around the corner. Now the engine revved as Leon stepped on the gas and aimed toward her and Michelle with a velocity unfit for the gravel lane.

Not a moment too soon, Caprice grabbed Michelle's arm to yank her out of harm's way. The truck whizzed by, brushing the flap of Caprice's bellbottoms. She hardly stopped to think about how lucky they'd been. Instead, still pulling on Michelle who seemed to be in shock, she encouraged her to run and run fast. Michelle had mentioned that the events room was open. Would Neil direct them there if it wasn't?

Caprice only glanced over her shoulder once. The truck had continued down the lane but then screeched to a stop in a spit of gravel.

The door of the truck opened.

Still pulling at Michelle to hurry, they finally reached the events building. Caprice yanked the door open and pushed Michelle inside. After she locked the door, she said to Michelle, "Engage the security alarm. If it goes off, your monitoring service will send more help too."

Michelle, who seemed to come back to life again, looked like she was going to break down. "I canceled the service. But the alarm still works. Leon won't know I canceled it."

Quickly studying the door and the rest of the room with its pastel tablecloths and beautiful place settings, she directed Michelle, "Help me move that credenza in front of the door."

Seconds later she and Michelle pushed and pushed and pushed the heavy mahogany credenza in front of the entrance.

"We can run out the back entrance," Michelle gasped, out of breath from the exertion.

However, they'd run halfway through the events room when the French doors at the rear of the room exploded with the sound of a gunshot and the piercing alarm. Apparently, Leon was cunning . . . more cunning than they were. Aiming at a chandelier, he destroyed the glass shade with shards of it spraying over the tables. He obviously wanted to prove to them he had good aim.

After that terrorizing display, he pointed his handgun first at Michelle and then at Caprice. His eyes were glazed and his expression wild.

Caprice expected to be dead in a matter of seconds. Tears burned in her eyes as she sent Grant and her family all the love she could visualize.

"Leon, stop," Michelle yelled over the sound of the alarm. She put up her hands as if they could ward off bullets.

"No reason to stop. No reason at all. I missed Neil's heart when I shot him, and I knew someone at the house would have heard. He slipped behind that Coronet and I tried to shoot him through the window. Then I heard voices, so I figured I could run you down with my truck."

He waved his gun at Caprice. "But she was too quick," he complained loudly to be heard over the alarm. "I should kill *you* first."

Caprice involuntarily gasped. She felt sweat at the back of her neck as panic squeezed her heart.

Again, Michelle tried to reason with Leon even though she had to shout. "You can't kill us all. The police are going to catch you."

"The police can't figure nothing out. You two will be dead and I'll be out of here—"

Suddenly in the midst of the alarm sounding, they heard pounding on the front door. Jarrett yelled, "Caprice. Michelle. Let me in! I can help."

Leon turned toward the door.

Caprice knew she had to move fast because she might not have another chance. She wanted to

marry Grant. She wanted them both to be surrounded by family for years to come. She had to be
smart since she had nothing to use as a weapon.

Maybe Leon was drunk. Maybe he was just crazy.
He shouted at Jarrett, "Get away. Go back to that
clam shack."

In the time Leon gave that order, Caprice yanked
the rose tablecloth from the closest table. Dishes
flew as she pulled it free and threw it over Leon.

Michelle picked up the crystal vase from the
wedding party's table and conked Leon over the
head with it.

Outside, Jarrett had gone quiet and Caprice wondered if he was running around to the back door.
However, instead of Jarrett, Brett burst in the back,
patrol officers behind him. To her relief, delight,
and joy, Grant followed them in.

Still dressed in his suit from the rehearsal dinner, minus the jacket with a pulled down tie, Grant
took Caprice into his arms. The officers deftly relieved Leon of the tablecloth and cuffed him.

"He has a gun," Caprice called to them.

Brett picked up the gun which lay on the floor.
Leon was still out.

A patrol officer checked his pulse. "It's strong,"
he told Brett. He'll probably come around any
minute.

"How did you know?" Caprice asked Grant, gazing into his caring gray eyes.

"We were all at the Blue Moon when your message for Brett came in. Your dad and Dom are still
there probably pacing the floor. Why didn't you
call me and tell me you were coming out here?"

"Because we weren't supposed to see each other after midnight," she answered reasonably.

With a roll of his eyes, Grant tipped her chin up and whispered, "It's not midnight yet." When he kissed her, Caprice finally let the fear and panic go and reveled in the strength of her husband-to-be's arms.

Epilogue

The following day, Caprice's and Grant's wedding day, Caprice stood in the dressing room at St. Francis of Assisi church along with her mom, Grant's mother, and Nana. Bella, Nikki, and Roz readied themselves to walk down the aisle. Bella finished dressing first and fussed with Caprice's veil to make sure the headband fit just right in Caprice's upswept hair.

"I'm surprised you don't need more makeup," Bella said. "Everything that went on last night and then giving your statement to the police should have caused black circles under your eyes. Did you get *any* sleep?"

Roz joined Bella at Caprice's side and adjusted the pink sapphire necklace that Grant had given her as a wedding present. It matched the earrings he'd gifted her with for Christmas as well as her engagement ring. While she'd given her statement at the police station, Grant had sped to his townhouse, fetched the necklace, and given it to her right at the station. The reason? He wanted to make sure he left her by midnight. He had . . . about two minutes before twelve.

When Caprice had returned to her house, she and her aunt had talked for a long while. Still she'd managed about five hours of solid sleep and she felt wonderful this morning.

"It's a shame all your plans and decorating are wrapped up in crime scene tape at the events room," Nikki said, adjusting the train on Caprice's gown. "You are so fortunate to be Ace Richland's friend. With his connections he built you a wedding reception venue right in his backyard overnight. I'm not going to tell you what it looks like because I want it to be a surprise."

"I don't care what it looks like," Caprice maintained. She glanced at her mother, who was attaching a corsage on Nana's dress. "I'm just so thankful Ace offered when Mom called him."

Finished with the corsage, her mother now came closer, adjusted the flutter of one of Caprice's sleeves, and slid her hand over the ruching at Caprice's waist. "I was afraid I was overstepping, but Ace didn't even hesitate. I just asked him if we could borrow some picnic tables and arrange them in his backyard. But he took over."

Grant's mom carefully arranged the lace-edged cathedral-length bridal veil over Caprice's train. Finished, she came around Caprice and asked hesitantly, "Can I give you a hug?"

Caprice was surprised but so delighted. She opened her arms wide and didn't care if she wrinkled anything. As Diane hugged her, her mother-in-law-to-be whispered in Caprice's ear, "I always wanted a daughter."

Tears brimmed in Caprice's eyes, and all she could say was, "Thank you."

Nana brought Caprice her peony-and-rose-laden bouquet. A tear rolled down her cheek as she hugged Caprice and whispered, "Be happy, *tesorina mia.*"

Roz opened the door so they all could enter the vestibule of the church. There Brett waited to escort Grant's mother down the aisle. Brett gave Caprice a thumbs-up then did his duty admirably.

Roz, Bella, and Nikki lined up in front of Caprice while Vince walked Nana and his mother to the front of the church. Caprice's gown swished around her as she made her way to her dad who offered her his arm.

As organ music swelled, Caprice walked down the aisle on her dad's arm toward Grant.

Grant had arranged for a horse and buggy to transport him and Caprice from the church to the reception. Caprice wouldn't have cared if they traveled by bobsled or hot air balloon. She was just so happy to be married to Grant she couldn't stop grinning.

She and Grant sat close, holding hands as the horse clomped along a back road to Ace's estate. At the security gate, the driver of the horse and buggy tapped in the code to open the gate.

"Are you sure Ace won't mind the buggy messing up his lawn?" Caprice asked as the horse was led around to the back of the mansion.

"Ace is the one who told us to do it," Grant offered. "He's been so terrific about everything."

"I'll have to decorate Marsha's house for free."

The driver of the open buggy stopped at the fire pit where Grant had proposed to Caprice. "This spot will always be memorable," Caprice murmured.

"I'm sure Ace will let us borrow it now and then," Grant assured her.

Grant exited the buggy first, then held out his hand to help Caprice step down. When she did, she faced Ace's yard. "Oh, my gosh," she said to Grant. "Look at the tents and the flowers! It's my color scheme."

"Now that's all important," Grant remarked with a chuckle.

"But it *is*. It's what we were supposed to have in the events room down to the smallest detail."

"Ace cares about you and your family. He wouldn't let you down."

And he didn't. Ace even played Master of Ceremonies, announcing Grant and Caprice under the flowered arch, escorting them to the wedding party's table. There were two wedding cakes—the more traditional one had layers with edible flowers drifting from the top layer to the bottom layer, as well as a groom's cake that was covered in chocolate frosting with two cocker spaniels who looked remarkably like Lady and Patches as a cake topper.

The wedding party had been introduced before Grant and Caprice. Her family and his were waiting for them, and there were hugs all around. Holden and Grant's dad even let her hug them. Not very long hugs, but it was a start.

Grant kept his hand at Caprice's waist as if he

was afraid she'd flutter off if he didn't hold on. While all the guests were finding their seats, Brett tapped Caprice's shoulder. "Do you want to be brought up-to-date or do you want to forget everything except your wedding reception?"

When Caprice glanced at Grant, he gave a nod. After all, he did know her very well. "Catch me up," she murmured.

"Leon confessed. He calmed down after he came to and we had a doctor check him. He insisted he wasn't paying out of his pocket for a lawyer."

"Did you find out why he murdered Travis?" Grant asked.

"It all had to do with the classic cars," Brett explained. "Leon murdered Travis because Travis discovered he wasn't using authentic car parts in the restored vehicles. Leon claimed that he *was* so he could charge more. His business and his life would have been ruined if word got out. Leon was also the one who hired the teenager to ruin Rambling Vines' wine."

"What did Neil have to do with it?" Caprice asked. "And how is he?"

"The bullet went clear through Neil's shoulder. It will heal after some physical therapy. He apparently knew about the unauthentic auto parts so he was blackmailing Leon for a cut when Leon sold the vehicles for Michelle. Leon even confessed to sending that virus to Caprice's computer through a website on the dark web. That adds terrorist threats to the charges of assault with a deadly weapon and second-degree murder. My guess is that Neil Allen will dispute Leon's claim that he was going to be blackmailed. It's a he-said, he-said situation and no crime had been committed yet. Neil is planning to move out of state."

Suddenly Fred and his wife, Agnes, appeared by Caprice's side. She hugged them both and introduced them to Grant.

The first thing Fred asked Caprice was, "Do we have to sign anything to keep Grayson? Because we definitely want him. That pooch has been essential to Agnes getting well."

Caprice was delighted with the assessment. "I suspected the three of you would get along. No, there's nothing to sign."

"I have other news, too," Fred said. "I'm going to be making wine at Rambling Vines. Michelle and her mother-in-law are going to run it, and they want me to create the wine."

"That's wonderful news!"

"When Michelle called me this morning, she said you'd invited her to the wedding but she wasn't going to come. She said something about starting to put her life back in order."

Caprice guessed that meant bringing Dion Genet into her life more fully.

All at once, everyone began clapping and laughing.

When Caprice looked in the direction of the pool and pool house, she spotted the reason.

Ace waved to them, stooped, and let Patches and Lady off their leashes. The two cocker spaniels made a beeline for Grant and Caprice. Before she'd left for the reception, Bella had helped her change veils and detach her train so she could move around more easily.

Now she stooped down to pet both dogs and Grant did the same.

"If Ace could figure out how to bring Mirabelle and Sophia here, he would have," Grant told her. "Ace said he had a talk with them and they preferred to stay at home."

Before Grant and Caprice could stand, the guests began clinking their spoons against their glasses.

Caprice knew what that meant, and she smiled. Grant stood first and put his hand under her elbow to help her straighten. Gazing into those gray eyes that had always mesmerized her, Caprice wrapped her arms around his neck. Then Grant kissed her. She knew she'd never forget this moment . . . this day. Perfect happiness didn't come around that often. She was going to savor it while she could.

ORIGINAL RECIPES

Three Cheese Rotelle and Pepperoni Casserole

1 pound ground beef
½ cup chopped onion
½ teaspoon salt
⅛ teaspoon black pepper
1 clove garlic, grated
24-ounce jar spaghetti sauce (I use *Prego Flavored with Meat*)
3 cups Rotelle #124
2 ounces pepperoni (I use turkey pepperoni)
1½ cups grated Monterey Jack Cheese
1 cup grated mozzarella
½ cup grated Parmesan cheese

Preheat oven to 350 degrees.

Brown ground beef and chopped onions in a frying pan. Add salt, pepper, and garlic. Add the jar of spaghetti sauce and heat on medium high until the mixture begins to boil. Then turn to simmer until the pasta is ready. Cook pasta according to package directions, then drain. Put ½ in a 2-quart casserole. Mix in ½ of meat sauce. Top with a layer of pepperoni. Sprinkle ½ of each cheese on top. Spread in the rest of the pasta and cover with the remaining meat sauce and the remaining cheeses.

Bake at 350 degrees for 45 minutes.

Serves 4

Gourmet Chicken Salad

1 boneless whole breast
¼ cup chopped onion
¼ teaspoon salt
⅛ teaspoon pepper
1 teaspoon orange rind
⅓ cup chopped celery
⅓ cup dried cranberries
¼ cup pine nuts
⅛ teaspoon garlic powder
1 tablespoon mayonnaise
⅓ cup Ranch dressing

In a small roasting pan place chicken breast with chopped onion, salt, pepper, and enough water to cover the bottom of the pan. Bake at 350 degrees for about 1½ hours, until the meat pulls apart easily.

Tear chicken into small pieces in a bowl. Add orange rind, chopped celery, dried cranberries, pine nuts, garlic powder, mayonnaise, and Ranch dressing. Mix together. Refrigerate.

Serve in your favorite bun or on a bed of fresh garden greens.

Serves 4

Caprice's White Cake with Mascarpone and Strawberry Topping

White Cake

½ cup vegetable oil
1½ cups granulated sugar
5 egg whites
1 whole egg
½ cup sour cream
2 teaspoons vanilla
½ cup 2% milk
1 teaspoon salt
3 teaspoons baking powder
1 teaspoon baking soda
2½ cups flour

Preheat oven to 375 degrees. Grease and flour a 9 x 13" pan.

Mix oil and sugar. Add eggs, then vanilla and sour cream. Add milk, salt, baking powder, baking soda, and flour. Beat well and pour into pan.

Bake 25 minutes or until toothpick comes out clear.

When cool, top the cake with mascarpone and whipped cream topping.

Mascarpone and Whipped Cream Topping

8 oz heavy whipping cream
8 oz Mascarpone
3 tablespoons powdered sugar

½ teaspoon almond flavoring
1 cup sliced strawberries (for topping)

In a chilled bowl, whip heavy whipping cream until thick. Add Mascarpone and whip with the cream until smooth. Add almond flavoring, then add powdered sugar a tablespoon at a time. Spread this mixture over the cake. Spread sliced strawberries on top.

Connect with Us

Visit us online at
KensingtonBooks.com
to read more from your favorite authors, see books
by series, view reading group guides, and more.

Join us on social media

for sneak peeks, chances to win books and prize packs,
and to share your thoughts with other readers.

facebook.com/kensingtonpublishing
twitter.com/kensingtonbooks

Tell us what you think!

To share your thoughts, submit a review,
or sign up for our eNewsletters, please visit:
KensingtonBooks.com/TellUs.

Books by Bestselling Author
Fern Michaels

__**The Jury**	0-8217-7878-1	$6.99US/$9.99CAN
__**Sweet Revenge**	0-8217-7879-X	$6.99US/$9.99CAN
__**Lethal Justice**	0-8217-7880-3	$6.99US/$9.99CAN
__**Free Fall**	0-8217-7881-1	$6.99US/$9.99CAN
__**Fool Me Once**	0-8217-8071-9	$7.99US/$10.99CAN
__**Vegas Rich**	0-8217-8112-X	$7.99US/$10.99CAN
__**Hide and Seek**	1-4201-0184-6	$6.99US/$9.99CAN
__**Hokus Pokus**	1-4201-0185-4	$6.99US/$9.99CAN
__**Fast Track**	1-4201-0186-2	$6.99US/$9.99CAN
__**Collateral Damage**	1-4201-0187-0	$6.99US/$9.99CAN
__**Final Justice**	1-4201-0188-9	$6.99US/$9.99CAN
__**Up Close and Personal**	0-8217-7956-7	$7.99US/$9.99CAN
__**Under the Radar**	1-4201-0683-X	$6.99US/$9.99CAN
__**Razor Sharp**	1-4201-0684-8	$7.99US/$10.99CAN
__**Yesterday**	1-4201-1494-8	$5.99US/$6.99CAN
__**Vanishing Act**	1-4201-0685-6	$7.99US/$10.99CAN
__**Sara's Song**	1-4201-1493-X	$5.99US/$6.99CAN
__**Deadly Deals**	1-4201-0686-4	$7.99US/$10.99CAN
__**Game Over**	1-4201-0687-2	$7.99US/$10.99CAN
__**Sins of Omission**	1-4201-1153-1	$7.99US/$10.99CAN
__**Sins of the Flesh**	1-4201-1154-X	$7.99US/$10.99CAN
__**Cross Roads**	1-4201-1192-2	$7.99US/$10.99CAN

Available Wherever Books Are Sold!
Check out our website at www.kensingtonbooks.com

More by Bestselling Author
Hannah Howell

__Highland Angel	978-1-4201-0864-4	$6.99US/$8.99CAN
__If He's Sinful	978-1-4201-0461-5	$6.99US/$8.99CAN
__Wild Conquest	978-1-4201-0464-6	$6.99US/$8.99CAN
__If He's Wicked	978-1-4201-0460-8	$6.99US/$8.49CAN
__My Lady Captor	978-0-8217-7430-4	$6.99US/$8.49CAN
__Highland Sinner	978-0-8217-8001-5	$6.99US/$8.49CAN
__Highland Captive	978-0-8217-8003-9	$6.99US/$8.49CAN
__Nature of the Beast	978-1-4201-0435-6	$6.99US/$8.49CAN
__Highland Fire	978-0-8217-7429-8	$6.99US/$8.49CAN
__Silver Flame	978-1-4201-0107-2	$6.99US/$8.49CAN
__Highland Wolf	978-0-8217-8000-8	$6.99US/$9.99CAN
__Highland Wedding	978-0-8217-8002-2	$4.99US/$6.99CAN
__Highland Destiny	978-1-4201-0259-8	$4.99US/$6.99CAN
__Only for You	978-0-8217-8151-7	$6.99US/$8.99CAN
__Highland Promise	978-1-4201-0261-1	$4.99US/$6.99CAN
__Highland Vow	978-1-4201-0260-4	$4.99US/$6.99CAN
__Highland Savage	978-0-8217-7999-6	$6.99US/$9.99CAN
__Beauty and the Beast	978-0-8217-8004-6	$4.99US/$6.99CAN
__Unconquered	978-0-8217-8088-6	$4.99US/$6.99CAN
__Highland Barbarian	978-0-8217-7998-9	$6.99US/$9.99CAN
__Highland Conqueror	978-0-8217-8148-7	$6.99US/$9.99CAN
__Conqueror's Kiss	978-0-8217-8005-3	$4.99US/$6.99CAN
__A Stockingful of Joy	978-1-4201-0018-1	$4.99US/$6.99CAN
__Highland Bride	978-0-8217-7995-8	$4.99US/$6.99CAN
__Highland Lover	978-0-8217-7759-6	$6.99US/$9.99CAN

Available Wherever Books Are Sold!

Check out our website at
http://www.kensingtonbooks.com

Romantic Suspense from
Lisa Jackson

Absolute Fear	0-8217-7936-2	$7.99US/$9.99CAN
Afraid to Die	1-4201-1850-1	$7.99US/$9.99CAN
Almost Dead	0-8217-7579-0	$7.99US/$10.99CAN
Born to Die	1-4201-0278-8	$7.99US/$9.99CAN
Chosen to Die	1-4201-0277-X	$7.99US/$10.99CAN
Cold Blooded	1-4201-2581-8	$7.99US/$8.99CAN
Deep Freeze	0-8217-7296-1	$7.99US/$10.99CAN
Devious	1-4201-0275-3	$7.99US/$9.99CAN
Fatal Burn	0-8217-7577-4	$7.99US/$10.99CAN
Final Scream	0-8217-7712-2	$7.99US/$10.99CAN
Hot Blooded	1-4201-0678-3	$7.99US/$9.49CAN
If She Only Knew	1-4201-3241-5	$7.99US/$9.99CAN
Left to Die	1-4201-0276-1	$7.99US/$10.99CAN
Lost Souls	0-8217-7938-9	$7.99US/$10.99CAN
Malice	0-8217-7940-0	$7.99US/$10.99CAN
The Morning After	1-4201-3370-5	$7.99US/$9.99CAN
The Night Before	1-4201-3371-3	$7.99US/$9.99CAN
Ready to Die	1-4201-1851-X	$7.99US/$9.99CAN
Running Scared	1-4201-0182-X	$7.99US/$10.99CAN
See How She Dies	1-4201-2584-2	$7.99US/$8.99CAN
Shiver	0-8217-7578-2	$7.99US/$10.99CAN
Tell Me	1-4201-1854-4	$7.99US/$9.99CAN
Twice Kissed	0-8217-7944-3	$7.99US/$9.99CAN
Unspoken	1-4201-0093-9	$7.99US/$9.99CAN
Whispers	1-4201-5158-4	$7.99US/$9.99CAN
Wicked Game	1-4201-0338-5	$7.99US/$9.99CAN
Wicked Lies	1-4201-0339-3	$7.99US/$9.99CAN
Without Mercy	1-4201-0274-5	$7.99US/$10.99CAN
You Don't Want to Know	1-4201-1853-6	$7.99US/$9.99CAN

Available Wherever Books Are Sold!
Visit our website at **www.kensingtonbooks.com**